KILLER ON ARGYLE STREET

A PAUL WHELAN MYSTERY

MICHAEL RALEIGH

DIVERSIONBOOKS

Also by Michael Raleigh

Paul Whelan Mysteries
Death in Uptown
A Body in Belmont Harbor
The Maxwell Street Blues
The Riverview Murders

Diversion Books
A Division of Diversion Publishing Corp.
443 Park Avenue South, Suite 1008
New York, New York 10016
www.DiversionBooks.com

For more information, email info@diversionbooks.com

First Diversion Books edition February 2015.
Print ISBN: 978-1-62681-766-1
eBook ISBN: 978-1-62681-621-3

For Cate and Brian,
my sister and brother,
my lifelong friends

Prologue

The totem pole was made of red cedar and stood perhaps twenty feet high. A gift from the Kwagulth people of the Northwest, it bore a great bird with red, green and white plumage and a grinning sea monster with a man riding on his back. The brass plaque in front explained that the totem pole intended to portray Kwanusila the Thunderbird and other denizens of Northwest Coast mythology. The pole had arrived in 1929 and had stood in the park where Addison met Lake Shore Drive for so long that residents of the neighborhood rarely gave it a second look.

An occasional visitor or confused suburbanite ran the red light while staring at the pole but it had more or less become part of the background for all but children and the tourists.

A man in a small felt hat stood in front of the totem pole and peered up at it. He was a tanned man of indeterminate age, perhaps fifty, perhaps sixty, lean and sharp-featured and trim in a light coat and gray slacks. There was something foreign about the hat and the pattern in his slacks. The giveaway was the pair of sandals he wore over thick cotton socks. After a moment, he made a slow circuit of the totem pole, looking up and down its length and shaking his head in obvious admiration. As he studied it, he fumbled at the camera hanging from his neck. The rare April sunlight had attracted several groups of picnickers who huddled around their bottles of wine and plastic coolers and tried to ignore the knifelike wind and pretend that something like spring might be coming. Occasionally one of the picnickers looked up at the strange man, who seemed to be having trouble deciding how to focus the camera. A small boy stared at the man, his notice attracted by the man's odd footware on such a cold day.

Once or twice the man looked around, smiling as though hoping to engage a native in conversation, but these early sun worshipers seemed preoccupied with their cold chicken and cans of beer. Returning to the front of the totem pole, he backed up and focused. A heavy mass of gray cloud moved in and smothered the sun, and the man lowered his camera and made a little gesture of exasperation.

He adjusted the shutter speed, took several shots of the totem pole, then looked up again as the sky seemed to darken once more. He gave a little shake of his head, adjusted the shutter speed and took several more pictures, then replaced the lens cap and walked north, in the direction of the tennis courts and the parking lots.

There were three vehicles in the parking lot, two of them empty. A man sat in the third, a black Ford pickup. He was a big man going to fat, perhaps thirty, with sandy hair thinning at the front. He had spent several moments watching the other two vehicles for signs of occupancy but was now satisfied that they were as empty as they looked.

He sat with the window rolled down and listened to a country music station, drumming with his fingers on the door. From time to time he looked in the sideview and rearview mirrors, and he made a regular survey of the walkways and the baseball fields to his left. It wouldn't be a total disaster if he were taken slightly by surprise, but he'd have to come up with an explanation fast.

From the edge of his vision he caught movement. He turned in the seat to watch the newcomer. A tourist. From the looks of him, a German tourist: camera and a reddish brown tan and light brown sandals over his beige socks. The tourist seemed to be interested in the lone pair of tennis players. Craning a little out of the window, the man in the truck got a better look at the tennis players and decided that the tourist had good taste: they were a pair of tall slim young women, ignoring the cold, their legs red against white tennis skirts.

He climbed out of the truck, pushed the door closed and then leaned against it. From a pocket in his denim jacket he took out cigarettes and a disposable lighter and had a smoke. The German tourist had moved on from the world of young tennis players and now stood where the park suddenly sloped into a wide saucerlike depression to create the baseball fields. The empty fields seemed to confuse him and after shaking his head and peering around, he consulted a map.

Then as the big man stared at him, the German tourist suddenly looked up from the map and smiled directly at him. The big man recognized the pale blue eyes and even white teeth, the wolfen smile.

He was startled, and for a moment he did not know how to react. Then he took in the rest of the man's appearance, down to his ruddy tan, and laughed in spite of himself.

Like a goddam chameleon. He shook his head and waved to the tourist, who now folded up his map and came forward, still smiling.

The big man grinned and told himself that you had to hand it to the guy: a little out of it, too old for them to take him seriously any more but a smart guy in his way. The tourist was only a few steps away now and for just a sliver in time the big man felt nervous. This was the first time he'd met with the other man alone and he wasn't sure why he'd agreed to it. No, there was always the same reason you did things.

The big man shivered. "You oughtta be wearing a coat. It's cold."

The tourist gave him a look of mild contempt. "It's nice out. It's windy, that's all. I lived here for a long time. It's spring, this is what they call spring here."

The big man laughed and shook his head. "I lived here all my life, there *ain't* any fucking spring here. It's spring in your imagination. And you look like something out of the Alps. Where'd you come up with this getup?"

The tourist flashed a shy smile. "It's easy. Changing your appearance is no trouble at all. I've done it a thousand times."

"You're a whaddyacallit, a chameleon."

"Yes, I sure am."

"So, you, uh, you got a proposition for me."

"What's the hurry?" He looked around, took off his alpine cap and replaced it on his fine, straw-colored hair.

The younger man looked back toward the street. "Come on, let's get in the truck, fuck this outdoor shit."

Shaking his head, the tourist walked around the front and climbed into the cab, and the big man pulled himself up and slid behind the wheel.

They both lit cigarettes and smoked as they began their conversation. Fifteen minutes later, the tourist climbed out of the truck. He paused with the door open for several seconds, staring at the other man, then closed the door. As he walked away from the truck, he kept his head down and when he reached the sidewalk near the tennis courts again, he pulled out his map and began to study it. When he left the area, he was still staring at his map.

Inside the truck, the big man sat with one hand on the wheel and stared straight ahead in the direction of the lake. He was bleeding from a small chest wound just to the left of center, and he was dead.

One

Paul Whelan paused outside his office building and stared at it. A storm had blown out an entire window on the first floor. And since the absentee landlord wouldn't be likely to have it fixed for another six months, the tenant, a church-run social service agency, had covered the big hole with tape and several black plastic bags. Whelan thought it made the place look like a weary man with an eye patch.

A foot or so from the front door, a dead squirrel lay directly in the center of the sidewalk. The few people likely to enter the building to do business with the Korean importers or the flyblown travel agency or the social workers or Paul Whelan Investigative Services would have to step over the little gray corpse if they were serious.

Whelan stooped to look at the squirrel. He was mildly surprised to see a dead squirrel, having long assumed that if a squirrel could survive in Uptown it would have to be immortal. He had never quite figured out what squirrels found to eat in Uptown: the closer you went toward the lake the more barren the neighborhood became, trees grew scarce, lawns disappeared. Birds could fly away looking for food; squirrels were stuck here. Whelan looked for cause of death and found no marks, no bruise from a fall or collision, no tiny hole from a little maniac with an air rifle. Just a dead squirrel on his doorstep. Whelan cast a suspicious glance a few feet to his left, at the new tenant on the ground floor of the building, Mr. Cheeseburger, a dank, tiny hamburger stand that had already earned a dark reputation on the street. Had the poor squirrel gone rooting around in Mr. Cheeseburger's dumpster and died eating bad things?

He looked across the street. The pool hall had gone under,

replaced now with a large day-care center. The squadrons of kids and grown men who'd congregated on this corner had been greatly reduced in number but you could still find a few leaning on cars and watching people go by. There were two of them now, teenage boys, both black and neither having the slightest notion how he'd spend the day. Whelan waved, got their attention, motioned them across the street.

They did the gangster walk in slow motion, a couple of young dudes who couldn't be hurried, and when they reached Whelan, the taller of the two pointed his chin at Whelan.

"Morning, guys," Whelan said.

"Wha' sup," the tall one said.

"I need a favor." He pointed to the dead squirrel behind him. "I need that gone."

The smaller boy snickered and looked at the other boy out of the corner of his eye. The tall one went another shade of sullen.

"That right?"

"Yeah. Can you take care of that for me?"

The taller one stared, looking to see if his manhood was somehow being ridiculed. Whelan pulled a five from his pocket. "Buy yourself a Coke."

The tall boy's gaze rested on the bill for no more than a half second, then he shrugged. "Whatchoo want *us* to do with it?"

"Get a piece of newspaper and wrap it in that, and toss it in a garbage can for me. And don't let this guy see you," Whelan said, indicating Mr. Cheeseburger with a nod. "He'll make burgers with it."

The smaller boy grinned and Whelan thought he saw amusement in the tall boy's eyes. Still, the kid wasn't moving or taking the five.

"How come you don't do it youself, man?"

"I'm supposed to be a businessman. Be bad for my image."

And now the tall boy allowed himself a smile. He reached out casually and took the bill, then looked down at his companion.

"Go get some paper, man."

"Thanks, guys."

The tall one made the most noncommittal of nods and the small one went scurrying off to find newspaper. Whelan went inside.

He could hear Nowicki before he reached the second-floor landing. Mr. Nowicki's presence was proving to be a mixed blessing: on the one hand, Whelan was no longer the sole occupant of the second floor, a position he had occupied for more than a year. This meant that the building's miserly owner now saw fit to turn on all the hall lights and even open the rest rooms on the second floor, bringing these most basic trappings of respectability to Whelan's business. On the other hand, Nowicki was already becoming an irritant. He was a sallow man of average height, with a pronounced stomach and light brown hair, and greeted Whelan effusively whenever they met on the stairs.

Officially, his business was called A-OK Novelties, and an amateurish pink sign on the door to his office boasted TOYS, GAMES, FAVORS, NOTIONS, FOR EXPORT AND IMPORT. A-OK Novelties occupied the suite across the hall from Whelan, and through its clouded glass door Whelan was privy to the many passionate conversations of Mr. Nowicki. It was not only the proximity of A-OK that allowed Whelan to hear what went on across the hall, but also the loud, grating quality of Nowicki's voice and his intense manner of speaking, as though each conversation might end before he used up his nickel. Profanity was a salient feature of these conversations, a rather dull, uninspired profanity, and this much told Whelan that Mr. Nowicki had not gone to the better schools. Still, he managed to use the same three or four obscenities in imaginative ways, including the use of the word "fuck" as four different parts of speech. A large number of Nowicki's conversations seemed to be with someone named Lou, and Lou was apparently unreasonable and bad-tempered.

Whelan had never seen anyone but Nowicki going in or out of the office, and though he had all his long life wondered what "novelties," "favors," and "notions" were, Whelan was pretty well convinced that Mr. Nowicki didn't sell any.

At the moment, Nowicki was calling someone on the other end of the line an "ungrateful fuck." Whelan paused to listen and then realized that his own phone was ringing.

It kept ringing as he fumbled with his keys at the outer door. He crossed the room, set down his coffee and picked it up.

"Paul Whelan."

"You made it in to work!" a voice said, a loud, raucous female voice with a laugh built into it. "We can call off the search parties, Paul Whelan's at work."

"Good morning, Shelley. It's ten after nine, for crying out loud."

"More like twenty after by my watch, but what the hell, you came in and that's the main thing." He could hear her taking a long hissing drag on a cigarette.

"I take it I've had calls already."

"Of course. They've been lining up on the pavement to see you. Yeah, hon, you had a call. A Mrs. Evangeline Pritchett. Said she came in to see you and you weren't there."

"That means she saw the dead squirrel."

Shelley laughed. "She didn't mention it. She was at your office at eight-thirty, sweetheart, and you weren't there, so she went home and called your office."

"Did you tell her I was in a meeting?"

"I told her you were barely conscious at eight-thirty. I've got her number." Shelley's laughter rumbled into the phone. "Says she was referred to you by your cop friend Bauman."

"Oh, Lord. This can't be good news. Give me the number, Shel." He wrote it down. "Thanks."

"Don't mention it, babe. Oh, and we may have a personnel change around here."

"You're leaving?"

"No, but Abraham is."

Whelan felt his mood brighten. One of the great trials of his professional life was the fact that his answering service chose to relieve Shelley with a chirpy little man from India, whose perennial struggles with English grammar and idiom had resulted in something close to a new language. Phone conversations with Abraham could open an ulcer.

"Wait—don't tell me he got that job as a police dispatcher?"

"No. But he got another one. Says he's going to work at the end of the month for a cab company."

"Oh, Lord—*driving?*"

"No. Dispatching cabs to the far corners of our fair city."

"God help those who need cabs," Whelan said. "Later, Shel."

"Toodle-oo."

He called Mrs. Pritchett and apologized for being away from the office when she came by.

"Should I come by now?" the woman asked.

"No, it's my turn. Where do you live?"

She gave him an address on Wilton, less than a half mile from his office.

"I'll be there in fifteen minutes." He didn't leave immediately but crossed the room and stood before his newest purchase, the one intended to catapult his agency into something close to the twentieth century: a tall, gleaming, silver-and-blue water cooler. He poured himself a paper cup of icy water that hurt his teeth. The cooler gurgled and he resisted the impulse to pat it.

A couple of men in a car gave him the look as he pulled up in front of the building on Wilton but Whelan ignored them. At the top step, a white-shirted security guard moved aside for him to pass.

Mrs. Pritchett lived on the third floor. The hall was chilly and the narrow strip of carpet that ran timorously down its center was stained and smelly, but somewhere on this floor there was a genuine cook at work. Whelan thought it smelled like gumbo, or at least some exotic species of chili. He could also make out the faint but familiar odors of pork chops fixed the way Grandma Whelan used to make them, breaded and then tossed into their own molten pool of Crisco: little warheads of cholesterol, but to Whelan's way of thinking the way God intended pork chops to be cooked. He smiled at the memory of his grandmother, a permanent nemesis to his parents and the person who had introduced him to coffee, Pepsi-Cola, and the concept of a piece of cake after a breakfast of waffles.

Mrs. Pritchett's door was the third one down and he could hear a radio playing old music in the background. He knocked twice and waited. Someone cut the radio and scuffed quietly toward the door.

"Yes?"

"Mrs. Pritchett? It's Paul Whelan."

"Yes, sir, just one moment." It was a pleasant voice with the faintest hint of an accent.

The door opened two inches on a brass chain and a light-skinned black woman in her late fifties or early sixties peered out at him. He held out his wallet to show his identification.

"I believe you, sir. I just need to see folk before they come into my home."

Whelan heard the other message in the voice, that she wasn't some senile ancient who could be swindled out of her savings or talked into a truckload of aluminum siding. The chain dropped, the door opened and Mrs. Pritchett looked him over. After a moment, she stepped back from the door. "Come in, sir."

Whelan followed her in, feeling much as he had when called into the principal's office in the days of his barbarous youth.

He saw her run a quick glance over the little living room to see if it was in proper order to receive guests. It was a cluttered room, with stuffed chairs and a sofa and several tables and standing lamps, and in the far corner of the room, a few feet from the television, a Victrola perched on a tall narrow table. The big brass trumpet gleamed from a thousand polishings.

"Does that work?"

Mrs. Pritchett glanced at her antique and gave him an amused look. "It does if somebody cranks it up, but I'm too old to be getting exercise every time I want to listen to a record."

"My grandfather had one. My grandmother hated it."

"She probably had to clean it."

"She didn't share his taste in music, either. He liked comedy records, she liked nice music."

Mrs. Pritchett was nodding. "Men always like silly music. Sit down, sir."

"Thank you." He took the nearest seat, an old armchair.

"Can I get you something?"

"No, thanks. You mentioned that Detective Bauman referred you to me."

"Yes," she said, and paused. Her face clouded and she seemed to be running through something in her mind.

"And if you survived your contact with Detective Bauman, you can handle anything."

She smiled and nodded. "He was nice to me, Mr. Whelan, but he is a very intimidating man."

"He is."

"I can also tell you he's not a very healthy man. He's a candidate for a heart attack. If that man came to see me when I was working in the cardiac unit, we'd have slapped his butt into a bed and strapped him in."

"You're a nurse?"

"Yes, sir. Why you look so surprised? I look too old to be a nurse?" Mrs. Pritchett gave him a slightly belligerent look and he realized he was out of his league. Start singing, Whelan.

"No, ma'am," he said. "You're…you're in your forties or thereabouts."

"Sir, you are a liar." Then she laughed. Her laugh was a deep rolling sound, lower than her voice, a Pearl Bailey kind of laugh, and Whelan liked her. "My forties!" She shook her head. "Wish I had them *back*. Had a different life when I was in my forties, young man."

She allowed herself to sit at the edge of her couch, then took a very quick look at her watch.

"Are you due at the hospital soon?"

"No, this is my day off. Anyway, Detective Bauman was polite to me but he seems very hostile. And I know a drinker when I see one. He smokes too. I could smell it on him." She gave Whelan an appraising look. "I can smell it on you, too."

Whelan blinked but said nothing.

"He said you were very good at what you do. And that finding people is your specialty."

"He's full of surprises, Mrs. Pritchett. He'd never say those things to me. Tell me about your case. I assume it's a missing persons case."

"Yes. It's about a boy. A missing teenage boy."

"Your son?"

"No. He's not mine, but I took care of him for a while. He's not a black child, either, sir. He looks white."

"Looks white? What is he?"

"His father was white, his mother was an Indian."

"They're both dead, then."

"Yes—least I think so. Father run off when the boy was very small. Nobody ever heard from him again, not even his people. They were very poor, I guess they lived in a lot of different places. The boy's name is Tony. He's sixteen. They had two other children that died very young. So the boy has had a hard life, not much of a childhood at all."

"And where has he been living?"

"A lot of places, Mr. Whelan, including the street. He lived with me for a while and now he's missing and I want to find him, make sure he's all right. And," she took a deep breath and let it out, "...I'm not sure he is."

"What brought it to your attention that he was missing?"

"The police came to ask questions and told me he hadn't been seen in a while. Wanted to know if I'd seen him. There was some...trouble involving some people he had been, you know, running the streets with."

He thought about the pause before "trouble" and leaned forward in the chair. "What kind of trouble, Mrs. Pritchett?"

"Very bad trouble. They found some men killed. Three of them, and they were people who Tony knew." Mrs. Pritchett gave him a wide-eyed look of distress, and it was clear that the second fact was the greater shock for her. "I sure don't know how he'd know these people. Mr. Bauman seemed to think

Tony ran errands for them, and when the police went looking for him, you know, to ask him questions, they couldn't find him anywhere."

"And they think he may be in some danger himself."

"Mr. Whelan, that boy was in danger from the day his mother died. He was sure enough in danger when he left here."

"How long did he stay here?"

"A little under six months." Whelan waited a few seconds and the woman added, "Leona was a very nice lady. We worked together."

"Where?"

"Cuneo Hospital. She was a nurse's aide. One of my aides."

"How did it come about that you took Tony in?"

"After Leona died—the boy went on up there to Wisconsin to live with some people that knew his mama. They weren't kin, though."

"Reservation?"

"Yes, sir. 'The Rez,' he called it. He didn't like it much up there. He's a city boy, y'understand. So he came back here and stayed with some relatives on his father's side. But they couldn't handle him. He's a moody boy, got a temper, and this family couldn't do anything with him."

"His mother had no family?"

"She told me once she had some people in the South, Alabama, she said. But I don't know where in Alabama. Said she had a couple of aunts down there, told me one of 'em didn't even speak English."

"What tribe was Leona?"

"Some tribe I never heard of. Said a lot of the old folk still speak their old language."

Whelan remembered something Abby at St. Augustine's Indian Center had told him once about a boy living with his grandmother who spoke only the ancient tongue, an old woman just up from the south. Chickasaw, maybe. No, Choctaw.

"Choctaw?"

"That's it, Choctaw. You know about them?"

"Not enough to be helpful, but I know some people who

might be able to find the family. So—what happened after that?"

"Went from one thing to another. He wound up in a group home run by some agency. Wasn't happy there either, but he stayed for seven months and he was getting himself together. Then he ran away. I saw him on the street one day and told him he could stay with me for a while. 'A while' turned into six months. I had him in school for most of it, you see. But this is no life for a young man and I don't think he was ever really comfortable with me. I'm not his family and there's no way you can change that. Didn't matter how I treated him, he still acted like he was just visiting. He wouldn't hear of going to live with a foster family, and I wasn't going to force him. I really didn't know what to do about him, and finally he made the decision for me. Told me he was moving into an apartment with some friends, or a friend and his older brother."

"How long ago was this?"

"In the fall. October. Never told me who these people were."

"Do you know the other people Tony was hanging out with, the ones the police are concerned with?"

"No." Mrs. Pritchett looked down, as though embarrassed not to have information.

"You never saw them?"

"I saw him with other boys a couple of times. On the corner. You know. But never with any grown men."

"How about names?"

She nodded. "Detective Bauman told me three or four names but the only one I heard is 'Jimmy.' I know he did some work for a man named Jimmy, odd jobs, just pocket money."

"Do you know how he got involved with these people?"

She made a visible effort to come up with this connection and began to shake her head, then she stopped. "I think it was the garage. He worked for a garage over on Broadway. I think he met them there."

"Where on Broadway?"

"Up near that street where you find all the Vietnamese places."

"Argyle Street. Okay. Get the name of the garage?"

"Roy's. Tony worked for Roy, oh, maybe four months."

"Did he ever seem to be frightened or anxious about anything when he was here?"

She lowered her head to look at him over her glasses. "Boy with no family, drops out from school, living with a stranger. Wouldn't you be scared?"

"I'd be scared of a lot less."

She nodded. "He was scared all right. But he didn't say anything. Pulled his little self up into a shell, didn't say anything, didn't show any feelings. Watched TV, played those fool games down at that arcade, that's all he did."

"So if he was afraid of something in particular, he wouldn't have said anyway."

"That's right."

Whelan sat silent and let her continue.

"I did hear him say one time that this man Jimmy had a new partner, an older man, and I think Tony ran some kind of errands for this other man, but he never said a name."

"How long ago was that?"

"This was just before he moved out."

"In the fall, then."

"Yes." For a moment, Mrs. Pritchett was no longer in the room with him. Her eyes moved around her little apartment and she blinked in her confusion, and she looked ten years older. Finally she met Whelan's gaze.

"I just don't know where to look for him."

Whelan thought for a moment. "You've looked yourself, haven't you?"

"Yes. I went to some of the places that I know he went to, a couple of places where I ran into him. But…"

"You looked, Mrs. Pritchett. He's not your boy, but you went out on the street looking." Lady, you're all right, he thought.

"Detective Bauman said you could help me."

"Maybe. There's no way of telling till we try it."

"He said you cost money though."

"Well, we…"

"A lot. He said you cost a lot." Mrs. Pritchett's face registered a mild disapproval.

"He *said* that? Now, that's...it's not exactly true, ma'am. I work for a fee but..."

"I have some money, Mr. Whelan—what are your fees, sir?" Mrs. Pritchett drew herself up into an erect position and faced her financial fate.

For a moment Whelan couldn't say anything. Then he shrugged, promised to have his revenge on Bauman someday, and said, "My fees are decided on a case-per-case basis, ma'am. I'm sure we can work something out."

Her hand went to her lips and she appeared on the verge of biting her nails. Then she seemed to come to a decision. "I have five hundred dollars I can pay you. Will that be sufficient, sir?"

Sure, Whelan thought, that will cover my fee for two working days, lady. To Mrs. Pritchett, he said, "Yes, ma'am. Five hundred will do it. Now, the real business: what does he look like?"

The woman smiled and a faint blush of relief came into her cheeks, and Whelan hoped he'd find this boy. "He's about five seven or five eight, kind of thin, boy never eats. He's got sandy colored hair and wears it long, sometimes he ties it back. Let me see now, he's got a little scar here," and she touched her chin, "and he has this nasty tattoo of some kind of comet on his right forearm. Paid good money to some fool to put marks on him," she said with distaste.

"What name does he use?"

"Tony Blanchard. Blanchard was his father's name."

"Fine. And I'll need those corners where you saw him and any other place where he used to hang out. You mentioned a video arcade—which one?"

"That one over by the college. On Wilson. Sometimes I think he went to this area where a lot of young people congregate at night, but I don't know where it was. He mentioned a doughnut shop somewhere up by the ballpark once but that's all I know. And he used to go hang out at a little restaurant over by the Uptown Theater."

"What kind of a boy is he?"

"He's a g— —Oh, you must hear that every time somebody asks you to look for a child, but—he is a good boy. He's quiet, and he's very smart, and he's thoughtful about things."

"And when was the last time you heard from him?"

"Christmas. He came by with presents for me. That little Oriental vase on the table, and a bottle of champagne. It was very nice champagne, too." She smiled proudly. Whelan looked at the vase on the side table: Chinese, maybe Vietnamese. The garage she'd mentioned was up near Argyle, and Argyle Street was full of shops. "But I haven't seen that boy since." Her concern had come back.

He looked around at her tidy apartment for a moment. "Mrs. Pritchett, I think if I were a street kid in trouble, I might think about coming back to a place like this and a person like you. It would give me a little edge just knowing I could come back here. And there's a chance he will. If he does, get in touch with me, or with the police."

"I will." Mrs. Pritchett seemed on the verge of asking another question, then caught herself but he read the question in her eyes.

"If something had happened to him, we'd have heard by now. And you said he was smart."

"But he's just a little boy: all these little boys always be thinking they're smart."

Yeah, they all think they're smart, Whelan thought. They're all streetwise.

He stood up and held out his hand. She reached for his hand and then stopped. "Do I pay you something in advance?"

"Not necessary. It'll keep." Now she shook his hand and walked him to the door.

When they reached it, she turned and looked him up and down again as she had when he entered her house. "No scarf, no hat. Men wonder why they get sick so much. At least you had the sense to wear a decent coat."

"I came out in a hurry. Besides, it's supposed to be spring."

"Feel like spring out there to you?"

"I'll do better next time."

Mrs. Pritchett smiled and shook her head.

• • •

He found a pay phone half a block away on Broadway and called Area Six. The detective who answered said "Violent Crimes" the way somebody might announce a flower shop.

"Bauman around?"

"No, sir. Take a message?"

"Yeah, tell him Paul Whelan called. Ask him when he started referring business to me."

There was a pause as the detective wrote down the message, and then a chuckle. "This isn't gonna make him mad at me, is it?"

"Bauman? When did Bauman ever get mad at people?"

"Right," the cop said, and hung up.

It wasn't ten-thirty in the morning yet but the video arcade across from Truman College was packing them in. There were more than a dozen kids crowded into the little box of a room, all of them huddled around video games, the ones with no quarters fixated on the video adventures of the ones with money. Most of the kids were black, some were Latino, a couple white. About half of them looked as though they belonged in school.

A couple of the older-looking ones watched Whelan enter, and he saw one give an elbow to his companion. The second kid turned from the game he'd been staring at and gave Whelan the look. Whelan ignored him.

I'm a busy man, he thought. No time for badass teenagers.

He walked over to the register, where a Middle Eastern-looking man was arguing with a small boy over the probability that a machine had eaten three of the boy's quarters. The man seemed to think it was unlikely, the boy insisted that the machine was alive and ravenous. At Whelan's approach, the man broke off the debate and turned to him.

"Yes, sir? Can I help you?"

"Maybe. I'm looking for someone."

Several of the older kids nearby turned to stare at Whelan and he looked back at them.

"Who you are looking for?" the man asked. "A kid?"

"Yes," Whelan said, still watching a tall black kid who had turned his attention back to a game in which rockets threatened the earth. "His name is Tony Blanchard. He's about sixteen, light-colored hair, wears it long, has a tattoo of a comet on one arm."

The man nodded and looked knowledgeable. "The police were here about him. I know this boy but he's not here. He don't come in lately. Ask them," he said, indicating the kids in his room.

"I will."

Whelan made the circuit of the room and drew one-word answers or blank looks. One kid, no more than thirteen, swore at him when his pinball game ate the last ball.

Whelan handed him a quarter. "Chill out, kid, it's only a game." Mollified, the boy mumbled something and took the quarter.

"Tony Blanchard," Whelan said to him.

The boy shook his head. "Ask Ricardo."

"Which one is Ricardo?"

"The brother over by the door," he said without looking.

Whelan patted him on the shoulder and crossed the room. Ricardo proved to be the tall one who'd been watching him, and now the boy folded his arms and went into one of his poses. He probably had a dozen: this was the "Whatchoo-want-wit-me-now-cop" version.

"Ricardo?"

The boy made a little jerk of his shoulders and looked across the room at the young one who had given up his name.

"Easy there, slim. I'm not a cop."

One eyebrow lifted and told him that Ricardo was a hard sell.

Whelan fished a card out of his shirt pocket. "That's what I do."

Ricardo studied the card and the eyebrow went back to its parking space. He looked at the card longer than he needed to and Whelan knew he was buying time. This was a first for

Ricardo: he'd probably been rousted by every kind of cop and guard and security man, brought in for two dozen offenses, real and imaginary, but never buttonholed by a private detective. The boy's face was a road map of life on the streets: he had fresh scratches on one cheekbone, a slightly swollen left ear and more scar tissue than Tony Zale. It was a bad year for the children of the poor, particularly if they were living on the street. You had to dance faster than the next guy, faster than guys you hadn't even imagined yet.

"I'm looking for Tony Blanchard. I know the cops were here and left empty-handed, and I'm sure everybody had a few chuckles over that. But now it's different. I'm working for a lady that wants to find him. Her name is Pritchett."

Ricardo finally looked up from the card. "That black lady he used to stay with?"

"Yes. She wants to find him."

Ricardo shook his head. "That boy don't want nobody to find him."

"Have you seen him?"

"Nope. Ain't nobody here seen 'im."

"Why do you think he's laying low?"

Ricardo gave him a sardonic look. " 'Cause somebody gon' shoot his ass."

"You know who?"

Ricardo put up both hands as though to ward off trouble. "No, man, I don't know nothing about that shit."

"Who would?"

Ricardo shrugged and looked around the room.

"Any of these kids hang around with Tony?"

"Nobody here."

"Who?"

"White boy named Marty."

"Does Marty come in here?"

"Not no more."

"Where would you look for Marty?"

"I don't look for nobody."

Whelan rooted around in his pants pocket and came up

with a couple of singles. He put them in Ricardo's palm. Ricardo looked at the singles, then at Whelan.

"Got a cigarette?"

Whelan gave him a smoke and a light, and the man behind the counter yelled that they had to go outside if they wanted to smoke. Ricardo pushed his way out onto Wilson Avenue and Whelan followed him out.

"You've got my number on the card. If he shows up, use it."

Ricardo glanced up and down the street and tried to look bored. Another pose, and the kid had this one nailed, too.

Two

The day had gone raucous in his absence. A *Sun-Times* delivery truck had tried to pass a cab on Lawrence and had taken off a few layers of the cab's paint. The cabbie and the truck driver stood a few feet apart and gesticulated dramatically for the crowd that assembled hoping to see a fight or something exotic. Two doors west of Whelan's building, Sam Carlos and a dark, curly-haired man stood next to a fruit market truck and bellowed into each other's faces. In his right hand, Sam held a bruised nectarine or peach as a prop, and as Whelan watched, the devious little grocer squeezed the fruit till its pulp squirted out between his fingers. He held it up and pointed to it and the other man shook his head and yelled something in what sounded like Greek. Their noses were almost touching, an Uptown Eskimo kiss, and finally Sam broke off the discussion by tossing the nectarine at the window of the other man's truck. He missed. The nectarine sailed on over the truck and found its own target with a wet splattery sound. From the knot of people watching the other altercation Whelan heard an angry yell and grinned over at Sam.

"Nice shot, Sam."

Carlos said "Oh-oh," looked at Whelan, waved and went back into his notorious little grocery, where nectarines like the one he'd just flung at a neighbor went for a buck apiece on a good day and buying meat could be an adventure. In the grocery store of Sam Carlos, an Armenian passing himself off as a Puerto Rican, once a food item hit his shelves, it gained eternal life.

The coffee in his bag was probably getting cold. Whelan took one last look at the cabbie and the deliveryman and went inside his building. At least the squirrel was gone.

He hadn't opened the door yet before he realized he had company. The air in the dusty hall was ripe with the smells of Right Guard and bad cigars. He sighed.

The man in the guest chair in Whelan's inner office gave no sign that he was aware of Whelan entering. He went on smoking, as he'd apparently been for some time and, predictably, without opening a window. The man sat in the chair as if it belonged to him. And, Whelan knew, the man probably believed that he owned it as he felt he owned the streets. Whelan closed the door behind him, crossed the outer office to his desk and slid into the chair. He set the bag with his cup of coffee on the desk. His visitor was a big man, with brush-cut brown hair shot with gray. He wore a thick gray wool coat with dust on one shoulder, and beneath it, a brown polyester sport coat with lapels like a pair of wings, a jacket out of style mere minutes after it came out of a factory in Korea. Smiling slightly, the visitor stretched, showing a vast expanse of stomach just barely held in by the orange knit shirt.

"Got a new water cooler, huh? Prosperity's a helluva thing."

"Right, and you've got a new shirt."

"Yeah. Like it?"

"Sure. You look like a three-hundred-pound sunburst. The last time I saw that shade of orange, it was on a pumpkin."

A smile played at the corners of the man's mouth but he swallowed it. "Yeah, and I'm wild about your clothes too, Whelan. Salvation Army had another sale?"

Whelan didn't answer. He got up and opened the window onto Lawrence. A chill pushed its way into the room and brought with it street noises and the smell of diesel fuel from a passing truck.

"Hey, you wanna gimme a cold?"

"I figured if I let it get cold, you'd be more inclined not to dick me around and you'd come to the point faster." Whelan pried off the lid and took a sip of his coffee. It was still scalding, and he set it down quickly.

"Whatsamatter, Whelan? I can't visit my local private operative to shoot the shit?"

"You got my message?"

"Yeah, I got your message. What's there to tell? I send you a nice lady who's got a runaway for you to find and you wanna know why?"

Whelan took out his cigarettes, Bauman shook his head. "Dogshit habit. Those are bad for you," he said. His big hand went inside the sport coat and came out holding a pack of skinny cigars.

"Oh, no. Here, wait," Whelan said. "I bought you a present."

"You missed Christmas by four months."

"For next Christmas, then. Just don't light up one of those little nasty things."

"Aw, you're gettin' fussy on me."

"That's right. They smell like snakeshit. Here." He slid open the desk drawer and came out with a cigar in a long narrow silver case. He slid it across the table at Bauman.

Detective Albert Bauman squinted at him, tilted his head to one side and said, "What's the deal, Shamus?"

"I already told you. You don't want it, leave it, but don't light up one of those things. After you leave, my office always smells like somebody died in it."

Bauman picked up the cigar case, studied the label, then opened it. With the air of a man settling down to a fine dinner he held the cigar to his nose for a moment, took it away, then sniffed at it again. He made a little nod toward Whelan.

"That's nice. Maybe I don't care what the catch is."

He bit off the end, took the wet tobacco in his fingers and deposited it carefully in Whelan's ashtray. Then he raised his eyebrows and grinned. "What? You thought I was gonna spit it out on the floor, right?"

Whelan smiled. "Wouldn't have surprised me."

Bauman shook his head. "You're gonna smoke these things, you have to do it properly. Same with drinking. You want to drink good booze, you better know how to act."

Whelan studied the little red splashes in Bauman's cheeks, the swollen red tissue of his nose, and decided not to answer. He watched Bauman hold a match to the far end of the cigar and puff away. In seconds the office was filled with the powerful aroma of genuine leaf tobacco.

"So where'd you park Detective Landini and his gold chains and his pungent gentleman's cologne?"

"You don't like the way he smells either, huh, Whelan? I sent him on an errand. I just told him I was coming up here to look up my friend Paul Whelan the Sleuth and he decided to go check out a couple people we need to talk to."

"He's not real fond of me."

"Don't take it personally." Bauman indicated the office with a wave of the cigar. "Nah, it's this. He don't know why he has to associate with somebody livin', you know..."

"On the fringe? The lunatic fringe, maybe?"

"I guess you could call it that. He still don't understand a guy that was wearing the blue and pretty good at it, and then just dropped it for this."

"And you do?"

"Do I care?" Bauman made a little shrug and took a long pull off the cigar. After a long moment, he exhaled; thick gray smoke came out of his mouth and both nostrils.

"You're not supposed to inhale cigars, Bauman."

"All of a sudden you're an expert on cigars, Whelan? Or you're a doctor maybe? Lotta people inhale cigars."

Whelan put up both hands in an "I surrender" pose. "Okay, let's talk. How come you sent Mrs. Pritchett to see me?"

"So she could, uh, avail herself of your hot-shit detective skills. How's that? Your legendary, uh, cognitive powers." He grinned. "To get her outta my hair, all right?" Bauman puffed at the cigar, took it out, looked lovingly at it. "That's real nice, Whelan. Need a nice whiskey to go with this—but it's a little early."

"For you?" Whelan snorted. "All right, tell me about this kid."

"He's dead." The cigar went back into his mouth and smoke came out.

"Did you tell her that?"

"I told her what the real skinny was, Whelan. I told her

there was a good shot that we ain't gonna find this kid. This Tony Blanchard, he was no choirboy. Street kid."

"I know that much already. And most of them are harmless."

"Some of 'em. But this kid wasn't hanging around in the record stores, Whelan. He was a runner for a bunch of fucking thieves. Bad things happened to the people he was hanging around and now nobody's seen him."

"*Things?* You mean like homicides?"

Bauman shrugged. "Hey, it comes from writing reports. Interferes with my beautiful command of the language. Yeah, we got three, four homicides that we think are connected."

"*We?* Walking the party line on this one? That's a new wrinkle."

Bauman made a half shrug. "They gotta be right sometime."

"And Tony Blanchard worked with these people."

"More or less."

"What does *that* mean?"

"Like I said, he was a runner. Errand boy."

"And do we have a theory about why these guys were killed?"

"Everybody's got theories, Whelan."

"And would you like to share one with me?"

"No."

"Might help."

"Don't see how. Got nothing to do with you."

"But you think the boy is dead."

"No question. All the grownups he was hanging around with wind up dead, what are the chances he's still around? He was supposed to be smart, Whelan, but none of 'em are that smart."

"So you sent me this nice lady, and I'm supposed to take her money and look around for a kid that's dead, and then I'm the one that breaks it to her."

"You'll do a better job checkin' it out than we will. We got no time for street kids, Whelan. I'm looking for the guy that took out all these other people, I got no time to look for this nice lady's kid. It's not even her own kid, for Christ's sake."

Whelan sat back and watched Bauman for a moment. A familiar feeling had come to him, a feeling from poker games, an unpleasant feeling usually associated with the loss of money, self-esteem, intellectual balance.

"*You* think the kid's alive."

"I don't *think* shit, Whelan. If this kid is alive, I think I sent this lady to the right guy. This is you, Whelan, this is right up your alley, roamin' the streets and playin' in the mud makin' new friends among the street guys and lowlifes. Figure it this way, if he's dead, somebody'll probably find a body and then we'll be the ones that gotta tell the lady. If he's still around, you'll find out—and then you can tell me and maybe it'll do me some good."

"What'll it do for me?"

Bauman grinned. "You'll earn the gratitude of the Department. Maybe get an honorary badge or something." Bauman seemed to have an afterthought. "And as for taking the lady's money, if you find the kid, you won't feel bad about it. If you don't...you're a grown man, Whelan, you got a conscience."

Whelan sighed, stared at Bauman and said, "Last seen?"

A long slow shrug. "Four, five weeks."

Whelan said nothing and Bauman took a puff at the cigar, then stole a quick look at him.

"Well, you're right. It doesn't sound too promising, Bauman. You give me a kid who's known to associate with several people that have already wound up dead and then you tell me he hasn't been seen in maybe a month. Sounds like this boy's dead."

"Like I said. So. What else you need from me, there, Shamus?"

"I got a description from Mrs. Pritchett. Any place you think I should look?"

"He's a kid, Whelan. Look wherever fine youths congregate at night. We looked but you oughtta look yourself. Sometimes people don't wanta talk to me. Maybe they'll talk to you, Whelan."

"Gee, why wouldn't they want to talk to you?" Bauman gave no sign that he'd heard but Whelan knew better. Bauman got to his feet. He stared for a moment at the almost two-inch cylinder of ash about to drop from the end of his cigar.

"Supposed to be the sign of a good cigar, you know. How long you can keep the ash from falling off." He made an all-but-imperceptible movement and the ash fell onto Whelan's carpet.

"Whoops!" he said, happily. "Well, I'll be in touch, Whelan."

Whelan stared at the little cone of ash on his floor and didn't look up till Bauman was at the door. "Okay, Albert."

The detective paused with the door half open and glared at Whelan for a two-count. "Don't call me that."

Whelan smiled. "I keep forgetting."

Detective Albert Bauman was still glaring when he left the office.

Whelan sipped at the coffee, staring at the list of names and addresses, and wondered just what kind of con Detective Albert Bauman had going. "Only one way I'm going to find out," he said to the office furniture.

The first stop was not a known hangout for street kids: the Sulzer Library just west of Uptown. On the second floor, he cast a quick glance at the younger of the two librarians, a willowy young woman with auburn hair. He'd noticed her before and the look he saw in her eyes seemed to suggest that she'd noticed him. Turning toward the microfilm section, he put the thought from his mind. Who needs more trouble, he thought.

In the past year and a half, Whelan had experienced two moments when it seemed that a woman was coming into his life for something more serious than the occasional exotic dinner. The first, a cheerful, even-tempered woman named Pat, had faded from his life when her ex-husband had come back to her after an absence of more than seven years. He thought about her seldom, primarily from a sense of self-preservation.

The second person to break into his bachelor preserve was an introspective woman named Sandra McAuliffe, whom he'd known for seven months. There were times when they seemed to be gravitating toward something permanent, and others when her deep mood changes or his long hours of silent preoccupation drove wedges into their evenings together and made them glad to be rid of one another. She was a tall, big-boned woman with dull blond hair shot with a trace of silver:

she was also two years older than Whelan. Her age made no difference to him but he thought it bothered her. She was intelligent, well read, laughed easily when the mood was on her and was the best company in bed he'd ever had. There were moments when his years of solitude seemed to catch up with him and he was desperate to be alone, but in the months he'd known her, he hadn't made it through a day without thinking of her. She loved his restaurants and the odd city places he showed her; she made him laugh, introduced him to new writers and cooked for him. She also drew into herself once a month and picked fights without warning. A brief, sharp argument a week ago had put distance between them once again, and he hadn't called or heard from her.

Whelan allowed himself a quick look at the red-haired woman. She met his gaze for a moment and then looked past him, and he told himself it was time to go to work.

It took him no time at all to find what he was looking for: the kind of story he was interested in always ran within the first half-dozen pages. In twenty minutes he'd found the story in both the *Tribune* and the *Sun-Times*. In another half hour, from references in the first story he'd tracked down the earlier ones.

The homicides—Bauman's "things"—had occurred in the last week of February and the first three weeks of March.

They were young, these dead men, one of them little more than a teenager: Mathew Makowski, 20, Barry "Chick" Nelson, 32, Rory Martin, 30. Northwest-side addresses were given for Makowski and Nelson, but the initial information on Martin was vague. That the killings were related was obvious from the circumstances—the three knew each other, all had previous records and were believed to have been involved in an organized form of burglary and occasional car theft. Police were said to be investigating a related matter, the possible homicide of the group's leader, a man named Jimmy Lee Hayes. Hayes's blue Grand Am had been abandoned near a small strip of park along the Chicago River. An anonymous tip had given the police the car's location and the paper hinted without really saying it, that the body had been pushed into the river.

Makowski, the first victim, had been shot at close range with a .22 caliber gun; the other two had been stabbed to death with what was described as a long thin blade—but just in case the reader missed the connection, both papers ran helpful leads, referring to a "string of brutal knife murders" and "a bloody series of gangland executions."

Whelan almost missed the final piece of information, and soon wished he had. He was going through the various accounts one last time when he noticed a slight change, given without further explanation. In the *Tribune* account of April 12, the dead men were listed with aliases: "Mathew Makowski, also known as Mathew Blair, Barry Nelson, and Rory Byrne, also known as Rory Martin," and Paul Whelan felt the wind leave his lungs.

He sat back in the chair and looked out the high window where he could see the heavy gray sky. In his mind's eye he saw a group of young boys sitting on the rocks at Addison, surrounded by baseball gloves and a half-dozen battered Louisville Sluggers. One by one, the boys peeled off sweaty T-shirts and dove into the cold lake, then crawled out onto the rocks again, hyperventilating from the icy water. Even at this distance, he could make out the faces of a young skinny Paul Whelan and the handsome Bobby Hansen and Artie Shears and a half-dozen others, including a moody boy named Mickey Byrne, along with Artie Shears one of his favorites, always one of his favorites. A thin dark-eyed boy given to long thoughtful silences and almost always shadowed by his baby brother, Rory. Parents died early and the boys went to live with an elderly aunt, and from near-poverty to the real thing. A pair of troubled children with no luck. And now they were both gone: Mick had come back from Vietnam with a mind on the verge of collapse. A year after his discharge he'd been in a mental hospital in Seattle, and a little later, Whelan had heard from a mutual friend that Mick was living in alleys and gangways. Later, news reached him that Mickey Byrne had made it to Portland, and he was going to go no farther: Mick had been admitted to a VA hospital for tuberculosis.

What Whelan remembered most about Mickey Byrne was his fierce loyalty, to his friends and especially to his little brother, a pugnacious boy in constant trouble. He wondered how Mick would have taken this final hard news.

He couldn't be certain how Bauman had made the connection between himself and Rory Byrne but he was certain Bauman knew. Why he had decided to involve Whelan was still an open question, but there could be no mistake about his intentions: there was no such thing as coincidence where Detective Albert Bauman was involved.

Whelan gave a distracted nod to the woman at the circulation desk as he left. He went across the street and into Wells Park, found an empty bench and had a cigarette. He hadn't been close to Rory Byrne—there had been too great a difference in age between them, but the news was disturbing. Again and again his thoughts went back to that little knot of boys sunning themselves on the rocks, hard-luck boys some of them, and he was reminded of the death of Artie Shears, who had been his closest childhood friend. He thought about Artie, dead in an Uptown alley and Rory Byrne and Mickey, and by the time he'd finished his cigarette, he'd begun to shiver. He realized that he was angry as well, and fought his sudden impulse to call Bauman: plenty of time for that later. First, he wanted to see if he could come up with something that Bauman didn't know.

Logic said to hit the group home next, but one of the places Mrs. Pritchett had mentioned was a sandwich shop that Whelan had been in once or twice, a little place on Broadway a couple doors from the Uptown Theater, and Whelan had a hunch about it. As he drove east from the library, he remembered stopping in the place once in the evening and seeing a group of teenage boys crowded into a back booth. None of them could have been more than sixteen or seventeen, and he wondered now if one of them had been Tony Blanchard.

The smells of an overworked deep fryer and a grill in constant use struck Whelan as soon as he pulled open the door. A double row of green Naugahyde booths ran parallel to a gleaming white counter with perhaps one patron for every three stools. On the far side of the counter a thin pale man scraped at the grill surface and bopped to the country music coming from the jukebox. He had three patties of meat sizzling in the center of the grill, with the buns lined up alongside them. A few inches away, he had three eggs taking shape. A huge pile of onions sat to one side and slowly went opaque.

He took a seat across from the grill, for the sheer enjoyment of watching a short-order cook at work. Down the counter, a middle-aged woman with dyed red hair in a net tore off a bill and put it down in front of a man who just nodded when she called him "Sweetie." She moved soundlessly down the counter to Whelan.

"Coffee, hon?"

He nodded. Any place where the help called you "hon" was worth the support of the community. "Sure."

She padded off to the coffee machine and came back to pour his coffee. A little blue tag on the front of her blouse said her name was Helen. "Can I get you anything else?"

"No, but I'd like to ask you a question." He took out his business card and laid it on the counter. Helen studied it for a moment and lines appeared on her forehead that hadn't been there before. "It's not about you," he added.

She shot a glance at the cook, more to see if her orders were up than to see if he was listening, then gave Whelan a short nod.

"I'm looking for a boy who hangs out around here. His name is Tony Blanchard. Know him?"

She met his eyes for a moment and then said, "I know a Tony."

"Average height, light brown hair that he wears kind of long, tattoo of a comet on this arm." Whelan tapped his right forearm and looked at her.

She pursed her lips and seemed on the verge of shaking her head when her honesty got the upper hand. "Right. What about him?"

"Have you seen him lately?"

"What's 'lately'?"

"Last couple of weeks."

"No," she said quickly and relaxed. "Haven't seen him."

"Would you tell me if you had?" He raised his eyebrows and the waitress fought off a smile. Whelan took a sip of his coffee. It was scalding and black and thick, and the little place had his attention. "Well, now," he said to himself. To her, he said, "Good coffee."

"We grind our own beans," she said. "And no."

"Pardon?"

"No, I wouldn't tell you." She pointed to the card still lying on the counter. "That don't mean anything. You're not a cop, I don't have to talk to you. People usually talk to you when you show them that card?"

"Yeah. But first they say they've never met a real private eye before."

"My ex hired one. And he was an asshole, pardon my French."

"Burgers up," the cook muttered.

"The detective, or your former spouse?"

"The both of 'em," she said, and smiled.

"Burgers up," the cook said, louder. He stirred and scraped a little pool of eggs in the center and half turned to stare at her.

"And so's he," Helen said and jerked a thumb in the cook's direction. She looked at Whelan expectantly and then laughed. "Excuse me. If I don't jump when Napoleon here tells me to jump, he's gonna have a baby."

She turned slowly and met the cook's stare, and soon he found the scrambled eggs interesting. The waitress picked up the three plates waiting at the grill's edge and walked down the counter, sliding one plate toward each of three waiting diners. A moment later she returned to Whelan.

"So what do you want with that boy?"

"I want to find him."

"Why?"

"It's what I do. My specialty. People come to me and ask me to find somebody. I don't follow people's wives and I don't peep into keyholes. If you don't want to talk to me, somebody else will—eventually." After a second's pause, he added, "I hope."

She leaned up against the counter and studied him, and he had a chance to do the same. Up close he could see that she was nearer to sixty than forty but she'd probably been something special in her time.

"And when you find him, then what?"

"Then I tell the lady who hired me. And I have to tell the police. They'll want to question the kid but as far as I know he's not a suspect in anything."

She was shaking her head as soon as she heard "police."

"But I don't think I'm going to have to talk to them, because I don't think I'm going to find him."

"Why is that?" she asked, pretending to sort her checks.

"Because I think he's dead."

The woman blinked twice and then looked away. Some of the color was gone from her face and the heavy makeup now just made her look older.

"Maybe I'm wrong. But the police have been looking for him and he hasn't turned up in weeks so…" When she said nothing, Whelan took another sip of his coffee.

"He's just a kid. He's not sixteen yet, I don't think."

"I know. I think he started hanging around with the wrong people, and several of them wound up dead."

"Who were they?"

Whelan recited the names to her. "Ring any bells?"

"No. These are kids?"

"No. Adults. Grown men. Youngest one was twenty."

She nodded as though confirming a suspicion. "I never saw him with no men. Just other boys."

"Like who?"

She shot him a quick look but it was too late. "I don't know their names."

"You know him but you don't know anybody he hung out with? That make any sense at all to you?"

She looked past him and seemed to be watching something out on the street. Whelan fed her a line.

"I know he was living with another boy for a while, or with

the boy and his brother." Something moved in her face and she looked away.

"Who was that boy, Helen? Was that Marty?"

She met his eyes finally. "Yeah, Marty. He stayed with Marty sometimes. He didn't have no family, Tony. He stayed with different people sometimes. This boy Marty lives with his brother over on Winthrop." He wanted to ask her about the other boys but had a feeling that she'd given him the most likely place to start looking.

"Got an address or a last name?"

Helen hesitated and then said "Wills" in a resigned voice. "I don't know his address." She shook her head and Whelan wondered whether she was more upset over the possibility of the boy's death or the fact that she was giving out information.

"If it helps any, Helen, I'm good at what I do. If he's out there I'll find him and nothing'll happen to him, and that will be because you helped me."

She nodded and looked around. Then she seemed to have an afterthought. "How come people got you looking for him? How come the cops can't find him theirselves?"

"Hard to say. Sometimes people talk to me when they won't talk to a cop."

"Maybe that's smart. We get the beat cops in here, they're okay. But one time a detective comes in here and starts pushin' everybody around, and I told 'im to go piss in the wind. Big fat one, this was."

"Crew cut, ugly clothes."

"That's the one. You know him, huh?"

"Yeah, I sure do."

"Ain't he a damn blowhard."

"That's a pretty fair assessment. He could use a little more polish."

"Honey, I know what *he* could use, and it ain't polish." Helen allowed herself a hard smile and then moved away as a diner a few feet down the counter held up his empty coffee cup.

When Whelan finished his coffee, he left her a couple of singles for her trouble. In the chilly little space between the inner and street doors, there was a pay phone with a phone book. He paged through it rapidly and found a Daniel Wills on the 4700 block of Winthrop. As he pushed his way out onto the cold street, Whelan reflected on the waitress's spirited description of Detective Albert Bauman and understood why Bauman had left this particular interview to Whelan.

Three

There were trees on this block of Winthrop, three of them, and one of them looked as if it might still be alive, but they were the only things that grew here. The green had been scoured from what had once been lawns, and windows were patched with masking tape and the flaps from cardboard boxes, and doors hung loose from their hinges. The buildings lining both sides of the street were big, heavy brick affairs that, like much of Uptown, had once been showpieces, the homes of the upper middle class and even the well-to-do. Now the buildings were owned, like the dog-eared office building where Whelan himself rented space, by people who lived as far from the city as they could get and counted money for their hobby, never venturing into town till the city managed on the rarest of occasions to summon them for court appearances to explain a thousand and one violations.

There were people in many of the windows, some of them white, most of them black. In one window, a group of big-eyed brown skinned children sat with an older woman dressed in a sari. The people in the windows stared at Whelan and he thought a few may have wondered about him, but most were probably just wondering when their luck would change.

The address he was looking for proved to be a red-brick apartment building of six units, with rounded sides and turrets at the north and south ends of the roof. The gray marble around the front door and the scrollwork just under the roof told him that it had once given itself airs but now realized it was just another Uptown tenement. He parked and went up the stairs.

At the door, he rang the bell marked WILLS—1B and got no answer. He tried the door and it opened immediately. Nothing like a little security if you lived in a tough neighborhood. At the door to 1B he listened for a moment. Inside someone was listening to rock music. Whelan waited and then knocked twice.

Over the music, a man's voice yelled out "Yeah? Who's there?"

"Dan?"

"Yeah…who's that?"

"It's Paul Whelan."

"Paul who?"

"Whelan. It's about Tony."

The music died and Whelan heard nothing for several seconds. Then a chair scraped along linoleum and he heard several footsteps in the direction of the door.

"He ain't here. He don't stay here no more."

"We know that, sir," Whelan said calmly. "We'd like to ask you some questions."

The man's confusion was audible, then he crossed the room to the door and opened it six inches. A pair of large dark eyes looked Whelan up and down. "Yeah?" the man asked, a little more quietly.

"I need to ask you a few questions about Tony, Mr. Wills."

The eyes moved down to Whelan's hand, as though expecting to see the badge.

"I'm not a cop. And none of this is about you."

The door opened wider and Whelan got a look at the man inside. He was in his middle to late twenties, medium height, with a blotched complexion and dark uncombed hair that hung down his face and nearly obscured one eye. He was thin and there were dark brownish circles under his eyes and he smelled of cigarette smoke.

The picture of bad health, Whelan thought. "Can I come in?" he asked.

"If you're not the Man, I don't have to talk to you."

"No, but this would be a good way to save yourself trouble down the line. If you don't talk to me, you *will* talk to them sooner or later."

The man muttered something like "Aw, fuck me," and

swung the door open. He walked back into his home and fell rather than sat on a sofa. Whelan followed him in and pushed the door shut behind him. On the floor near the sofa was a can of beer. Wills noticed Whelan staring at it.

"I'm fucked up from last night."

"You look pretty sick. Okay, let's make it fast, then. Your brother Marty hangs around with Tony Blanchard and Tony stays here sometimes."

"No, man, he don't flop here no more. Got his own crib."

"Where?"

"I don't know."

"Does Marty know?"

"I don't know, ask him." Wills shook his head and took a sip of his beer. He groaned and lay back on the couch.

"Okay, where can I find him?"

Wills squinted up at him and tried to retrace his steps. "No, he don't know nothing about Tony, man. I just. . .you know. Hey, I'm real sick." He lit up a cigarette. Whelan shook his head: great hangover remedy. Beer and a cigarette before lunch.

"I told you before, I'm not a cop. Somebody wants to find Tony, and if I can't find him, this person will probably bring in the police, then you'll be talking to them. I need to find Tony. I have no other interest in you or your brother. This person I'm working for didn't come right out and say it, but he thinks Tony may be in some trouble. The kind that affects a guy's health."

Wills stared at him and then nodded. He took a pull at his cigarette, a sip of his beer, then belched. "He's in trouble, all right. He been running with wrong fucking dudes and some bad shit went down, and now the shit's hittin' the fan, you know what I'm saying?"

No, I speak only English, Whelan thought. "Yeah," he said. "Jimmy Lee Hayes. Those people."

Wills pointed a finger at him. "There you go, man. And I ain't gettin' into that shit, no way I'm gettin' into that shit. I never had nothing to do with their whole fucking program."

"Nobody thinks you did. Now Marty—"

"Marty didn't do nothing for them. Tony did, and now he's

in deep shit. Look, man, Marty can't tell you where Tony is."

"He might be able to give me somebody who can. Where can I find him?"

Danny Wills sighed. "He's at work. Works at that place across from the Jewel. The cajun chicken place."

"Larry's? On Montrose?"

"Yeah."

"Thanks, Mr. Wills."

"Keep him outta this shit."

"I will."

"Okay, man. Cool." Wills nodded and then, apparently experiencing a relapse, fell back on the couch.

"Hope you make it," Whelan said as he left.

He drove the long way, back up Lawrence and onto Broadway, a route calculated to take him past the melancholy site of his favorite local establishment, the most bizarre of all restaurants, the late, lamented House of Zeus, now shut down by order of the City of Chicago. What he saw there made Whelan pull into the first parking space he found. Then he got out and crossed Broadway to take a closer look.

The audaciously purple curtains were open, the orange lights were on, the smells of Greek, Persian and American food battled and rose in a gray cloud from the tiny grill near the back, dazed-looking customers stood at the counter waiting forever to order: the House of Zeus was open—again.

Things are looking up, Whelan told himself.

The last time he'd walked down Broadway, a notice from the Board of Health had been affixed to the door and the House of Zeus had been closed, a casualty in a bloody but ultimately one-sided conflict between the restaurant's mad Iranian owners on the one hand, and the City of Chicago on the other. Or, if you listened to the proprietors, Rashid and his cousin Gus, the conflict was between good and evil, or between the ancient and cherished culture of Persia and the tasteless barbarism of America. They tended to lean heavily on the good-versus-evil theme, for the other seemed insincere even to them, given their "Streets-paved-with-gold-or-at-least-dollar-bills" attitude toward their adopted country.

The trouble had come as no surprise to Whelan, arising as it did from what he saw as the natural conflict between the City of Chicago's health code and the Persian boys' murky notions about cleanliness. Whelan himself had witnessed the start of the problem, a brief but memorable encounter with a health inspector. The boys had tried out a few of their more outrageous excuses and alibis on the inspector, a pinch-faced man with the animation of a cadaver, and that gentleman had responded by citing the House of Zeus for several dozen health violations, notably the absence of any rigorously applied plan of hygiene and the sale of rotten meat. A guerrilla war had ensued.

Gus and Rashid had hired *their* cousin Reza to sue all manner of government entities, including the governor of Illinois, on the grounds of harassment—though what sort of harassment was never made clear. City inspectors overran the House of Zeus, violations were tabulated, citations made, additional suits were filed by the tireless Reza, suggesting racism, anti-Iranian feeling, corruption and malfeasance. A half-hearted attempt by a minor inspector to glom onto a little extra cash became a flashpoint. In Reza's febrile worldview, all human interaction was nothing more than dueling conspiracies, one cabal colliding with another, and the dapper little barrister was quick to label the inspector's request for a handout as a vast extortion scheme reaching to the fifth floor of City Hall.

The mayor lost his temper: more inspectors showed up, in squadrons. They examined the pipes and the cracks in the ceiling, the sidewalks and the stairs, the lead content in the paint and the condition of the boiler.

After a month of citations and accusations, letters to the editors of all possible newspapers, appearances on local newscasts and even a feeble show at picketing outside the mayor's office by a tiny group of Iranian women, mostly relatives of Gus and Rashid, the City shut down the House of Zeus. A last-minute attempt by the cousins to secure an appearance on *The Oprah Winfrey Show* was fruitless. Thus Chicago's only Iranian-run Greek restaurant fell before the unleashed might of City government. Like its predecessor, the Persian A & W, the House of Zeus was but a culinary memory, and Paul Whelan had thought his heart would break.

One winter morning, Whelan had run into Reza downtown, and had asked what was going on with the restaurant. Reza, resplendent in a leather coat and matching cap, took a colorful pose in the middle of the crowded sidewalk, hands on his hips, feet wide apart, and told Whelan and anyone within twenty feet that the war was far from over.

"You have not seen last word of this one, Mr. Detective Whelan. I have more tricks up my coat, yes. We will fight this one out in courts of America, one little business run by political refugees standing up to fight entire government of city."

"Well, good luck."

"We will have good luck, and more important, excellent legal counsel. First-rate counsel."

"How can you lose?" Whelan asked.

Whelan had watched the little Persian lawyer trot off, smiling to himself over his grand plan to bring down the government.

And now the House of Zeus was open.

Whelan stepped inside, smelled the familiar, slightly rancid odors of the grill, the deep fryer whose oil was never changed, the huge conical chunk of *gyros* turning slowly on a spit. He looked around and reassured himself that it was all still here: the ugly leatherette chairs, the little plastic red food baskets left over from the old A & W, the bloody murals on three sides showing Persian warriors butchering Greeks.

At the counter, people were murmuring about the service and Rashid was shouting at them from the grill, and Gus ducked his head out from the back room. He had a cleaver in one hand and a look in his eye that bespoke hatred for either his fellow man or his cousin.

"Hi, Rashid. Hi, Gus. Just like old times, huh?"

Both of the proprietors turned at once and grinned at him.

"Hello, Detective. You see we are back!" Rashid yelled. His little paper cap chose that moment to slip from his hair and fall onto the cheeseburger he was making, and Whelan heard a man at the counter mutter, "Damn, I'm glad I didn't order a hamburger."

Gus emerged with his cleaver and Rashid approached the counter with the hamburger on a spatula. He tossed it in a basket on top of a mound of fries and handed it to a middle-aged woman without looking at her. She frowned at her burger and walked away with it, shaking her head.

Rashid showed his many teeth in a grin and threw his arms open wide. "You see! We are back on top."

"That's one way of looking at it."

"Hey, how 'bout some service here?" a man at the counter growled.

Rashid gave the man a look that suggested they belonged to different species and then pointed to Whelan. "You cannot wait for one moment while I talk to my friend? This man is detective, he is important man in community."

The five people left in line all turned on cue to have a look at Whelan. From their facial expressions, he could tell they weren't impressed.

"I don't care who he is," the first man said.

"I don't care if he yo' mama," a young black man said.

Rashid faced the line of customers with his hands on his skinny hips and stared at them, giving them the full force of his contempt. He glared, showing them the anger of ancient Persia. They were unmoved. Whelan could almost hear Rashid's thought processes: half a dozen customers at four or five bucks a pop. Rashid relaxed, showed them all his teeth, shrugged and said, "Everyone is in hurry in Chicago. Okay."

He took orders and continued to grin, and Gus came over to the counter. "He's gonna lose all our customers, this one. Then we'll be closed for good."

"But I'm glad you're back. What happened?"

"It is the will of God," Rashid yelled over from the grill.

Gus sneered at him. "There was problem, we fixed. Little problems, no big deal."

"Seemed like a big deal when you were trying to sue the mayor and the governor at the same time. I think I heard the word 'conspiracy' a few times."

Gus laughed. "That was Reza's idea. He is lawyer, they are not normal. Lawyer's mind is not normal mind. Lawyer's mind is like…" Gus looked off into the distance, groping for more English and finally gave up. "Lawyers, they are strange. All lawyers, everywhere."

"So how did you 'fix' the trouble?"

Gus shrugged. "We fixed all trouble. We clean up kitchen, we buy new coolers, we fix pipes in toilet so now this one, it can flush, even in cold weather." He scratched under his paper cap, considering the many improvements. "We took class in restaurant management, class in hygiene so this *poisoner*…" Here he turned to stare at his cousin, who shot him an evil look. "… can't kill people with his food."

Rashid straightened up from his grill and pointed at Gus with a spatula. "You want to see poison, Gholam? You want poison? Look in your lunch today. You will see poison. I will spit on your food, I will put slime from under stove on your—"

"Hey, I'm trying to eat here," a customer yelled from a side table.

Gus leaned closer to Whelan and lowered his voice. "It is true. He is poisoner. The health inspector, the one who made all trouble, Rashid tried to poison him. Tried to give him bad food here."

Rashid, scraping the surface of the grill, said nothing, but his grin showed that he had heard.

"Rashid?" Whelan said.

"It is joke," he said, still scraping at the grill. "He makes jokes. Who dies from my food? Name one."

Whelan stared at Gholam for a moment and shook his head. "So you fixed the place up and behaved like good boys? You're telling me that's all it took? Nothing else, Gus?"

Gus sighed. "Maybe we pay a little money."

"Fines."

"Yes, fines and…you know…" Gus made a motion as if peeling bills off a stack.

Whelan laughed. "The Chinese call it 'squeeze.' The hoodlums call it vigorish. A fine Chicago tradition: a modest gift of currency to your favorite local officials."

Gus hung his head and Whelan saw that the "gifts" had not been so modest.

"It's okay, Gus. You made it through, you're in business, and the city teems with folks who've never had Shalimar kabab. Speaking of which, I need lunch. I'll have a falafel sandwich and an order of rings, and a root beer."

When he was finished, and reasonably certain that the universe had stabilized itself, Whelan strolled out onto Broadway, and lit a cigarette. He walked a few paces and stopped to peer into the window of the African import shop. The window displayed crafts from a half dozen or so different African countries, including kente cloth caps and handbags, beadwork, little statues in a dark wood and boats of various sizes carved in a light wood and peopled with little crew members. Whelan was toying with the idea of buying the biggest of the boats, a two-foot-long affair with a dozen rowers on each side, and trying to get a better look at the price tag. The tag proved to be upside down. The store was in darkness, so he checked the hours posted on the door and decided to come back another time. As he turned, he saw the car and wondered how long it had been on his tail.

"Well, here's a surprise," Whelan said.

The gray Caprice was parked in a good spot, on the far side of Broadway and halfway up the block. Only somebody used to seeing it would actually have picked it out, but Whelan was used to seeing it. Even at this distance, the two figures in the front seat of the Caprice were a mismatched pair, the one on the passenger side a lot bigger and heavier than the driver. The Caprice was positioned to pull out into traffic as soon as Whelan drove past.

Whelan looked at his car, then shrugged. He pretended to watch a couple of kids arguing over money, then moved on to the corner on foot, where he made a sharp turn onto Leland. The Caprice was still a couple of car lengths past the corner, so they'd have to go around the block to head him off. He shook off the impulse to duck into the alley: a few feet down this alley, in another time, they'd found the body of Artie Shears. Instead he walked on and found a sunken gangway between an apartment building and a two-flat and went down the steps. After a ten-count, the Caprice came up Leland and he could see Landini peering over the steering column. Bauman, a little more used to Whelan's ways, was just shaking his head and looking into the gangways and halls.

"See you guys later," Whelan said to himself. He watched the Caprice turn south on Broadway and then emerged from the steps.

The signs painted on all the windows of Larry's Dog 'n Chicken Shack bragged of a menu of broasted and Cajun chicken, ribs and rib tips, burgers, Polish, hot dogs, and corn dogs, the latter labeled "specialty of the house." The faces behind the counter were Korean, all but one, for there was no Larry running "Larry's." This was after all Uptown, where a couple of deranged Iranians could run a Greek restaurant, and a Vietnamese family could run Chop Suey Kitchen, and the New Yankee Grill had a Greek guy dishing up the Denver omelets, and Whelan reflected that the populace would be less than likely to buy corn dogs and Cajun chicken from "Kim's Dog 'n Chicken Shack."

The one non-Korean face behind the counter was a younger, just barely healthier version of Danny Wills's. Marty Wills was filling a juice dispenser. Whelan got a coffee from the Korean woman taking orders and then found himself a stool along the window. Marty Wills came out from behind the counter and began busing and scrubbing the outer counters and refilling napkin holders and saltshakers. Whelan sipped at his coffee and watched the traffic till Wills was a couple of stools away.

"Marty?"

The boy stiffened and looked at Whelan but said nothing.

"Dan told me where to find you. My name's Whelan. I'm a private detective and I'm looking for Tony Blanchard."

Marty Wills gave a quick shake of his head. "Don't know where he is. He don't stay with us no more."

"I know that. But I need to find him."

"I don't know where he is, man."

"But you do know he's in trouble."

Wills shook his head again and jammed a wad of napkins into a holder.

"I need to know where he is, Marty."

"What do you want me to do about it?" the boy whined.

"I want you to give me some idea where to look. Maybe you don't know where he is, but you've got some notion where he might go. Your brother said Tony's got a place of his own, but I don't think so. There aren't a whole lot of people who rent to a sixteen-year-old. I think he's staying with somebody or he's out on the street."

Marty Wills said nothing for several seconds. Finally, he shot a quick look at the Korean woman, then faced Whelan. "He don't have no crib. He, like, stays sometimes with this old black lady."

"Over on Wilton, in the high-rise?"

Wills nodded.

"He's not staying there now."

"Maybe not, but he could show up there if, like, he needs a place to flop."

"But where would you look for him?" The boy hesitated and Whelan pushed. "It might save his life, Marty."

"I don't know."

"Yeah, you do. Would he ever go back to the garage?"

Marty rolled his eyes in the look all adolescents reserve for their retarded elders. "No way, man. Roy sucks."

Whelan thought about Mrs. Pritchett's present and threw his knuckler. "I know he was spending some time up on Argyle Street. Is he still hanging around there?"

The boy blinked in surprise, then recovered quickly. He

pursed his lips and shook his head slowly. "Nah, he don't hang out in Chinatown."

"Chinatown's on the South Side, Marty. I said Argyle Street."

"Hey, like, I don't know what you call it. He ain't there, that's all I know. Why would he hang out in a place like that?" Marty sneered but his eyes had a panicked look.

"Okay, you know more about this than I do. But he was up there before. I know that."

Marty wrestled with this and finally made the faintest shrug. "For a little while, maybe."

"Why there?"

"Man, I don't know every little thing about the guy's life. I think he knew this guy at one of the joints up there."

"And let me guess, you don't know which place." The boy gave a sullen shake of his head. Whelan took a sip of his coffee. "Did you know the guys he was hanging around with? Jimmy Hayes or any of the other ones?"

"No, man. If I did, I'd be fucking out of here, I'll tell you that. They're all dead, man."

"Do you know why?"

"They fucked with somebody and they got wasted."

"So you think Jimmy Lee Hayes is dead, too."

"Absofuckinglutely." Marty forced a last wad of napkins into the holder and slid it across the little table.

"Something they did or..." A thought struck Whelan. "... something they took? I keep hearing they were into cars and stereos but maybe this is about something else. Drugs, maybe."

"Beats the fuck outta me," Marty said, but something in his eyes told Whelan that the boy had the same suspicion.

"You have any idea who—"

"Nope," the boy said, getting there seconds before Whelan.

Whelan studied the kid for a moment. The boy poured four ounces of salt into a three-ounce shaker and shot a quick look at Whelan.

"Maybe you heard Tony mention a name or something."

"He mentioned some names. He talked about Jimmy, mostly."

"What other names?"

An irritated shrug. "All the ones that got wasted, man. Matt Makowski, this dude Chick Nelson, Rory Martin. This little dude Sonny that got took out last year."

"I don't know about him. Got a last name on him?"

"No but...that was before any of this other shit went down."

"Did you ever meet any of the guys that Tony was hanging around with?"

Marty shrugged and tried to scoop the spilled salt back in through the spout. "I seen a couple of 'em around."

"Which ones?"

"I seen Jimmy Lee a couple times. I seen Matt Makowski. Matt was younger than those other guys. I knew him, kind of."

I bet you did, Whelan thought. "How did you know him?"

"We had, you know, a couple brews together. That's all."

"Did you work at the garage with Tony?"

"Nah, I don't need that shit."

"Tony must have told you a little about why he hung around with these guys."

Marty recovered some of his scorn. "*Bread,* man. Cash. Whaddya think?"

"He tell you what kinds of things they asked him to do?"

"Naw, he never said."

"Cars? Apartments? What?"

"He never said."

"And you never did anything with them? You weren't interested?" Whelan looked around the grill as though assessing Tony's source of income.

"Maybe with Tony, yeah. But not with nobody else, man." The boy screwed the top back on the saltshaker and looked ready to move on. Whelan stared till the boy met his eyes again.

"Let me try something else out on you. Jimmy Lee Hayes had a partner, an older guy. What was his name?"

"I don't know nothin' about any partner."

"I can't believe Tony never mentioned the guy's name. He lived in your house, you were running buddies. I want to know the guy's name."

"He never told me shit, man."

"Yeah, he did, and if you don't want to be doing this same dance with the boys at Area Six, you really ought to think about talking to me. I need to know about this guy."

Marty looked past Whelan for several seconds, breathing through his mouth. His eyes moved rapidly from one distant object to another and Whelan could almost hear him measuring his chances in one scenario against those in another. Finally he looked over his shoulder at the Korean man, who was talking to a woman at the counter. "I gotta go back behind the counter. They're gonna think I'm pulling some shit here."

"Fine, I'll come, too. You can give me another cup of coffee, to go this time, and the name of this guy."

Marty grabbed a styrofoam cup and a lid and set them down on a back counter. With his back to Whelan, he mumbled something.

"What? I didn't catch that."

Marty turned around to face him, holding a half-filled coffee pot.

"Maybe you're talkin' about Lester. I think that's who you want. Lester. He wasn't Jimmy's partner, though."

"What was he?"

Marty moved his skinny shoulders in a half-hearted shrug. "Just a guy they worked with."

"Worked with how?"

"When they had, like, radios, car radios, he could get rid of 'em."

"He's a fence."

"Whatever."

"He's the one you moved all your stuff through?"

"Not me, man. I never moved nothing. I told you, I didn't have nothing to do with that shit. This guy Lester, he wouldn't know me from fucking Adam."

Whelan nodded. "Where would I find him?"

"Beats the shit outta me."

Somebody ought to, Whelan thought. To Marty, he said, "I think you've got some idea."

The boy looked down. "I think I heard Tony say they used

to meet this guy at this place up on Irving." He gestured with his chin to indicate south.

"This *place?* Could we maybe narrow it down a bit?"

"It's a restaurant, man, I don't know the fucking name. It's on Irving, that's all I know."

"Irving's only about ten miles long. That's really helpful."

The kid sighed. "Up there by the El station."

"Irving and Sheridan, okay. What's he look like?"

"I don't know, man, how would I…"

"Quit whining. I think you know what he looks like."

Marty rolled his eyes. "He's old, man. He's skinny and he wears this, like, fedora thing, got all kinda stains on it like he pissed on it, which wouldn't surprise me, and this ratty blue coat, and he's got yellow teeth and he's got fucking hair growing out of his ears and his hair is gray and it sticks up on top."

"You were attracted to him."

"What?" Marty curled his lip.

"Just kidding."

Marty turned back to pour coffee into the cup. He fumbled with the lid, spilled some of the hot coffee on his hand and cursed. He wiped his hand on his apron and set the coffee in front of Whelan without looking at him. "You finished, man? Can I get back to work?"

The boy's face had taken on a greenish pallor and for a moment, Whelan felt sorry for him.

"Here, this is for the coffee," he said, and handed Marty a single. "And this is for you." He slid a five toward Marty. The boy's hand snaked out and the five disappeared. "I might be back. I might have to ask you more questions."

Marty dared a quick look at Whelan, then stared down at the table.

"It'll be just between you and me."

"Yeah, right," the boy muttered, and a stricken look came into his face.

Outside, Whelan lit a cigarette and decided that this evening he would visit the lair of the redoubtable Albert Bauman to see what the good detective could tell him.

Four

There were three customers inside the Alley Cat, each sitting at least five stools from the others and all doing their best to ignore one another, and although one of them was a stout crewcut man in a plaid sport coat, he wasn't Bauman.

Ralph, the aging bartender, just shook his head when Whelan asked whether Bauman had been in.

A half hour later, he pulled up across the street from the Bucket O'Suds and crossed the street. The lights out front weren't on yet but there were two cars parked in front and one belonged to Joe Danno, the owner. The other was Bauman's Caprice.

Whelan pushed open the door and inhaled the smells that told the newcomer that there were three hundred opened bottles of liquor here and a kitchen where wonders took place.

Two men sat in semidarkness at the far end. The stuffed marlin still hung over the upright piano, the ossified sea turtle still swam forever over a row of bourbon bottles and the dead merganser still flew across the bar. If you looked close, Whelan had decided, you could see confusion in the dead duck's eyes. At the center of the bar was another odd creature, drinking a stein of BBK and a shot of bourbon. He'd shed the coat and plaid jacket, and the orange shirt lit up the area. Across the bar from him, Joe Danno held court.

Joe was holding up a bourbon bottle and pointing out something about the label and Bauman was nodding. Only Joe turned when Whelan entered.

"How you doing, Paul?"

"I'm okay, Joe. But I'm tired and thirsty and my horse died."

"Can't do a thing about the horse, but you we can take care of."

From the back room, Fena appeared carrying two pizzas to the men at the far end. She set down the metal plates, looked up the bar, noticed Whelan and waved. "Hi, hon."

"Hi, Fena. Joe, how about a beer. And a shot of G & U for Mr. Personality here," and he tapped Bauman on the shoulder.

"Coming up." The bottle was already at the edge of the bar in front of Bauman. Joe ran a hand through his white hair and poured a shot into Bauman's glass. He held up the bottle. "How about yourself, Paul?"

"Not yet, Joe."

"Hello, Snoopy," Bauman said, and knocked ash from his skinny cigar, then took a puff. He still hadn't looked at Whelan.

"We've got a problem, O Detective of Detectives."

Bauman looked at his cigarillo and said nothing.

Joe returned with a stein of BBK that sported an inch and a half of foam. Whelan took a pull at his beer and then stared at Bauman for a moment. The earlier anger was gone and it was probably just as well. Anger would not move this hard-drinking hard-skinned man. Anger, Bauman could relate to. Confusion might be more effective. "I called Mrs. Pritchett, so you'll probably hear from her again. I'm out of it."

Bauman turned slowly to look at him. "Why is that? You runnin' out of gas? I thought you never quit anything. Isn't that you, or am I thinkin' of some other *sleuth?*"

"First time for everything, Bauman. You can find this poor teenage stiff yourself."

Bauman leaned back and squinted at Whelan. "Is that right? So, what's your hard-on this time, Whelan? Lemme guess, you're pissed off because you saw us tailing you this afternoon. Is that it?"

"Come on, Bauman, I lost you in five minutes—I wasn't even inconvenienced. You're the one that ought to be pissed off, you and your hard-guy partner." He grinned. "You lost face. In Japan, you and Landini would have to cut each other's fingers off. But I suppose if I stopped to think about it, I would be a little irritated that you decided I had to be followed. What does that mean, actually? Is there a message there?"

"Aw, your feelings are hurt. You think I don't trust you 'cause I had old Landini there tailin' you."

"I was thinking along those lines, yeah."

"I trust you as much as I trust anybody, Whelan. I just know you got certain habits, you got this one habit in particular of keeping things under your hat till you think there's a pattern. I told you if you found anything to give it to me, but I got a feeling I'll hear from you when it's all over. And I don't need that here. There's other things involved here. So, yeah, I was tailing you to see if you come up with anything I ain't got yet. Besides," he grinned and belched up bourbon, "it's good practice for Landini. He's really dogshit at puttin' the tail on somebody."

"He's not real slick but I've seen worse."

"Who?"

Whelan smiled again. "Mark Durkin."

"That's 'cause when Durkin tails somebody, he wants to run 'im over." Bauman tossed the shot off at a gulp. "Thanks for the drink. So. You feel better now, or do you still have a hair up your ass?"

Whelan looked at the other man and saw the expectant gleam in his eyes. "Yeah, I do. The tail was the easy part. The other part is more complicated. One of the dead men was a guy I knew, and you sucked me into this thing without telling me. You sent this lady to see me and then laid back to see what I'd do, and I'm not even sure why."

Bauman shrugged. "I didn't know for sure if you knew this guy. What—you wanna be questioned like all the other people that knew any one of these guys? That make you happy?"

"You could've said something up front so I'd know you made a connection."

"I didn't make any connection. And I didn't have no plan to screw you, Whelan. We had people all over the North Side looking for this kid and this old babe comes to me like I'm some kinda youth worker, and I figure it's a good spot for Paul Whelan."

"You already knew I was acquainted with one of these men."

"Yeah, yeah, we found out you knew one of the three

stiffs but I don't get the idea he was a bosom buddy of yours. Thought it might make things interesting, that's all. And it did, am I right?"

"Yeah, it made things interesting all right. Makes me wonder what else you're not telling me."

Bauman gave him a sly look and a little smile came to life.

"We're even…for the stuff you're not telling me."

"No, we're not even."

"Suit yourself, Snoopy. I don't have time to argue with you. I spend half my fucking day arguing with Landini."

"You deserve each other."

"Maybe we do. Come on, I'll buy you a drink."

"I've got one."

Bauman ignored him. "Hey, Joe? We need a couple shots here." Joe interrupted his conversation at the far end of the bar and came down to pour them a pair of shots. He was humming to the jazz coming from one of his many tapes.

"Thanks, Joe," Whelan said. "Who we listening to?"

"Dexter Gordon." Joe looked at Bauman's pile of money, shrugged, took four singles and padded over to the register.

"Tell me how you made the connection, Bauman."

"Like I said, there was nothing solid. This guy Byrne, we got not one, but *two* files on him." Bauman held up two stubby fingers. "We got his sheet, which is not exactly short but mostly small time, and we got a personnel file on him."

Whelan frowned. "Rory was a copper?"

"Naw, but he was one of these 'Police Community Aides,' remember them? Those kids that worked out of the stations and did odds and ends?"

"Yeah."

"Well, this guy was one of them for a couple months. And on his application for the job, he had to list references."

"He listed me?"

"No. Art Shears. Your friend. Shears was with the *Trib* then. From that, and from the address this guy Byrne give us, up in your old neighborhood there by the ballpark, I figured there was a pretty good chance that our boy Whelan knew him."

"Kind of a stretch. I didn't know everybody Artie knew."

"You know just about everybody in your neighborhood now, you know people that live in doorways, and I'm thinking you probably always been that way."

Whelan drained his whiskey. On an empty stomach, it burned its way down. "I knew him, but we weren't friends. He had an older brother, though, who was a good friend of mine. The whole family's gone now—parents died when the older one was about fourteen. He kind of came apart after Nam, living on the streets for a while, then he got tuberculosis."

"Hard luck family."

"Yeah. I never really knew what Rory Byrne was into. He was no worse than most of the kids around there. It's hard to believe he eventually got himself into something that would kill him."

"Well, he did. Him and a bunch of other guys. Happens all the time, Whelan."

"You have theories."

"Yeah, I do."

"It might help me out if I knew more about this Jimmy Lee Hayes."

Bauman sighed. "You're not *lookin'* for Jimmy Lee Hayes."

"I'm looking for anybody that knew this kid, so why not him?"

Bauman gave him an irritated look. "He's a sleaze. And now I think he's a dead sleaze. He met an untimely end. Just a small-time hood, that's all he was."

"What flavor?"

"A thief. I mean, they're all just thieves, but old Jimmy Lee was a genuine full-time thief. He stole cars, cameras, electronic stuff, jewelry. For a while, he was heavy into cars, had his own shop up there by the river, on Elston. You'd park your car on Sunday night, and by Monday afternoon it would be a pile of parts on the floor of Jimmy Lee's chop shop. But that got him into heavy shit, he was cutting in on somebody else's business. He got sent up for heisting a truckload of VCRs, probably saved his ass. While he was inside, one of his partners seems to have developed an insatiable need to swim in the Chicago River in November. When old Jimmy came out of the joint, he wasn't in the car business anymore."

"Sounds like a good career move."

"Yeah. Went back to stealing small shit and selling it."

"You think he got big ideas again, and went foraging in somebody else's backyard?"

"That's one theory."

"But not yours. What do you think happened?"

"I think it's personal."

"Why?"

"I just do. It's my opinion, all right?"

Whelan said nothing. He patted himself down for his cigarettes and came up empty. "Damn."

"Here." Bauman shoved the little thin pack of cigarillos along the bar with the edge of his hand.

"God Almighty." Whelan shook out one of the long dark things, looked at it, sighed and lit it up. He puffed at it once, then inhaled. A rasping filled his lungs, as though someone had stuffed sandpaper into his chest. He coughed and it was worse coming out. "Holy shit. These are terrible, Bauman. How can you inhale these?" He took several deep breaths. "I think I'm gonna die."

Bauman watched him in amusement. "Glad you like 'em. I got stronger ones at home."

"Might as well smoke inner tubes. No, you've probably smoked inner tubes already."

Bauman took the rest of his whiskey in a gulp, then a swallow of beer. He lit one of his cigarillos and blew smoke up toward the dark ceiling of the bar. He had the contented look of a man who's just had a fine meal, and Whelan laughed.

"What's so funny?"

"Nothing. Just the weird company I keep these days."

For a moment neither said anything. Whelan turned on his stool and studied the back wall, covered with labels of distillers and famous whiskeys long gone. He was going over ways to get Bauman to open up when Bauman spoke again.

"There's talk that a shipment of drugs come in about a month ago, and the big bad city swallowed it up before it could get to the people that owned it, and these people are a little put out. That's what the idea is now. Me, I think somebody a lot smarter took that shit off the street and we ain't heard the last of it. Bad shit, new blood coming in to take on the old. Jimmy Lee Hayes couldn't pull something like that off. But Jimmy Lee did something every day of his adult life to piss somebody off, and I'm thinking that's what this is about, Whelan. He pissed somebody off and now he's fertilizer."

"Pissed off how?"

"Jimmy Lee Hayes was the Deep Throat of the North Side. He informed on everybody."

"You ever use him?"

"I talked to him, but I put everything he told me through a strainer, and when I took another look, there was nothing left. He'd tell you whatever you wanted. You wanted a new name for the Kennedy assassination, Jimmy Lee Hayes would give you one. You wanted to bust his ma, Jimmy Lee would give her up. Just a simple country boy, old Jimmy Lee Hayes, carrying on a family tradition. Old man was a hood, too. Some of these families, Whelan, they carry on in that scumbag tradition. I read a book once, said when they got Pretty Boy Floyd back in the thirties, one of the guys with him was this old fuck that rode with the Daltons or somebody like that, and his father rode with one of these other gangs and it went all the way back to Jesse and Frank James. This old guy kinda taught the new guys the ropes."

Bauman took a slug of his beer and belched. "Yeah, old Jimmy just wanted to be left alone to make a few bucks. Thought he was a pretty smart fella, and a big-time hood. Some guys wanna be president and some guys wanna be Elvis and some guys wanna be hoods. Kinda like your old friend, the late Harry Palm. Even liked to use different names, like Harry: James Lee, Leon Hayes. Like that."

"Harry Palm. There was a piece of work. I sort of miss him."

"Jimmy Lee had that same, you know, outlook, only he didn't have Harry's nice taste in clothes."

"Maybe we'll find Jimmy Lee Hayes in the lake, too. Like Harry."

"The river, is what we think. We'll find 'im sooner or later, I know that. And he won't be tellin' stories no more."

Whelan watched Bauman for a moment and then let it drop. "I heard he had a partner. An older guy."

Bauman showed him nothing. He drained his beer and shoved it out onto the edge where Joe could see it. When the tavernkeeper made his way down again, Bauman took Whelan's half-empty glass and shoved it out, too.

"Put a head on Whelan's beer, there, Joseph. And give us a couple more shots, and then I'll order us a pizza from the lovely Fena, that *artiste*."

"Slow down, Bauman. I haven't finished the last round."

"Drink faster."

Joe grinned at Whelan. "You fell in with that fast crowd your mother used to warn you about." A row of paper plates hung from the top of the back bar, just above the Chinese brandy with the snake in it and the Mexican stuff with the dead scorpion. Each of the plates bore a portrait of Joe: an art class had taken to coming into the Bucket and each half-inebriated student took his shot at the definitive sketch of Joe Danno.

Whelan stared at the array of shots and beers in front of him and shuddered, remembering other lost evenings when he'd gone drinking with Bauman. When he looked up, Bauman was staring at him.

"You were sayin'."

"I think I was finished."

"No. You were tellin' me stories. You were holdin' me fucking spellbound. You were tellin' me about a partner. Tell me more."

"I think I've exhausted my store of knowledge. Mrs. Pritchett said she heard Tony talking about doing something for a partner of Jimmy's. She said she thought he was an older man."

"You know, Whelan, you got this gift. You get answers

where other guys strike out. Now, I talked to that lady—nice lady, too, although I don't think she liked me."

"She thinks you're a paragon of poor health, and she's a nurse."

"Whatever. Anyhow, she didn't tell me about no partner. That's a funny thing, ain't it? I bet she gave you a name, too."

"No. I was kind of hoping you'd supply the name and anything else that you conveniently left out when you set all this up."

"Hey, you know what I know, probably more," Bauman said, and neither man believed him. He smiled, a little glint in his eye. His cheeks were flushed now from his whiskey intake and his breathing was audible.

Bauman pursed his lips. "Listen, Shamus, I'm just wondering, if you got this one item, what else did you get? Not that this piece of information is gonna change the world. 'Cause as far as we know, the only partners old Jimmy-the-Sleazebag had are in the joint or fertilizing the tulips in our fair city."

"Now I'm disappointed. I thought I had a new angle, somebody new to look for."

"No, brother, they're all dead. If they were partners with Jimmy Lee Hayes, they're dead. If he had a real partner, you'd just be givin' me another stiff to look for. Whoever this guy was, he wasn't no partner." Bauman filled the air around him with a dirty gray corona of smoke. "See, Whelan, old Jimmy was forty-five goin' on fourteen, and all the guys he surrounded himself with were half his age, guys that would kiss up to him and treat him like some kinda Mafia Don. He didn't work with a real grownup partner in a long time. Long time," Bauman said, and then stared off into space.

"What about this garage, Roy's? The kid worked there. Is there a connection between the garage and these guys?"

"Yeah, they used to meet there. But Roy got nervous and made them find a new clubhouse."

"He wasn't a club member himself?"

"Nah, Roy's just an old fuck. They threw a few dollars his way and he thought it was great. Then back about six, seven months ago they stopped using his garage. Jimmy Lee felt the need for a little more privacy, I guess." After a moment's silence, he smiled at Whelan. "So, you gonna help me with this pizza I ordered?"

"Not this time. If I stay any longer, Joe'll have to let me sleep in the kitchen tonight. Got any last-minute suggestions for me?"

"Do what you want. Mostly, I want you to find that kid for that lady."

"You've got me looking for a body."

Bauman took out another of his little cigars and stared at it. "Do what you can, Whelan. You don't find him, then maybe he is dead." He spoke quietly, as though tired of it all.

"Anything else you want to tell me, Bauman? Anything that maybe slipped your mind?"

"Nah. Settle down, Whelan. Nobody's running a game on you." Bauman watched him for a second, then said, "Take it easy, Snoopy."

"See ya, Paul," Joe Danno sang out, and Whelan waved as he left.

The night had crept in while he'd been in the Bucket and a bitter wind knifed its way up the street. It had passed across the lake, and Whelan thought instantly of Sandra McAuliffe. He got into the icy front seat of his car, fumbled getting the key into the ignition. He was light-headed and a little giddy, and he realized he was in no condition to visit Ms. McAuliffe. After their most recent evening, the last thing, the very last thing they needed now would be Whelan showing up at her house breathing whiskey on her and mumbling. The Jet, his rusting hulk of a car, started on the second try, the radio came on with Randy Crawford singing of the "Street Life," and Whelan decided that this was a night for food with teeth.

Thirty minutes later he was home with a miniature Mexican feast from the gaudy but dependable Campeche restaurant across from the wide white hulk of Wrigley Field. The Cubs were due back at the end of the week after a week and a half in the east, where they'd lost considerable blood and self-esteem. On Thursday they would limp back like the remains of Napoleon's Grande Armée, hoping never to see New York, Philly or Pittsburgh again.

He was tunneling into the second burrito when the phone rang.

"Hi. It's Sandy," she said unnecessarily, and he was glad to hear her voice.

"I knew that. How are you?"

"Oh, I'm all right. How are you? You sound like you have a cold."

"Not really. I just came in and it's nasty out." He relaxed a little, happy to hear her voice and surprised.

"Oh," she said. She sounded disappointed.

"What's wrong?"

"Nothing. I mean…you just came in, you probably don't want to come out again."

He suppressed a sigh. He was tired, his feet hurt, he'd had too much liquor and too much fighting the spring winds to want to go out again. He thought of inviting her over but she didn't like to do that for reasons she'd never given but which he thought he could guess. In her own place, she was a woman receiving guests, not a visitor or a transient spending a night.

"Well, I suppose I could—" he began and her laughter cut him off.

"It took you about a ten-count to answer. I think I get the message. It's okay, we can get together some other night. I don't blame you for wanting to spend a quiet night. Maybe I haven't been very good company lately anyway."

Whelan looked around at his darkened living room and the television that was going to be his only company. He stared at the burrito in his hand.

This is crazy, he thought. I'm spending a quiet night at home with a burrito and reruns of *Gunsmoke.*

"Actually, I was going to call earlier but I had a few drinks in me and I wasn't sure you'd be all that wild about *my* company."

"You don't sound drunk."

"I'm not. I had a burrito and about a quart of hot sauce. I might be dying of indigestion soon, but I'm not drunk."

"Come on over. I can pick you up if you want, I don't mind."

"Best offer I've had in days."

"I'm on my way," she said, and hung up.

He had enough time to wash up, put on a clean shirt, and toss a few things into closets before she showed up. He stood back from the door to let her in and she took two small steps in. The confusing Ms. McAuliffe had put on mascara, her only concession to makeup, and she was wearing a pair of jade earrings, his first present to her. She was smiling and the green eyes held a little light as though she knew something secret that hadn't occurred to him yet.

"Hi," he said, and was about to say something else when she shook her head.

"Men spend most of their day saying stupid things," she said. She moved toward him, then put her arms around his neck and kissed him hard. Her lips and cheeks were cold and she smelled as though she'd just left the shower, and just as he was about to break off the kiss, her tongue found its way into his mouth.

She took a step back and he saw her reddish glow: the only woman he'd ever known who blushed when she kissed.

"I'll be ready in ten seconds. Less than that, even."

Eventually they made it to her place, and had a beer and made quiet contented small talk through the first half of an old movie. Whelan was gazing around her tidy living room when he realized she was watching him.

"What?"

"I was a little worried."

"About what?"

"I think we were both actually angry last time."

"People get mad, it's not the end of the world. It doesn't have a significance of its own."

"I know that, that's not what I was worried about. I think people get angry and let something unimportant become an issue and then they have to take a position. Sometimes, early in a relationship, people look for an excuse to fight, just to establish for themselves that they're still, you know, free."

He looked at her for a long moment. "You think that's what I was doing?"

"Yes."

"Can't I get pissed off?"

"Sure, and I'll give you more reason than anybody you've ever been with, but you can't make little things into something more than they are."

"I wasn't."

"You didn't call me. How long were you going to go without calling me?"

"It wasn't something I planned out."

"How many days do you punish somebody for pissing you off?"

"I was going to call you tonight but, like I said, I had a couple drinks in me…"

"It was probably *because* you had a couple in you that you even thought about calling me."

"Are we gonna fight again?"

"Might be healthier than what we were doing." She moved closer to him on the couch. "Correct me if I'm wrong, but I thought you cared about me."

"I do."

"You ever gonna tell me?"

"Sure." He looked away from her.

"Afraid to talk about it?"

"No. I'm not." He studied the label on his beer. It said the beer was made from natural products and ingredients. "I'm not afraid to talk about it."

"You're afraid to tell me you care about me."

"No, I'm not."

"So do it."

"Don't you know by now?"

"Know what?" She seemed on the verge of laughter.

"All right, have a few laughs at my expense." A moment later he said, "I care about you. I'm glad you called me."

"This ends our first lesson," she said, and put her arms around him.

When he woke the next morning, she was in the kitchen, singing in her bent voice to an old Beatles song on the radio and making her uniquely cheery but raucous kitchen clatter. He shook his head: a woman given to long silences, who cherished quiet afternoons sitting in a window sipping tea but could rouse the ghosts of her ancestors with her noise in the morning.

Eventually the smell of coffee pulled him out of bed and he padded to her bathroom.

Still crooning, she was scrambling eggs when he made it out to the kitchen. She smiled. "Morning, sunshine."

"Morning." She was wearing a brightly flowered blouse and dark blue slacks. He shook his head.

"You look like Donna Reed."

"I do not. I'm dressed for work. You've caught my act on a Saturday morning once, I believe." She gave him a sardonic look. "Did I look like Donna Reed then?"

"As I recall, you looked wonderful and burned an omelet in an attempt to impress me."

She laughed. "There's coffee. Get it yourself."

"You're not going to wait on me?"

"Lincoln freed the slaves. All of them. Put some toast in, why don't you."

He poured himself a cup of coffee and carried it back to the table, then put four slices of whole wheat into her ancient toaster. In seconds, she came over with the pan full of eggs and scraped some out onto his plate and the rest onto hers.

She sat down across from him and put salt and pepper on her eggs, then looked up at him. "What are you waiting for? I even put out a bottle of ketchup. My concession to your odd tastes."

"I saw. I'm deeply moved."

"So eat."

"I was watching and listening to the toaster." From the fat, boxy old toaster a steady whirring noise could be heard, then something that sounded like the coiling of a spring. Little plumes of steam rose from the dark openings at the top. He shook his head. "Maybe it's time for a new toaster."

"It was my mom's. I intend to use it till it incinerates my toast."

"Your mom's? 'Nuff said."

They ate quietly for a few moments and Whelan told himself this was a fine way to begin a day. The sound of her quiet laughter brought him out of his reverie.

"What's so funny? What did I miss?"

"You are one of the few people I've ever met who smiles at his food."

Embarrassed, he said, "I was just thinking…"

"You were thinking about your food. You smile at your food a lot. You smile at *pad thai,* you smile at burritos, you smile at *bibim bop.* Paul, you smile at hot dogs."

"But today I'm just in a good mood."

She raised her eyebrows slightly. "Some people like waking up with someone. Folks do it every morning."

"I know."

She picked up her coffee and took a sip. Then she leaned forward, still holding the cup in both hands, and regarded him over the cup. "About what we were saying last night. I just want to make one little point. It's not a plea on my own behalf or anything like that, because I think you know I kind of like being single. In a lot of ways. But if we were together, it would be a nice life, nicer than both of us have most of the time." She looked at him with something like defiance and took another sip of her coffee. "I know you, some mornings you'd be in a hurry to leave for work and get away from me, and some mornings I probably wouldn't want to talk to you, but every morning we'd be together. Some people think about the nights, I always think about the mornings. Starting the day."

He sipped at his own coffee and thought about the difference it would make in his life, and nodded slowly. "I'm thinking. I'll admit I'm thinking."

"Fair enough," she said. Then she looked at the bold red stripes of ketchup across his eggs and shuddered.

Five

It was 9:20 when he finally made it into the office but he was only mildly irritated at the slow start.

A logical man, Whelan told himself, would be back looking for the boy, but Detective Albert Bauman had complicated things, and Whelan realized he was already deep into a different process. The boy would keep. The boy would keep because he was dead.

The restaurant was on the northwest corner of the street, directly across from the King's Palace, where there was a FOR SALE sign out front.

"Say it ain't so," Whelan muttered. The King's Palace, the ultimate lounge and home of the Hightones, three middle-aged men with dyed hair and white shoes who couldn't sing, dance or play but for almost two decades had been mining the music of their betters. Whelan had long assumed that the King's Palace would outlast Chicago, that in some post-nuclear-Armageddon Chicago there would be this one building, and in it, till the end of time, there would be these three guys doing their Beatles medley and their Tribute to the Motown Sound. If the King's Palace went under, what would become of the Hightones? The other sign was still there, the miniature marquee that screamed out DIRECT FROM LAS VEGAS, THE HIGH TONES! Well, not exactly direct. They'd been playing here in 1967. He took another look at the newly vacant little lounge and went across the street.

The restaurant was a twenty-four-hour diner that boasted ice cream specialties. Whelan had been there several times:

roomy booths and a long laminated menu, soda fountain, cheap dinners and two dozen kinds of sandwiches, breakfast any time—all the signs of a Greek-run Chicago eatery. He waited outside and peered in through the window for a minute or two.

Four customers sat at the counter, one of them an unshaven older man who sat jotting things into a small spiral notebook and shooting sour glances at the other patrons. A sweat-stained fedora rested beside his cup like a pet rat, and Whelan could see a folded newspaper peeking out from beneath the man's plate of sausage and eggs.

Whelan went in and slid onto a stool beside the old man. The notebook disappeared into a pocket of the blue raincoat, but Whelan thought he saw the names of baseball teams and dollar amounts. The waitress finished taking an order from two men in a booth and came back behind the counter. She was a fiftyish woman with a round face and the bearing of a grandmother.

"Be with you in a sec, sir." A moment later she was poised to take his order.

"You have a lot of ground to cover."

She lifted up one foot to show her new sneakers. "That's why we wear track shoes, dear. Breakfast today?"

"Just coffee."

While she went off to get the pot, he turned slightly on the stool and looked at the old man. "What do you say, Les?"

The other man rammed a forkful of sausage in his mouth and stared at Whelan. It was a sallow face, with the pinched look of a mouth caving in on itself after a lifetime of bad teeth. Up close there was a hardness in the face that Whelan hadn't seen earlier. This one had seen the elephant, and it had been a lot more intimidating than Paul Whelan. He chewed a couple of times and the sausage became a lump in one unshaven cheek. "You don't know me."

Whelan slid a business card along the white countertop. "Paul Whelan. I'm a private investigator. I live a few blocks from here."

The waitress came to pour his coffee and then warmed up the old man's. She seemed about to say something, then caught the look passing between them and just walked away, tucking her check pad into a pocket in her apron.

"So? So what?" Les said.

Not bad, Whelan thought. Openly hostile within ten seconds.

"So I thought you might be able to help me with some information. I was told you know a lot of people and that you might be able to give me a couple of names I need."

"Told by who?" He chewed slowly, mouth open, his eyes never leaving Whelan's face.

"Somebody that, all of a sudden, nobody can find."

Les stared at Whelan for a moment and then bought a few seconds by taking a sip of his coffee. He took his sweet time setting down the cup, wiping his bristly chin with a soggy napkin and poking at his eggs with the fork, then looked straight ahead. Slowly, almost imperceptibly, his head began to shake. "I got nothing for you, I don't care who you are."

"I want to find Tony Blanchard, that's all."

"I don't know anybody like that."

"Well, yeah, you do. You know a lot of people, and a lot of people know you. That's how I know you, that's how I knew where to find you. It's how I know you're a fence, how I knew you moved some stuff for Jimmy Lee Hayes, among many others." The old man looked down at the food going cold on his plate. Time to push. "I can tell you who busted you, and when. I can tell you which cops have come by in the last month to question you, I can tell you—"

Les held up a skinny hand, as if to ward off his many troubles. "I don't know nothing about that damn kid, I can tell you that."

"I didn't mention his age, Lester. You know he was a kid, you just admitted you knew him. That's a start."

"But I ain't seen him or none of them, not in weeks. Months, maybe."

Whelan nodded and took a sip of his coffee. It was burnt, coffee that had died a slow death in the pot. It made him long for the wonderful brew he'd had the day before up on Broadway.

"And you're not going to see any of them again, you know that, don't you?"

Les dipped his head slightly and punctured a piece of hash browns with his fork.

"Matt Makowski, Chick Nelson, that guy Rory what's-his-name?"

"Martin," the old man muttered. "Called himself that, wasn't his real name."

"No, let me think. Byrne, that was it. Rory Byrne."

Lester turned slightly to look at him, then looked away.

"You know they're all dead."

"I can read."

"And Jimmy Lee."

This earned him a shrug.

"Jimmy Lee's history, Lester, he's floating with the catfish in the river."

"They ain't found him yet."

"You think he's still alive?"

"How do I know?"

"You did business with them, Les."

"This shit's got nothing to do with me."

"Jimmy Lee is feeding flies someplace, and somebody took out all these guys who worked with him, even this kid Makowski who was a gofer, he was nobody, and you," Whelan pointed a finger at the old man. "You moved his goods, Les, my man, you made money for him. And you made money for yourself, and whoever decided Jimmy Lee should bite the big one, he's gonna get around to you eventually."

The old man turned on the stool, the fork gripped tightly in a fist. For a moment Whelan wondered if Les would stab him with it.

"Lighten up, there, Les."

"Goddamit, I told you this hasn't got nothing to do with me, I told you that, I told those asshole cops that..." Lester's voice grew louder and from the corner of his eye, Whelan could see people at some of the booths looking at them.

"Take it easy."

"Don't tell me to take it easy."

"You're gonna have a heart attack and die in your scrambled eggs." Whelan fished. "The cops—Harrison and Gentry? That who you talked to? White guy and a black guy. Or Bauman and that Italian kid?"

"Him. Bauman. I ain't moved nothing in six, eight months. I got no money comin' in or nothing, I'm livin' like a damn dog. I ain't doing any business with anybody." Whelan thought about the little notebook with the day's wagers and said nothing. "Somebody has a problem with Jimmy Lee Hayes, it's got nothing to do with me."

Whelan shook his head. "You're being logical. This thing, it's not logical. I think you're in trouble, and you know it."

The old man looked down at his cold breakfast and his entire body sagged. He shook his head. "There ain't any reason for them to come after me. There's other people oughtta be sweatin' now, instead of me."

"Such as?"

Les's bony shoulders moved slightly in a shrug. "Jimmy Lee had a couple people working with him that I didn't know. This kid you're talkin' about, for one. He's just a name to me, that's all."

"Who else?" Lester seemed to be ignoring him, and Whelan was about to prod the old man some more when Lester pointed his deadly fork again.

"I'll tell you who oughtta be thinking about gettin' the first bus back to Tennessee. His brother, that's who." Lester nodded in agreement with himself.

"Whose?"

"Jimmy's." Lester allowed himself his first smile. "Didn't know about him, did ya? Didn't know he had a brother."

"We didn't socialize. I don't know his family tree, Les."

Lester nodded, his superior knowledge confirmed. "Name's Bobby."

"Same last name?" Lester nodded again. "Where's he?"

"How the hell should I know?"

"Where would you look for him?"

"I wouldn't. I don't give a shit where—"

"Where would you look if you didn't want to bother old Lester any more?"

"Tavern where he hangs out."

"Which one?"

"Place up on Clark Street, up near Lawrence. By a park." Les pointed his fork north.

"Does it have a name?"

"Ed and Somebody, I don't know. Anyhow, that's who oughtta be sweatin' now, not me. Picked a helluva time to come back to town, didn't he?"

"Just got back?"

Les nodded. "Couple weeks ago. Maybe a month. That's what he said."

"Did you tell him about any of this trouble?"

"Naw. I didn't say nothing about any of that. Got nothing to do with me, and anyways, I wouldn't trust this Bobby Hayes far as I can throw him."

"You didn't talk about Jimmy Lee at all?"

"Naw. And I wasn't gonna say nothing either. People talk. This was a tavern, for Chrissake. People talk."

"When was this?"

"What's today—Wednesday? This was maybe a week ago. I forget."

Whelan finished the bad coffee and zipped up his jacket. Then a new thought struck him. "When did you talk to Bauman?"

"I dunno. Couple weeks ago."

Excellent, he thought. "And the kid? You can't tell me anything about the kid?"

Lester shook his head and watched Whelan. Whelan signaled for the waitress. When she arrived, he nodded toward Lester.

"Give me his check, too. See you around, Lester," Whelan said, and then walked to the register.

The jukebox in Ed and Ronda's was too loud, and there was no ventilation, so that cigarette smoke hung in the air forever, and a little bald man at the far end of the bar was singing a Johnny Cash song while the box played Barbara Mandrell, and the bartender was an untalented liar who said he hadn't seen Bobby Hayes in he-didn't-know-how-long. Other than that, Whelan told himself, it was a profitable visit.

SIX

Whelan made the turn off Broadway and saw the brilliant red-and-gold pagoda-style roof of the Argyle Street El station. Less than six blocks from his own home, but no longer on his own turf. You left Broadway and you weren't in Uptown anymore, you were in someone else's country. He'd had the same feeling in other places, on 16th Street where mariachi music blared out onto the streets, and Chinatown itself where you crossed under the dragon gateway and found all the street signs written in Chinese characters as well as English. But Argyle Street was still a Northside secret, still a tiny undiscovered pocket of foreign-born humanity known largely to cops and deliverymen and seekers of cheap restaurants. Even the nickname served to thicken the smokescreen: for "New Chinatown," as some called it, wasn't Chinese. There were Chinese living in the area and a scattering of Chinese businesses, but this little three-block stretch was a street lifted whole from South Vietnam and dropped with all its parts into Chicago.

When the first Vietnamese businesses had been established here, Whelan had come for a look, wondering if the sight of so many Vietnamese signs, Vietnamese people, would bring out feelings and memories he didn't want to deal with, but his reaction had been the opposite. He'd had dinner in a big brightly lit place called Mekong and then explored the street. The odd feeling of walking alone among hundreds of people of different race and culture, smelling the cooking smells and hearing the high-pitched nasal sounds of their language reminded him that he wanted someday to visit the country and see it in peacetime. The other feelings touched him when he saw a shivering wreck in khaki standing aimlessly on a corner puffing at other people's cigarette butts. At such times, he knew he was one of the lucky ones: all his wounds had been physical.

He made a long slow tour of the main strip, drove up and down side streets and realized he didn't know where to begin. At last, he parked at a meter near Sheridan, the eastern end of the strip. Across the street from his car, a little group of elderly Russians huddled in front of New Chinatown Bakery and Coffee Shop and debated whether to go in. Whelan sat in his car and watched them: this was a familiar sight in the area now, Russian Jewish immigrants, recent recipients of a rare Soviet leniency, wandering in groups in their heavy coats and outrageous fur caps, sightseeing in the damnedest places. From what he knew of them, the old Russians would stop wearing their winter clothes sometime in May.

Whelan looked up the street and saw that these Russians were the only other Caucasian faces to be seen. He admitted to himself that he had no clear idea what he hoped to find up here.

I'm a poor boy a long way from home.

He got out of his car and fed the meter. He found that he was parked in front of Thanh Phuoc Gifts: a poster in the window advertised a series of tapes, Chinese songs for young lovers. A few inches away, a colorful sign announced the triumphant tour of a popular Vietnamese recording artist. The woman in the poster had gone Western all the way: she was sexy and tough-looking in black leather and boots.

Looking up and down both sides of Argyle, he saw Hong Kong Fashion, Pho Xe Lua Restaurant, Hoang Kim Fine Jewelry, Sunny Supermarket, Viet Hoa Grocery, Mai's Fashion and Bridal Shop, Lucky Garden Market and a dozen more businesses, most of them Vietnamese. The people on the street were Vietnamese, and all ages. A young Vietnamese man pulled into the parking spot ahead of him, got out with a cigarette in his mouth, glanced at Whelan and went on his way.

Whelan crossed Argyle and started walking up the south side of the street. A group of young Vietnamese women passed him, laughing and talking in high girlish voices. One of them seemed to look for a second at his hair and then said something to her friends.

I know, he thought. You don't have a lot of redheads in your neighborhood.

No one else seemed to give him a thought as he walked against the wind and tried to decide where to begin. He peered into the window of New Chinatown Restaurant, tried the door, found it locked. He knocked and a young man inside shook his head and pantomimed that the restaurant wasn't open yet. In front of a place called Lucky Grocery Market he paused. A dozen people seemed to be milling around inside, and a Vietnamese man in a T-shirt was whacking away at a chicken on a thick wooden carving board. In the window, a half-dozen ducks, their skin gone reddish and oily from the smoking process, hung by their unhappy necks from a steel bar.

Good a place as any, Whelan told himself: if I strike out, I can always buy a duck.

The smells that assailed him were food smells of another world: teas and ginseng and other herbs, and over it all, the pungent odors of smoked meat. And cigarette smoke: the air was blue with it, half the customers were smoking and the man with the cleaver puffed away while hacking at the hapless chicken. If the bird hadn't been dead, the smoke would have killed him.

Whelan looked around for a while and then noticed a slender Vietnamese woman in her thirties watching him from behind a counter. She had large eyes and a flat nose, and would have been plain but for her improbably high cheekbones. He realized how out of place he looked and grinned, and when she flashed her own smile, it changed her face and lit up the rest of the room as well, and for just a half second, Whelan could only stare.

"May I help you, sir?" she asked in a high, clipped Vietnamese accent.

He went over to the counter and leaned against it. "I'm looking for someone. A boy, a teenage boy." He stopped short of saying "A white boy" and settled for "Not a Vietnamese boy."

"American boy?"

"Yes," he said, grateful. You're Americans, he thought, but nobody's willing to admit it to you yet. "Yes, a young American boy. Maybe sixteen years old."

"What he look like?"

"About this tall," Whelan said, holding his hand flat to estimate the boy's height. "Long hair, longer than yours." This information seemed to amuse her, for the smile returned and her eyes took on a dark little sparkle. "A small scar on his chin and a tattoo." She wrinkled her nose and the smile got nervous.

"A picture of a comet, or…a star, here," he pointed to his right forearm.

She shook her head. "I don't see him." She turned and spoke rapidly in Vietnamese to the man with the cleaver.

No, Whelan thought, I don't want to talk to anybody with a cleaver. The man squinted, looked at Whelan and shook his head, then lopped the unfortunate chicken in half and grinned.

"He don't see him either," the woman said, and the smile lit up the room again.

"Well, thanks," Whelan said, and left. He tried three more places and came up with nothing but smiles or blank stares.

Two doors from the corner of Argyle and Kenmore, a square-built man in his sixties swept the windblown newspapers away from the door of a restaurant. He wore a white apron and a T-shirt; Whelan could see the red edge of a scar emerging from under the sleeve. The windows of the restaurant were steamed and sweating. A paper menu in English and Vietnamese hung in the center window but the other signs were entirely in Vietnamese.

Must be the real thing, Whelan thought, and decided this would be the restaurant he'd try next time down here.

The man dug with the edge of his broom at a corner of the doorway, then noticed Whelan.

"I'm looking for someone." The man blinked and made a little shake of his head. "No English, huh?" Whelan tapped himself on the chest. "No Vietnamese."

He shrugged and went inside the restaurant. There were a halfdozen customers inside, all Vietnamese. A young couple looked at him in mild curiosity. The others paid him no attention. He advanced toward the woman behind the little beige counter.

She was in her forties, with pale skin and large eyes, and she flashed a quick hard smile and reached to take a paper menu from a pile on her left.

"Do you speak English?"

She winced, grinned, held up two fingers in a pinch and said, "Little bit English."

"I'm looking for a boy. An American boy. Long hair, scar here on his chin, a blue star tattoo on his arm here. A tattoo. You understand —a tattoo?"

"I know tattoo, ya. Ya. I no see this one. American boy he don't come in here."

"Have you seen any American boys—on the street maybe?"

She shook her head. "No. No American boy. Only Vietnamese boy," and she laughed. "Lot of Vietnamese boy."

"I bet." The old man came in, rubbing his cold arms and grinning. He said something in Vietnamese to the woman and she nodded. As he passed Whelan, he nodded politely, then went into the kitchen with his broom.

The woman watched Whelan for a moment, then held up the menu. "You eat? You like Vietnamese food? You like more better Chinese."

"I do like Vietnamese food."

"Yes? You like?" She indicated her kitchen with a little nod. "My cook, best cook. Food very nice."

"This is your restaurant?"

She nodded. "My restaurant."

"Nice place. I'll come back. Well, thanks."

She nodded and gave him a little wave as he left.

At the corner he passed a long white truck and stopped to watch a young Latino man unloading pig carcasses. The man was slightly built and the pigs looked to be industrial strength, but the man slung a deceased pig over a shoulder with no visible effort and smiled at Whelan.

"You want a pig?"

"No thanks. I ate already."

The man patted his pig and carted the carcass into a Vietnamese meat market. Whelan crossed back to the other side of Argyle again and found himself in front of Phnom Penh Jewelers, a narrow storefront bearing script in four alphabets on its windows. The man and woman behind the counter were involved in two separate conversations with customers. Neither looked Vietnamese: from the name, he assumed this place was Cambodian. The man was tall and a little darker than his customers, his features less Asiatic. He was going bald, and the retreating hairline emphasized the high dome of his forehead. At the moment, he appeared to be negotiating to buy a ring from the customer.

Whelan tried the door and found it locked. He looked at the man, knocked, and waved when the man looked up. The man peered at him for a moment, then pressed a buzzer under the counter and the door opened.

The man moved a few feet up the counter to greet him. "Can I help you?"

"Yes. I'm looking for somebody. An American boy."

The bald man pursed his lips and shook his head. "No boys come in here. All steal, all boys: American boys, any kind boys. I don't buzz in any kind boys." He touched the buzzer in demonstration.

"Maybe you've seen him on the street. About the same size as your customer there. Long hair."

He gave his head a quick shake. "You try Apollo." He pointed in the direction of the El tracks. "Maybe they see him."

"Apollo? Okay, thanks."

The Cambodian man was back into his delicate negotiations before Whelan made it through the door.

He crossed Winthrop, went past a market that boasted fresh ginseng and its own collection of dead ducks hanging in the window—Argyle Street was hell on ducks, apparently—and passed into the chilly shadow of the tracks, where he found the Apollo.

It was as close as one could come to a cave in the middle of the city, jammed under the concrete superstructure of the Argyle

Street El station and spreading back in the semidarkness to the alley. A squad car sat out front and the cop who belonged to it was sitting in the window of the Apollo reading a newspaper. On the window over his head were the words WE SERVE BEST OF FOOD.

Whelan walked into the steamy air and the heavy odor of bacon and ham steaks frying. It took a moment for his eyes to adjust to the sepia light in the Apollo and then Whelan saw that he'd found the place where the outsiders came to hide. White faces and black looked up when he approached the counter, with nary an Asiatic in the bunch.

I've found the Island of the Lost Gringos.

An angular man in an Army coat brushed past him on the way out and Whelan narrowly missed walking into the cop, who was heading back to the counter for a refill on his coffee. Eventually Whelan found himself an empty stool where the counter made a ninety-degree turn.

He slid onto the stool and a plump young woman with a Mediterranean face came to take his order. She appeared to be having a running battle with the cook, a potbellied man whose stomach threatened to touch the surface of the grill. They were speaking in a language Whelan didn't know—Assyrian, maybe.

"What you gonna have today, sir?" the waitress said, shooting one last venom-laden glance at the fat man.

"Just coffee." He waited for her to fill a brown mug from a small pot. When she returned, he said, "I'm trying to find a runaway boy. He's about sixteen, with long hair, brown, has a little scar on his chin and a tattoo on his right arm. Tattoo of a comet. Ring any bells?"

She started to shrug and her face was wrinkling up into a doubtful expression. Then she paused. "There was a boy I saw a couple times on the street. But this boy didn't have long hair."

"He could have cut it. Did he have the scar or tattoo?"

"This one had something on his arm but I don't remember if it was a comet. I don't look at tattoos. They're so ugly, you know? And most of the guys that got tattoos, they give me the creeps."

"You said you saw him on the street. Where?"

She pointed out the window with the eraser end of her pencil. "Right out there. Across the street. He was standing in the doorway with another boy. I don't know if it's the boy you want."

"What did the other boy look like?"

She shook her head. "I don't remember."

"A white kid?"

She nodded. "But I didn't see them real good. At night, this was. It was dark already."

Whelan drew a card from his shirt pocket and put it on the counter. "If you see either of them again, call me. I have an answering service if I'm not in. Okay?"

The waitress stared at his card and a little glow appeared on her face. She looked from the card to Whelan and then back to the card. The fat man at the grill said something Whelan didn't catch and she shot him a look over her shoulder that made her feelings plain. She looked back at Whelan and grinned.

"This is real?"

"Yep. So am I."

She held the card in the palm of her hand. "This is really cool."

"It would be cooler if I made a lot of money at it."

She shrugged one shoulder. "So who makes a lot of money?"

The cook rumbled again and a man down the counter called out for a refill of his coffee. The waitress sighed, held out her hand and said, "My name's Diana."

"Nice to meet you," Whelan said and shook hands. Diana went to fill the customer's cup and the cook was growling at her again. She muttered something in the Middle Eastern language and the cook shot something back and Whelan thought he heard the girl say "Oh, fuck you." He fought an impulse to laugh, finished his coffee and walked to the door. For a moment he toyed with the idea of asking the cop in the window if he'd seen Tony Blanchard but there was something willful and single-minded about the way the cop stared at his newspaper and made eye contact with no one, and Whelan let it go. He waved to Diana the Waitress as he left, and she winked at him.

Outside he stood on the sidewalk and looked up and down Argyle Street. Dozens of Asiatic people passed him and paid him no attention whatsoever. He thought about what the waitress had told him and realized that if he wanted to catch sight of the kid down here, he'd probably have to come back at night. Whelan sighed.

I hate working nights, he told himself.

Dolly Parton had replaced Barbara Mandrell and the singing drunk appeared to have gone home but the rest of Ed and Ronda's was the same bad dream it had been before. Whelan stepped into the dark little tavern and leaned against the nearest stool. A couple of the drinkers turned to look at him and then looked back at their drinks or their cigarettes. At the far end, a sharp-featured young man in a red knit shirt peered at him through cigarette smoke and then looked away. The bartender was bent over a large beer cooler, one arm lost from view as he reached for bottles at the murky bottom. He cursed and shook his head, and finally came up with a couple bottles of Hamm's, dripping from the pool of slush where they'd been living these past weeks. He wiped the bottoms on a bar rag, opened them and set them up in front of a pair of old men, then seemed to notice Whelan. The bartender stared at him for a moment, stole a quick glance over at the man in the red knit shirt and made the faintest nod in Whelan's direction.

Thanks, Whelan thought. Now we've been introduced. He smiled at the bartender and saw that the man already disliked him.

The man in the red shirt started to get off his stool, then squinted in Whelan's direction and seemed to change his mind.

The bartender ambled in Whelan's direction but Whelan ignored him and moved on down the bar. He put cigarettes and a ten on the bar and took a stool next to the young man in the red shirt. The other man busied himself with the complicated ritual of busting open a new pack of cigarettes. He tapped the pack on the bar, ripped open the cellophane, pulled out a smoke, tapped the filter end on the bar to settle the tobacco, flicked a monogrammed lighter and puffed away. He blew smoke out into the air and fingered his change, and his facial expression never changed. Up close, the man was not quite so young and he wore the marks of life in smoky taverns: dark patches under the eyes, crow's-feet at the corners, reddish pimples across his nose and a few appearing on his cheeks. He'd slicked his blond hair back with a year's supply of hair cream or motor oil that made it look darker than it probably was, but he wore his sideburns long and they were going gray fast. He smelled of his hair cream and cologne and he still hadn't looked at Whelan.

"Bobby Hayes?" Whelan asked and without waiting for an answer, said, "My name's Paul Whelan."

The other man shrugged and continued to stare straight ahead of him. Whelan tossed a business card in front of Hayes. "I need to ask you some questions."

Hayes looked down at the card for a moment, then picked it up and began tapping on the bar in front of him. "I ain't seen him," Hayes said. He spoke softly, with a noticeable twang. Hayes looked at Whelan for the first time. There was a washed-out quality to his pale blue eyes that made him look fatigued.

"Gee, you mean I came all the way here for nothing?"

"That's about the size of it, Bo." Hayes tried to look pleased with himself.

Whelan pretended to think for a moment, then looked back at Hayes. "Who haven't you seen, Bob?"

"Who says I'm Bob?"

"He did," Whelan said with a nod at the bartender. The other man squinted at the bartender in momentary confusion.

The drinker nearest the door called out "How 'bout some drinks here, Ed," and the barman lumbered away.

Whelan leaned closer. "So who haven't you seen?"

Hayes snorted and stalled and then said, "Jimmy. Who d'ya think?"

Whelan shook his head. The bartender approached and Whelan waved him away. "I'm not looking for him. Besides, talk is, he's dead."

Bobby looked away. "You think so, huh?"

"Yeah, I do. I think they're all dead."

"I'll have to tell ol' Jimmy that next time I see him."

"Next time you see him, Bobby, you'll both be able to fly."

Bobby Hayes picked up his glass and sipped at what appeared to be vodka and the remains of a couple of ice cubes.

"Can I buy you a drink?"

"What for?"

"So I can ask you about the person I'm actually here about."

Hayes turned and looked at him for several seconds, then shrugged. Whelan caught Ed's eye and pointed to Hayes's drink. The barman poured a long shot of vodka from the speed rack and dropped a handful of ice cubes on top. He looked at Whelan.

"You want a drink?"

"No, thanks. Take it out of here," he said, pointing at his money.

When he looked back at Hayes, he thought he could see confusion in the pale eyes. "What I really need, Bob, is information about Tony Blanchard."

Hayes allowed himself a slight shake of the head and Whelan pushed. "I know you didn't have much to do with Jimmy's operation..." Bobby was nodding now. "...but I think you can give me some idea where to look."

Hayes shook his head. "I ain't seen him. Only saw those kids a couple times."

"The other kid named Marty?"

"I don't know any of their names, buddy. They were just kids to me."

"Was the second one tall and skinny with black hair?"

Hayes frowned. "Nah. This was a little ol' boy. Had blond hair." Hayes held up the glass of vodka. "Thanks, son." He took a sip and smacked his lips.

Whelan watched him for a moment. "Tell me, Bob—when did the shit start to hit the fan for Jimmy?"

"Couldn't tell you, friend. I wasn't here."

He thought about Bobby Hayes's reaction when he'd first

come in. "Maybe so, Bob, but you've got the same trouble. Same folks looking for you as for your brother."

Hayes shot him a sudden look. "I wasn't here. Like I said before."

"It doesn't matter and you know it. That's why you have your friendly neighborhood bartender telling people he never heard of you. And that's why you got nervous when I came in, at least until you saw who it was. You were expecting somebody else."

"I wasn't expecting nobody. I come in for a little taste. I don't bother nobody."

"Maybe so, but I heard you have reason to worry."

The other man was shaking his head before Whelan was even finished. "That's bullshit, brother. Who'd you hear that from?"

"Somebody who did business with your brother on a regular basis and thinks you ought to be watching your back."

Bobby Hayes studied Whelan, his pale eyes wide and nervous. "Why should I be watching my back? Who's gonna give me trouble?" He made a little shake of his head. "I know what this is. You want something."

"I told you what I wanted. But there's a good chance the one looking for you is also the reason I can't find this boy. I want a name."

Bobby Hayes stared down into his drink as though it had disappointed him. His shoulders sagged slightly. Whelan took in the gold chain, the long sideburns, the heavy cologne, and saw a man who had been a step slow most of his life. Hayes lifted the glass and slurped at the melting ice, then turned to Whelan. He seemed to be on the verge of opening up, and then Whelan could almost see the fear steering him off. Hayes pursed his lips and looked up at the ceiling for a moment. "Got no name to give you, old buddy."

"Okay," Whelan said, and dropped the card back in front of Hayes. "Keep this anyway and give me a call if you change your mind."

Hayes blinked and grinned at him, the portrait of false confidence. "Change my mind? 'Bout what, son? I don't know who you're talkin' about, how'm I gonna change my mind?"

"Well, just in case. Maybe I can be of some help to you."

Whelan got up and walked toward the door. Behind him, Bobby Hayes's voice rang out, "Thanks for the drink, buddy." And as Whelan reached the door, he could hear Hayes telling Ed that Whelan was "a real gentleman for a Yankee."

The group home Mrs. Pritchett had mentioned was called Archer House and Whelan found it on Carmen, a narrow side street just west of Andersonville, the old Swedish neighborhood. The home looked much like the other houses on either side of the street, a squat redbrick structure with a small dark porch, a prime example of what passed for a bungalow in Chicago. There was nothing on the building to indicate that it was anything but a normal family residence.

As he approached the staircase, he realized he was being watched from the cover of Venetian blinds in the house next door. At the top of the stairs he saw a little brass bell plate that read ARCHER HOUSE. UNITED SOCIAL SERVICES GROUP RESIDENCE. He rang the bell and waited in silence.

He heard voices from inside and a moment later the door opened and he found himself facing a young white man in his twenties, a 1967-looking young man with curly light brown hair and rimless glasses and an expression in his brown eyes that said "Surprise me."

The young man raised his eyebrows in question. Whelan held out a business card and waited as the young man's gaze moved over it and a look of amusement came into his face.

"What can we do for you?"

"I understand that Tony Blanchard lived here for a while. I wonder if I could ask you some questions about him."

Before the young man could answer, a second man appeared behind him in the hall, sipping at coffee from a paper cup. This man was in his mid-thirties and the hair at the front of his head was going fast. His hair showed a cap line all the way around. The young man turned and indicated Whelan with a nod of his head.

"Wants to ask us questions about Tony Blanchard."

The older man frowned slightly. "Again? About Tony, or about those killings?"

"About Tony."

"Okay with us but—"

"I'm not a police officer."

"He's a private investigator," the young one said.

Whelan took out his wallet and showed his identification.

"Private investigator. Who are you working for? Or am I not supposed to ask that?"

"You can ask. Actually, I'm working for a woman that Tony lived with for a while. Mrs. Evangeline Pritchett."

The young man looked to the older one. The man nodded. "Right. I heard he was staying with a friend of the family for a while. That her?"

"Right."

"And…I don't mean to tell you your business but—are we sure she's, you know, all right?"

Whelan shrugged. "The cops referred her to me. I know the detective who's been working on the case. You probably made his acquaintance earlier, and if he's in a good mood, he'll vouch for me. You can call him over at Area Six if you want."

"That guy Bauman?" The older one made a face as though a bad smell had come in through the door. "Never mind, forget it, we'll take your word for it. I don't need to talk to that guy again."

"Had his party manners on when he was here, huh?"

"That's about it. He wanted to question all the kids and most of them weren't even here when Tony was."

"There was no point in some of the stuff he wanted to do," the young one added. "Pretty hostile dude."

"He is that," Whelan said.

The older man came forward, hand extended. "I'm Jack Mollan. I'm director of the home. This is Greg Purcell, he's our staff counselor."

"Paul Whelan." He shook hands with the older man.

"Come on in, Paul."

Whelan stepped into the hall and the men led him into a small, crowded living room filled with furniture that had seen hard use.

"Coffee?" Greg Purcell asked.

"Sure, thanks."

The three of them sat in the living room and sipped coffee from Styrofoam cups for a moment and made small talk to get themselves acclimated to the situation.

"I already know a certain amount about Tony Blanchard. What I need from you guys is anything that might tell me where to look for him, or how to look for him. When did he leave here?"

Mollan leaned forward. "A year ago, at least. And I want to make clear, he left here on good terms. He didn't run away."

"Mrs. Pritchett told me that."

"I just wanted to make sure you knew that. A lot of kids on the street are running away from their living situations. Some of them come from places so bad they'll live in abandoned buildings without heat and water rather than go back to abusive or violent situations. Tony was just a kid who had no place. He came to us, went along with the program, pulled his weight, got along fine. He wasn't the nicest kid in the home and he wasn't the worst either. He worked for a while when he was here, bagging groceries at the Aldi over on Broadway to pay for food and things like that."

"Is that standard practice here? The kids work outside the home?"

Mollan nodded. "They're not bums so we don't treat them like bums. They're expected to perform certain chores around the home and earn money toward their keep. Most of the money they bring in we put away for them. The majority of our kids finish school while they're here—Tony didn't, but he did everything else we advised him to do."

"You sound like you like the kids."

Mollan shrugged. "I don't know about that, but I understand them. I worked with 'em a long time, here and other places." He looked around the room.

A black teenager stuck his head in the doorway. "Can I have some juice?"

"Go ahead, Reynard," Mollan said.

"Me, too?" A grinning white boy poked his head around the black kid's body.

"Don't try my patience, Donnie. He's sick, you're not. Get some juice and get back upstairs."

Mollan looked at Whelan. "On a good day, there's nobody here between eight and three, they're all in school. Today we've got one home sick and one truant. I'm supposed to meet with his principal in about an hour."

"I think I can guess which one is the truant."

Mollan nodded and seemed to be distracted momentarily.

"He's a good kid, though," Purcell put in. "School bores him. After the life he's had, I can see how school would seem boring."

Mollan looked at Whelan. "When he came to us, he'd been sleeping in an abandoned car in a vacant lot. God knows what else was going on in his life." He squinted as though remembering something, then looked at Whelan. "Do you know anything about what happens to these kids on the street?"

"Not the way you do, but in general, yeah. Prostitution and sickness, malnutrition, random violence…"

"AIDS. Murder. Rape. People cutting them out of the herd so they can use them. There's people that go around looking for them, particularly the real young ones that haven't got any street sense yet. They—"

"People kill them," Greg Purcell broke in. "There's no other way to put it. They just kill 'em, like they're not real people." He seemed to catch himself and looked down quickly at his coffee.

"It's pretty goddam frustrating," Mollan said. "The cops find them in doorways and alleys, and most of them they have to bury." Mollan gestured toward the doorway where the young truant had just appeared. "An abandoned car," he said in a harsh whisper. "Can you see yourself living in an abandoned car? Me, neither. But can you imagine what a kid like this, what his days and nights are like?"

"No. I've known some homeless adults and I've tried to

imagine what that would be like for one of them, and I can't, so I wouldn't begin to understand what it would be like for a kid."

"Adults got a better chance to live. And some of 'em, at least, had a life before things got screwed up. Most of these kids never had what you'd recognize as a life. Most of them come from poor families or families where there was no father around. Some of 'em were abandoned. Lot of them have been abused, one way or another. Lot of them..." And Jack Mollan let his voice trail off. He stood looking down at the worn carpet and shaking his head.

"Every one of them's got a story," Greg Purcell said, as though needing to puncture the silence.

Whelan looked around the room. "Those two kids seemed pretty comfortable with you. This seems like a place I'd want to stay in for a while if I'd been on the street."

"Some of 'em, you'd like to keep forever," Purcell said. "But you can't, you know..." He shrugged and shook his head.

"You can't protect them all their lives," Mollan finished for him. "You can't live their lives for them. They can't stay forever, and some of them, to be honest, want to be on their own. I mean, they're like any teenager that way—they want a car and steady money and to call their own shots. And when they're ready to go it alone, when they've got a few bucks and some idea what they're gonna do, we say, 'Hey, God bless,' and they leave. And we cross our fingers."

"How long do they stay here?"

"Depends on the kid and whatever extra baggage he's got to deal with while he's here—but it's an average of seven months, maybe eight."

"And when Tony left, he was together?"

The young one nodded and Mollan made a shaky motion with his hand.

"You're not sure," Whelan said.

"With Tony it wasn't always easy to tell. He was quiet, for one thing, kept a lot to himself. And his situation was a little different—as far as we can tell, he didn't come from a bad home, just, you know, his life disintegrated when his mother died. It happened to him really sudden, he wakes up one morning and he's an orphan. He didn't have any other family. But there was no previous history of him leaving his home or being tossed out, no violence…"

"Could that have made him less prepared to handle his situation?"

"Absolutely. And that was part of his problem. He was pretty angry when he first came here, and very confused. He had a home once and now it was gone."

"And what is he like now, if he's out there?"

"Who knows?" Mollan said. "If you're asking me, is he violent? —no, I can't see it. I don't see that kind of a change. He wasn't violent before and he wasn't violent here, so I don't think he's out there stomping old people for SSI checks. But it doesn't sound like he was able to handle it on his own."

"What do you think happened? Old contacts?"

Mollan nodded. "I think he had to have somebody to give him orders and somebody he knew got him in with this…" He groped for a word and Whelan could see him trying to avoid the cliche "gang."

"Burglary ring, the police said."

"Yeah. I think somebody he knew was already in with these guys and it was easy for Tony to be sucked in."

"After he left here, did you ever see him or hear from him?"

"One time. I ran into him on the street. This was over by the ballpark. I think he was already in with these people. He seemed real uneasy, anxious for the conversation to end. I don't know what he was doing or what he was into, but he was embarrassed."

"Is there anybody from his life outside this home that he might have gone to?"

Mollan shook his head. "He didn't have anybody. Nobody we knew of, anyway. We weren't aware of the lady you're working for until, you know, later."

"How about anybody from here?"

Mollan blinked. "What? You mean the kids? No, he wasn't in touch with any of the kids."

"How do you know for sure?"

Mollan gave him an irritated look. "I don't know *anything* for sure. Do you? I just think between Greg and the other staff here and myself, we'd know if anybody here was in touch with Tony. If he was in touch with any of these kids outside the home, it would get back to us. But you're missing the point."

"Which is?"

"He didn't know these kids. It's a whole different group. He maybe met one or two of them just before he left us, but basically he was gone before these kids came into the program."

"Can you think of any of the kids who were here when he was here, anybody he might be running with now?"

"No. There was a kid who was here before I took this position. Sonny Portis. Sonny left the home in about Tony's second month here, and they may have known each other outside before Tony came here."

"Where can I find Sonny Portis?"

Mollan shook his head. "He's dead. He lasted about three months on the street. Not one of our, uh, success stories. Greg can tell you more about him than I can. I never knew him."

"How did he die?"

"Somebody stuck him. Drug deal gone bad," Purcell said. "In an alley up by Clarendon Park. He walked out our door and we never saw him again. It happens that way sometimes."

"Did you ever hear Tony talk about Argyle Street? New Chinatown, some people call it—Little Chinatown."

"I know what you're talking about. No, never." Mollan looked to Purcell. The young counselor shook his head. "Far as I know he never went there. Why?"

"Somebody told me I might have some luck up there. That Tony knew somebody there."

"News to me."

Whelan finished his coffee and stood. "Well, thanks for your time. And for the coffee. It's cold out there."

"Yeah, spring in Chicago. There's a word for that, you know? Two words together that contradict each other."

"An oxymoron."

"That's it."

Whelan handed Mollan his card. "If you think of anything, or hear anything, please give me a call."

"We will." Mollan shook his hand and opened the door. As Whelan was leaving, he opened his mouth to speak and then seemed to change his mind.

"Were you going to ask if I thought he was still alive?"

"Yeah."

"I don't like to give people false hopes so, no. It doesn't look real good. Everybody he knew turns up dead, we have to assume that the person or persons responsible wanted him, too. The fact that nobody's seen him in weeks makes me think he's not out there. The police are looking for him as well and he still hasn't turned up so…I don't think we're going to find him."

Mollan nodded slowly, the calm nod of a man who has just heard exactly what he expected to hear. "Thanks. Good luck."

Whelan waved and went down the stairs.

Seven

The sun was just setting and the dampness in the air made for a cold night, but he could smell the fish in the lake. Smelt season, old men with three or four nets in the water, sitting on the jagged rocks with lanterns and a couple of beers and waiting out the smelt. He sat in his car for several minutes and listened to the radio and turned it all over in his mind. It had occurred to him that much of the ground he had to cover had already been covered by the police. If he didn't find a way of doing it differently, he was simply wasting his time. He remembered what Mrs. Pritchett had said about the area where Tony hung out at night: a place where a lot of kids went, a place with a doughnut shop. Whelan put that together with the tattoo and thought he had a pretty good idea where to look.

There had always been something seedy about the strip of Belmont that ran from Sheffield to Clark. The neighborhood around it had undergone that familiar rebirth that always accompanied a massive infusion of money but Belmont itself had remained slightly disreputable, like the reprobate cousin who won't dress up for family parties. On the side streets around it, homes went for $200,000, but Belmont was still the far side of the tracks.

Over the past ten years, entrepreneurs of every stripe had jumped into the strip, and to the handful of quaint ethnic restaurants from the old days—Swedish, Japanese, Chinese, and Mexican—there was Muskie's hamburger stand, a video arcade, a punk nightclub calling itself "Berlin," and a leather shop, along with holdovers from the past—a pawn shop, a couple of junk shops, a greasy spoon under the tracks, an Army surplus store, a pair of tattoo parlors and a hotel for transients.

What Whelan was looking for, however, was at the eastern end of the street: a big, brightly lit, pink-and-white Dunkin' Donuts franchise where street kids gathered most nights. It was still a little early for them to congregate.

Whelan parked and went looking for dinner. He settled on Ann Sather's, an old-time Swedish diner where six bucks gave you your choice of about fifteen entrees and a dozen side dishes. As always, the place, recently converted from an old funeral home, was packed with a cross section of Northside humanity: young couples, groups of gay men, families with screaming kids, and at the counter, solitary men from the hotel across the street. He wrestled with the possibilities and settled on Swedish meatballs, mashed potatoes, creamed spinach and a side of stewed tomatoes. Here, they threw dessert in for the price of the meal and he had a peach cobbler.

The waitress brought him a bill for $5.71 and he shook his head. "I feel like I'm stealing."

"Good. Leave a big tip," she said and strutted away.

Night had taken over and the entire populace seemed to be on the street. A stiff wind licked off the surface of the lake a mile to the east and filled the air with the smells of water and fish. It was a cold wind but for as long as Whelan could remember he'd associated it with spring and for the first time he realized winter was finished. In the window of the transients' hotel across the street from the restaurant, a couple of men in their fifties sat in barrel chairs and watched the street life go by. Whelan shouldered his way through the crowd and headed for the corner. The kids were already gathering in front of the game room near the tracks, and he saw half a dozen standing outside a video rental store. When he was a few yards from the Dunkin' Donuts, he crossed Belmont against the traffic and earned a blast on the horn from a stressed-looking guy in a new Buick.

Just inside an alley near the corner, three kids put their faces together by a telephone pole and did business. He saw money change hands and a tiny plastic bag appear, and the flashiest dressed of the three kids walked out of the alley pocketing his money.

Just like old times, he thought.

He passed the tattoo parlor at the mouth of the alley and the junk shop beside it where a kid could dress in the height of adolescent fashion, and a shop that sold plaster statues and paints to decorate them, and turned into the parking lot of the Dunkin' Donuts.

There was no single spot where they congregated: the kids stood in clusters in the parking lot and on the sidewalk surrounding the place and at the bus stop and outside the entrances to the place. Inside, the ones with money lined the table along the windows and nursed coffee or hot chocolate and munched on doughnuts.

Whelan leaned against the wall of the plaster shop and lit a cigarette. For a minute he smoked and watched the kids on the street as discreetly as he could. Eventually it became obvious that there were several distinct groups here, and he thought he could make them out: city kids looking for a hangout, genuine street kids, and suburban kids here to imitate city kids and find adventure. The city kids, white or black, had a breezy raucous way about them, high-fiving and laughing and calling one another names; the suburban ones dressed to imitate the city kids, particularly the black ones—baseball caps worn at odd angles, baggy pants and shirts. The street kids were a group apart. A couple of them were already beginning to look like street people, a little more wrinkled, more unwashed than the ones who'd just left Mom and Pop in front of a TV set. These kids weren't as demonstrative or noisy, they watched everything—the other kids, the cars pulling in, the people passing by on the sidewalk. Twice while he studied them, Whelan saw kids watching him and he had no doubt that one or two of them had already made him for a cop.

He imagined street cops or a guy like Bauman trying to get information from the kids on what they fantasized was their own turf and shook his head. There had to be a way to do this.

Whelan tossed the cigarette into the street and went to the

doughnut shop. The air inside was steamy and smelled of sugar and things frying in oil, and cigarette smoke—they smoked, these kids, all of them—and cheap cologne and bubble gum, and a half dozen of them watched him walk in.

The girl at the register was having trouble ringing up doughnuts and coffee for three girls. A few feet from her, a serious-looking man put out bismarcks and longjohns in perfect rows. He seemed out of place, an accountant or computer programmer dropped into the world of doughnuts and coffee. Whelan watched him till the man noticed and turned. The man raised his eyebrows behind silver-rimmed glasses.

"Yes? Can I help you?"

Whelan could feel the eyes of several of the kids on him. He smiled at the man and said, "I'm lost. I need directions."

The man came over and Whelan stepped a few feet away from the nearest customers. He pulled out his business card and a pen and began drawing on the back of the card.

"Can you show me how to get to this address?" When the man squinted and bent over the card, Whelan said in a low voice, "I'm a private detective. I'm trying to find a boy who used to hang out here. Tony Blanchard."

The man never looked up from the card. He shook his head. "Don't know the name."

"White kid, long hair, tattoo of a comet on his arm. Average height, skinny, scar on his chin."

"Oh. I remember the tattoo. He hasn't been here in—oh, it must be a month."

"What I need is for you to look around—here or outside in your parking lot—and tell me somebody who you saw him with, or somebody he talked to."

The man leaned back and looked around the room. In an unnecessarily loud voice, he said, "A cab driver might be able to take you there."

"I'm driving," Whelan said. Quietly, he added, "Lighten up."

The man bent over again, grinning. Having an adventure break from the doughnuts. He pointed to Whelan's card and said, "Two girls in the parking lot. Black one and a white one, the black one wears those little tiny braids."

"Appreciate it," Whelan said. He slid his card under a napkin, stood back and shrugged. "Well, thanks anyhow."

Shaking his head, he left the restaurant. He took the long way through the parking lot, pretended to be looking at street signs, and then made his way toward the girls in a long loop. He never made eye contact till he was almost within arm's reach, but the black girl had already made him when he looked at them.

"This is who I am," he said, holding up a card for both girls to look at. "I need information, and..."

"I ain't telling nobody shit," the white girl said. She had large blue eyes and crooked teeth and dark hair dyed an unearthly shade of red, the color of cherries and tropical flowers. The black girl in the dreadlocks laughed.

"...and I'd appreciate it if you'd just listen to me for a second. It's not about you, and I don't need you to inform on any of your friends..."

The black girl looked ready to laugh in his face.

"...and it will be the fastest ten bucks either of you ever made."

The white girl opened her mouth and the black one nudged her with an elbow. "Listen up, girl. Man want to give us money." She looked up at Whelan over the blue plastic rims of her glasses and he saw a girl used to doing business on the street.

"Ten bucks each?"

Not what I had in mind, Whelan thought, but I'm making a whopping five hundred for this one. He nodded. "Each. But I don't have time for anybody to jerk me around."

"What you want to know?"

"I'm looking for Tony Blanchard." The white girl began to roll her eyes. "And if you don't have anything at all for me, you can walk, lady." The girl glared at him. "I'm looking for Tony Blanchard. Other people have been looking for him, probably here, and maybe they talked to you girls. But I want to find him and if I don't, he'll be in more trouble than he is now." The girls gave him a practiced stare, two would-be streetwise kids showing how bad they were.

"You hang out here every night?"

The black girl smirked. "I don't hang out nowhere every night. I move. I don't even stay in the same crib every night. I'm a poet. You want to hear some poetry?"

"No. For ten bucks I shouldn't have to hear any poetry. For ten bucks I want to find Tony Blanchard."

"Why?" She smiled coyly. The girl was missing a tooth on the bottom.

"I've been hired to find him."

"By who? He didn't have no family."

"By a woman he used to stay with."

The girl considered this and shrugged. "He ain't been up here. Don't nobody know where he at."

"Do you know where he might go to get out of trouble?"

The girl shook her head and Whelan told himself that ten bucks didn't buy much these days.

"Okay, let's try something different, then. If you can't help me find him, maybe you can help me find the person who's after him. If Tony hasn't been around here, he probably thinks this person knows this was one of his hangouts. He probably saw the guy here." Something changed in the white girl's eyes and she didn't look so tough now. The black girl refused to meet his eyes. He gave it a push.

"Maybe you saw this guy. I don't need much—a name, if you heard Tony mention one, a description. I know I'm looking for a white guy."

An almost imperceptible nod from the black girl. "Old *nasty* white dude."

"You have my complete attention."

"Glasses. Big teeth. Got teeth like a horse," she said, and the white girl giggled. "Little skinny-ass face, got those pinched-in cheeks like he don't eat. Stand with his hand in one pocket and suck on his cigarettes, like this…" The young street poet thrust one hand into her stained ski jacket, let her shoulders slope and pretended to be watching people on the street.

"Gray hair? White hair?"

"Got ugly hair, that's what he have. Ugly old white hair."

She picked up one of her tiny braids and held it straight up. "His hair stick up on top of his head like he just woke up and forgot to comb it."

"Tell him about the dude's eyes," the white one said. "He gots these weird eyes like somebody, you know, like hypnotized his ass." She looked at her friend.

"Look like he's dead, those funny eyes. Look like a zombie."

"He made a nice first impression, huh?"

The black girl gave him the over-the-rims look again. "Mister, this was one ugly-lookin' motherfucker. His mama shoulda kep' him home."

She glanced at her companion and the two girls gave in to their laughter. The black girl held out her hand, palm up, and the white girl ran her palm across it, and they shook their heads and just lost it.

Whelan waited till they could calm themselves and then said quietly, "Got a name?"

"Name oughtta be 'ugly,'" the black girl said and they started laughing again.

"I take that for a 'no.' Did Tony ever talk to either of you about this man?" The white girl gave her friend a sidelong glance and both kept their silence.

"He did," Whelan said, "but you don't want to tell me anything he said. Okay. Did Tony ever see this man when you were around?"

They nodded.

"What did he do?"

"What do you think, man?" the white girl said. "He booked. He ran down that alley." She tilted her audaciously red head in the direction of the alley behind the doughnut place.

Whelan thought for a moment. "When was the last time you saw Tony?"

"Ain't seen Tony in weeks," the white girl said.

"And when was the last time you saw the older man?"

The white girl looked at her companion and shrugged. "That night it rained?"

The black girl nodded. "Right. That big rain. He was just

standing out there in the rain."

Whelan felt a little flutter in his chest. He took out his money clip and pulled out two tens. He handed one to each girl. "Thanks."

The bills disappeared in microseconds. The girls grinned at him. "You see Tony, tell him Angie said 'Hey,' " the white girl said.

"And Jozette," the girl with the dreadlocks said.

"I'll do that. And here," Whelan said, handing them each his card. "If you see that guy around here, call me. If you see Tony, tell *him* to call me."

They stared at his card and did their best to look indifferent. Whelan nodded to them and walked away. When he was a dozen or so paces from them, the white kid yelled out, "Good luck with that old ugly man." She appended half a dozen obscenities in case Whelan didn't know how she felt.

Whelan didn't bother to turn around. As he walked, he could hear them, convulsed with their humor, assured of their own invulnerability. He shook his head. There were few things as pitiful as young girls trying to sound hard.

At the corner, he surveyed the groups of laughing, gesturing kids. The ones who were just slumming, the kids from middle-class homes or the ones who drove in each night from the suburbs, they'd be back in their beds by midnight. The other ones, the genuine street kids, would have darker prospects. He thought about the two tough young street girls and wondered if either one would see her eighteenth birthday.

On the way back, he rolled down his window to let in the wet lake wind with its half-hearted promise of spring. In his boyhood, on nights such as this, they'd gather on somebody's porch and talk baseball. He could still see the faces around him on the stairs: Artie Shears and Mickey Byrne and Hansie Becker and the others. Somebody bouncing a ball off the top of the porch and someone else swinging an old bat and talking about the hotshot equipment he'd buy when he saved up enough allowance: new bats, spikes, a glove, maybe. You were always going to buy a new glove someday, a Wilson A-2000.

On his car radio they were playing Cannonball Adderley's version of "Mercy, Mercy, Mercy," and Whelan felt good because the two little street girls had just given him his first good news in days, the first reason to believe that Tony Blanchard was alive. The big rain, the first occasion of the year when Mother Nature had decided to drop something other than snow on Chicago, had been less than a week ago.

The Koreans were closing up inside Larry's but there was no sign of Marty, and the apartment where Marty lived with his brother was dark. Whelan drove north on Sheridan toward Argyle Street. The signs of the local business kept the traveler posted as to the ethnic makeup of each section. He drove past St. Augustine's Indian Center, past the Burger King and McDonald's, past a new Mexican restaurant and a place proclaiming itself HOJAS OTONOS—AUTUMN LEAVES SUPERMARKET AND LIQUOR. A few more blocks and he was in Southeast Asia again.

The biting wind that said "Rites of Spring" to Whelan apparently still said "Demons of Winter" to the people on Argyle Street. It had driven most of the natives into hiding but he could see inside the steamy restaurant windows that business was good in New Chinatown. He parked where he'd parked earlier in the day and walked down toward the Apollo. The street bore a different set of smells now, the odors of things cooked in sesame oil and stirred in a wok, dough being deep-fried, meat on an open grill.

As he walked, he took note of the clientele of each restaurant. You could tell the best ones: they were full of Asiatic people. Lucky Grocery Market was closed, inhabited now only by the row of unhappy ducks. A few doors down, the square-built old man who'd been so busy sweeping that afternoon was now sitting in a table in the window of the little Vietnamese place, smoking a cigarette. Whelan waved to him and the man stared. Vietnamese sat at several tables along the wall but there was no sign of the woman who owned the restaurant.

The crowd at the Apollo was half of what it had been in the morning. His waitress was gone but the fat man was still working the grill. Whelan got a cup of coffee and took a seat in the window where the cop had been reading the paper on his last visit.

He smoked and sipped at his coffee and watched the street, and the only Caucasian he saw was the one reflected in the window.

After the second cup he ordered some soup, to justify taking up their window space, but no one seemed to care. When he finished the soup and the third cup of coffee, he picked up a discarded paper and began idly paging through it. In the sports section he found the annual story he'd come to love, the one where the manager of the Cubs, a man no more than a hairbreadth from unemployment, waxed ecstatic over the new faces in the Cub pitching rotation. A "solid rotation," the soon-to-be-fired manager said of the embattled knot of men who'd just been shelled by the East Coast hitters. Whelan shook his head and smiled, then stopped, aware that someone was watching him. He looked out at the street and caught the faintest trace of a figure moving out of his line of vision.

Whelan had only impressions but they were enough: a slender figure in denim, Caucasian, long hair. He tossed the paper on the counter, ran out of the restaurant and collided with a pair of young Vietnamese men.

"Sorry," he said, and shot past them. Up ahead of him, the slender figure was already a half block away and making for Kenmore. Whelan ran east on Argyle on a parallel course but could see he was close to losing the runner. In the middle of the block he dodged cars and crossed Argyle, reaching the far side just as his quarry crossed Kenmore and cut up the side street heading south. When Whelan finally made it to the corner, he crossed to the far side of Kenmore, stopped and scanned both sides of the street. A young black man walked toward him and dropped his eyes as he approached Whelan.

"Did you see somebody run up this street?"

The young man made a stiff shake of his head and kept his

eyes focused on the sidewalk.

Right, Whelan said to himself. He trotted toward the alley and then came to a stop. Nothing was moving in the alley, in any direction, but he had a sense that whoever he was chasing hadn't had time to make it any farther. He moved quietly into the alley, all the while telling himself this was a very bad idea.

Twenty feet in, a fat gray cat jumped out from a dumpster, gave him a disdainful look, and trotted away. Whelan moved a few feet farther, stopped and was about to turn back when he saw the movement from the corner of his eye. He spun to block it but the blow still caught him across the top of his head.

He heard himself groan and fell to the pavement. He heard the wooden clatter of something falling to the ground, the scrape of footsteps on the concrete, someone moving out of the alley fast.

He stayed down for a moment, cradling the top of his head in both hands and rocking back and forth. A searing pain, dizziness, a sudden rush of nausea. An egg was forming, quickly, a large hard egg and he thought he felt moisture. Eventually, he pulled himself into a sitting position and took long slow breaths to calm his stomach. When the nausea subsided, he looked around. His assailant was gone, the cat was gone, the rats in the alley were probably gone. A few inches away he saw what appeared to be a table leg. He reached over and pawed it toward him.

"Damn." He felt the egg again and looked at his fingers—a slight bloodstain but nothing melodramatic. No one appeared in any of the windows, no witnesses to his embarrassment. Whelan sighed and allowed himself the small indulgence of sitting in the alley for a while, hoping only that no one would see him.

When he was certain he could stand, he got up and left the alley and went up the street to his car, half expecting to find a shattered windshield or slashed tires. Nothing. The only damage to the Jet was the damage it bore in noisy dignity every time Whelan drove the car—rust, loose things rattling around under the hood, belts near death, something working its way to freedom in its undercarriage.

Whelan got in and started the car, then took a look at himself in the mirror. The egg wasn't that obvious—he just looked like a guy with a bad haircut.

He spent a pointless half hour cruising the streets and alleys of the area, then widened his search to include some of the Uptown streets where he'd seen kids huddled together in boredom. Eventually he gave it up.

He hit a couple of buttons on the radio and found a rock station playing an old Beatles tune, "Getting Better."

For you guys, maybe, Whelan thought. But as he drove away from Argyle Street he saw that there was another way to look at it. *I guess I must be doing good—two days on this, and I've already pissed somebody off.*

Eight

His lump hurt when he woke the next morning, and when he showered, and even more when he combed his hair. To compensate himself, he made a vegetarian omelet and bacon, lingering over his breakfast and three cups of coffee and listening to music. Eventually he went out to work. There was a crisp wind from the north and that hurt his head, too.

Whelan was sitting in his car outside Larry's at ten-fifteen when Marty Wills appeared up the street, struggling in to work. Whelan couldn't be sure at this distance, but he believed he was watching a young man in the throes of a murderous hangover.

Good. We're all walking wounded this morning.

He got out of his car and walked up the street to intercept the kid. The midmorning sun had burned off most of the chill, and he felt slightly uncomfortable in his canvas vest. Halfway up the block, he stopped and waited—Marty hadn't seen him yet. The boy walked head down with a slight lurch, stumbling once over a hole in the pavement. He was within ten yards of Whelan when he looked up. What he saw stopped him in mid-stride.

Whelan saw Marty mouth the word "fuck," and for a second he thought the boy would bolt.

Go ahead, Whelan thought. For once, I've got a guy I can outrun.

To the boy, he said, "Morning, Marty. I need your help."

Marty stared at him and said nothing. He breathed through his mouth like a man who has come a great distance.

"Not feeling so hot, huh?"

Marty gave him a sullen look and muttered, "I got the flu."

You got that mean ol' bottle flu. "Well, it's the flu season. I take tomato juice myself."

Marty turned slightly green and looked away.

"Or sometimes, if it's really bad, a raw egg." Marty gasped. "But a lot of people can't eat a raw egg. Tuna salad's good—high in protein, so it's good for the lining of your stomach."

"Aw, man, gimme a break."

"Just trying to be helpful, Marty. Listen, the other day when we talked, you told me about Les but I think the guy I need to find out about is a different guy entirely. I think you'd know this guy if you saw him. Older man, white hair, glasses, funny eyes, big teeth."

Whelan caught the look that danced across Marty's face. The kid tried on a couple of expressions, boredom, nonchalance, but Whelan had seen his eyes.

"You've seen him."

"I see a thousand people at work. I see a hundred old guys with glasses on the street. Fuckin' neighborhood's crawling with 'em."

"Not like this one. And I think if you saw this one walk into Larry's you'd shit in your pants. That's what I think."

Marty studied his shoes. Muddy high-top gym shoes, tongues out and laces undone. "I gotta go, man. I'm late."

"Is he after you, Marty? Or just Tony?"

A pleading look came into the kid's eyes. "He don't know me from fucking Adam. I wasn't in that shit."

"I heard different."

"I give a shit what you heard," Marty said, but he wasn't convincing.

"What's his name?"

"Like I know every old blow job on the street? Like we're friends or—"

"Chill out, Marty. Which would you prefer? For me to find him, or him to find you?"

Marty looked around for a moment, licking his lips and breathing through his mouth. Whelan shuddered and took a step back: wine breath. Muscatel? Richards? Thunderbird? What did the amateurs drink these days?

"Whitey, his name is."

"Got a last name?"

"No. I don't know, just Whitey. 'The old man' is pretty much what everybody called him."

"How well did you know him?"

"I toldja, I didn't know 'im."

"But Tony did."

"I don't know, why don't you ask him?"

"Whitey was the guy I asked you about, wasn't he? Jimmy's partner?"

"He wasn't nobody's partner, man."

"What was he, then? Competition?"

"He was an old fuckin' creep."

"What else can you tell me about him?"

The boy shot him a look full of venom. "He looks like a fucking skull, man. Like a corpse. The dude's face looks like somebody sucked all the juice out of it." He shook his head as though to clear it of the image.

"Tall?"

"Not as tall as you. A little taller than me."

That made the man about six feet tall.

"And his hair," Marty made a vague motion toward his hair, "it sticks up like…" He shook his head. "He's a freaky-looking dude."

"You know where he is?"

"I don't know where nobody is. I got nothing to do with any of this shit."

"Hope not. What's going down isn't very nice, and the bad part is, it's not over yet—but you knew that."

Marty nodded hesitantly. Then he shot Whelan a sly look. "Any luck with Tony?"

"No. You'd have been the first to know." He studied the kid for a moment. The slyness came back into Marty's face, and something else. Then he looked away.

"I gotta go."

"All right. Thanks, Marty. Hope you feel better."

He was back in his car, heading north, thinking about the look he'd seen in Marty's eyes. It was amusement—if only for a second, but amusement, nonetheless.

Glad you found something to smile about, kid.

Whelan parked across the street from the tavern but went around back. Two cars were parked in the yard, a little red Chevy and a dark blue Olds. A woman was just emerging from the apartment above the tavern. She was a slim weathered-looking woman in her late forties with dark reddish hair piled high and tight jeans that she filled well. She gave a start when she saw him, paused at the top step and then came down, looking past him.

He pushed open the sheet-metal rear door and entered the tavern. Bobby Hayes had changed his red shirt for a green one and had moved one stool closer to the television; other than that, nothing had changed at Ed and Ronda's. Hayes looked up briefly when the door opened and looked away quickly. Whelan moved past him and slid onto a stool beside him.

"How are things, Bob?"

Hayes looked up, blinked as though in sudden recognition, and shook his head. "Snuck up on me there, son. Pull up a stool and sit down—oh, you already done that. Hey, Ed. Get this Yankee a drink."

The potbellied man plodded over and looked at Whelan. "You want a drink?"

"Too early for me."

"Hell, it's nighttime in China," Hayes said, and tried on a smile that didn't take.

"In China, they put dead snakes in their liquor. I'll have a ginger ale."

"So what can I do you out of?" Hayes asked. He kept his left hand on his drink and fumbled for a cigarette with the other, shaking one out, picking it up, popping it in his mouth and then lighting it with the monogrammed lighter. "Still looking for them li'l boys?" He blew smoke out in the direction of the bar mirror, looked at himself through the cloud, and then turned for Whelan's answer.

"No, not kids this time. A full-grown man, old guy. Fellow

you probably did some business with yourself."

Bobby Hayes smiled and the smile looked real this time. He shook his head and pointed his finger at Whelan. "You're a smart ol' boy but I'm a smart ol' boy, too."

"That's us, Bob. Couple of Rhodes scholars."

"I don't know nothing about that, but I do know you been talking to folks, and I know who some of 'em are. I know you been talking to Lester. I like your style: you talk to Lester 'bout me and you talk to me 'bout Lester." Hayes took a sip of his drink and shook his head. The world was an amusing place this morning. "So whatcha want to know about ol' Lester?"

"Nothing." He took a sip of his ginger ale and took out a cigarette, and when he thought he'd made Hayes wait long enough, he said, "Whitey."

"Say what?"

"Whitey. I want to know about Whitey."

He turned and looked at Bobby Hayes. The smile died young. For a moment, Whelan was convinced Bobby Hayes was no longer breathing. Hayes watched him for a three-count and began to shake his head. He puffed up his cheeks and looked up at the ceiling as if trying to place the name and shrugged. Whelan would have laughed out loud if Hayes hadn't looked so terrified.

"Don't know any 'Whitey.' Sorry."

"You're sorry, all right. You're sorry you came back to Chicago and sorry your brother's people all started getting whacked in vacant lots and sorry your last name's Hayes, and you're probably sorry you can't run faster. But you know Whitey."

"No, sir, I sure don't, and that's a fact."

"Bob, I think every time that door opens, you expect to see an old guy named Whitey. All I want to know is, why?"

Hayes was still shaking his head, still refusing to look Whelan in the eye. "You're pretty far off base, Whelan. You're way out there in left field. I never heard of nobody named Whitey."

"Guess not. But if you run into anybody named Whitey, or figure out where somebody like me might find a guy named Whitey, you've got my card."

"Sure will." Bobby Hayes sank back into his chair and Whelan could see him begin to relax. Whelan climbed off the stool and patted Hayes on the back.

"Thanks for the ginger ale."

"Any time. Good luck finding this Whitey."

Whelan smiled. "I'm going to need it, Bob. I think he kills people."

The troubled look came back into Bobby Hayes's eyes and he looked away. When Whelan pushed his way out the front door, Bobby Hayes was singing with Linda Ronstadt. A little boy whistling past the graveyard, Whelan thought.

As he drove away from the bar, he went over the sketchy picture he had of this man and wondered what there was about this skinny man in his fifties or sixties that terrified everybody.

What do they know that I don't?

Lester the fence wasn't at his regular stool yet so Whelan left the grill and drove up Sheridan to the Carlos Hotel. He parked directly across the street and began reading the paper, from time to time glancing at the ornate white marble facade of a landmark from another time.

In a town filled near bursting with shady hotels, many of them famous, the Carlos held a unique place in street folklore. A small gray building two blocks up the street from Wrigley Field, it had passed into local legend in the 1930s, when a star Cub player had been shot in one of its rooms. The shooter was his distraught young lover. These days the Carlos was a hotel for transients. It was not known whether the current crop of Cub players held their assignations there anymore.

Whelan was finishing the sports section when Lester came out. There was no evidence that he'd changed clothes in the past two days. Whelan gave him a half-block start and then followed him on foot to a newsstand under the El station at Sheridan and Irving, where Lester bought the green sheet and headed for the restaurant. Whelan gave him a minute, then went in.

The old fence was bent over the green sheet, squinting, his

nose nearly touching the paper and his right elbow resting in a pool of ketchup. The nasty hat sat a few feet away and cast evil spells over other people's lunches. Lester circled one horse, shook his head, scratched it out and circled another.

Whelan watched Les doping his horses: The Poor Man's Pension. All over town, guys like Lester were hunched over the racing form and hoping to make a fast buck, maybe even The Big Score. Somebody somewhere had been telling them all that this was America, anybody could be rich, everybody had a shot at the big money, and they all bought it, every last one of them, and they'd all go to their graves clutching the green sheet or a lottery ticket or their daily number and wondering who had screwed them out of their payoff.

"Lester."

The old man cupped a hand over his picks and looked up, eyes wide with worry. He tried on a scowl but it didn't take. "What you want now?"

"I don't want your horses, Les. Relax."

"Don't tell me to relax."

"Okay, I won't." He sat down next to Les and gingerly shoved the hat away with his finger. Immediately Les grabbed it and slapped it on the counter away from Whelan. It landed in a little puff of dust and debris. Lester glared at him.

"I got a name to try out on you."

"I ain't giving you shit."

"This would be worth a couple bucks."

Lester sneered and allowed himself a hoarse whisper of a laugh. Whelan put his hand on the counter and let the corner of a ten show and Lester stopped to collect his thoughts. While Lester considered his options, a consumptive-looking waitress started toward Whelan. He gestured to the coffee pot she carried and she brought him a cup.

To his left, Lester grunted and rooted around in his dirty pockets and came up with what had once been a pack of Luckies. He lit one, looked again at the ten, and made a subtle nod.

Times *must* be tough, Whelan thought. He should have laughed at my ten dollars.

"I've got a guy I need you to tell me about."

Lester made a little bored shrug of his bony shoulders.

Whelan said "Whitey," and old Lester wasn't bored anymore. The old fence put on a nonchalant face but he couldn't quite get the stiffness out of his shoulders.

"Tell me about Whitey, Les."

"Don't mean nothing to me."

"If you knew Jimmy Lee Hayes, you knew Whitey. I need to know about Whitey."

Lester started to pull back into his shell and Whelan pocketed the ten. The old man looked at Whelan's empty hand and said, "Hold on a minute."

"I can't. Time is money, Les. You're a busy guy, I'm a busy guy. Give me something worth ten bucks. Who knows—maybe I've got another picture of Hamilton on me."

"He's just a guy."

Whelan laughed. It was genuine and he hadn't laughed in a while, and the feeling surprised him. "Les? This is not 'just a guy.' I don't know quite what he is, but he's not just a guy, he's somebody's nightmare. A kid I know is terrified to say this guy's name, another kid hits the bricks when he starts showing up in the neighborhood. A grown man watches the tavern door hoping Whitey won't come through it. And you want to tell me he's 'just a guy'?"

"I don't know what you want to find out about 'im."

"Let's start with him and Jimmy Lee. Partners?"

"Long time ago."

"And now?"

"Jimmy Lee don't need no partner."

"So they were partners a long time ago and—then what?"

"Then nothin'. He didn't tell me nothin' else."

Whelan decided to try a new angle. "When did Whitey start showing up again?"

"I don't know. I can't keep track of every goddam—"

"Stop bitching at me and try to make a couple bucks here, Les."

Les puffed at his unfiltered cigarette and put it down in

the ashtray, where the lit end rested on a discarded filter and sent up a plume of yellowish smoke. It smelled like somebody's hairpiece had caught fire.

"When, Les? I have to leave soon—it smells like a camel died here."

"A ways back..."

"Dance faster, Les, and drop the farmboy routine."

"End of the summer, maybe. September, like that. I know he was here during the Series, I remember that. I had a few bucks on the Series."

The sour look on Lester's face told Whelan how the World Series had gone for at least one small-time gambler.

"Did he start working with Jimmy Lee?"

"Nah. He come around and, you know, hung around waiting for people to throw money at him. They did a few jobs together but I know what he wanted. Wanted to take over, that's what. And Jimmy Lee wasn't about to let that sumbitch take his operation, after he built it up and all."

"Some operation. A handful of guys grabbing VCRs and boosting cars and running down alleys. Big deal, Les. What would Whitey want with that? What would anybody want with it? Jimmy Lee was a loser."

Lester stared at him for a moment. "Maybe you don't know as much as you think. Jimmy Lee was one smart fella."

"Smart enough to go into the tank, maybe. Smart enough to get all his people killed. A towering intellect, Les."

"You know so much, how come you're the one has to ask all these questions?"

"Never said I was smart, Les. Just rich. Is Jimmy Lee hiding from Whitey?"

Les chuckled and took up his Lucky again. He puffed and put it back, shaking his head. "What would he do that for? Run from some old man? He just knows when to lay low, you understand? He run into trouble with some people, is all."

"What people?"

"People that's afraid Jimmy's gonna get a piece of their operation." Lester gave him a knowing look and Whelan fought the impulse to tell him how completely and remarkably full of shit he was.

"Names?"

"Have to ask Jimmy 'bout them."

"You have any idea where I could find Whitey?"

"Uh-uh. Nope, I sure don't." Lester looked down at his ashtray and Whelan wondered if anything Lester said was true.

"Here's your ten."

"You said twenty."

"I didn't get twenty, so you don't either. Take it easy, Les."

The old man muttered "shit" and covered the bill with a dirty hand.

"If you come up with something you think I might be interested in, like, you know, the truth, give me a call." Whelan paid for his coffee and left.

He waited in his car fifty feet from the restaurant and watched Les through the wide window. The old fence got up and walked to the phone in the entrance way. He spoke to someone on the phone and hung up after less than a minute. When he emerged, he looked up and down the street and then began walking back toward his hotel. There was a little smile on his face and Whelan thought he looked like a man who has found money.

Lester emerged from the Carlos twenty minutes later and flagged down a northbound Checker cab. Whelan hung back three car lengths and followed the cab up Sheridan to Windsor and then went east. Near the corner of Windsor and a little street called Hazel, the cab pulled up in front of a small shabby apartment building flanked by bigger, newer ones. A small sign attached to the brown brick said it had been turned into a rooming house. The rest of the street seemed to be having trouble making up its mind what it was going to be. A couple of the buildings looked to be in fine condition and one appeared to be in deep need of a cash transfusion. The lot across the street from the rooming house was overgrown with a dense tangle of weeds.

The cabbie waited while Les went in; a moment later, Lester emerged, looking puzzled and tucking what appeared to be a note into his coat pocket. The Checker pulled out, made a U in the service drive of a building and headed back to Sheridan, then on to Broadway. It continued on Broadway all the way south to Diversey, where Broadway ceased to exist. The cab then went up Clark to Armitage, and from time to time, when he allowed himself to get closer, Whelan could see Lester shaking his head angrily in the backseat. At Armitage Lester got out across from the Academy of Sciences gesturing and yelling. From his angle, Whelan could see the cabbie gesturing back.

An unhappy transaction, Whelan thought: the cabbie had taken the longest, slowest way here and old Lester probably wouldn't tip him. Whelan smiled. A couple of small-time con artists trying desperately to screw one another. He waited till the cabbie moved off and then parked and fed a meter. When he crossed Clark to enter Lincoln Park, Lester was already crossing Cannon Drive and heading toward the Farm-in-the-Zoo.

He moved faster and entered the zoo area just in time to see Lester disappear into the nearest of the farm buildings. He hung back for a moment, then entered. This building held a group of sheep and lambs, a sow with a litter of five, and two goats. The goats stared at him. Over it all was the smell of animals and straw and the things animals do in straw. He found himself at the tail end of a school field trip, as a young woman in a khaki zoo employee shirt explained to three dozen giggling children the intricacies of animal husbandry.

Whelan thought the matter could have been simplified: we feed them and when they're fat, we eat them. He looked around the building and saw several adults at the far end but not Lester, and he realized that the old fence had just cut through the building, in one door and out the far one. Whelan followed. A few yards east of the Farm-in-the-Zoo lay the dark green expanse of what zoo people called the South Pond, but one of at least three little man-made bodies of water that the populace called "the Lincoln Park Lagoon." Whelan could see ducks swimming in a long line, and a couple of the little blue paddle boats were already out on the water.

The next building housed chickens and roosters and he waited at the door to allow a mother with two small children in a double stroller to enter ahead of him. The mother was explaining the chicken-and-egg relationship to the kids, who looked puzzled. Lester wasn't in this building either, and Whelan began to have a familiar feeling.

He went through the remaining buildings and found no trace of Lester, then left the Farm-in-the-Zoo. Just beyond it lay the figure-eight shape of the pond, cut in half by a bridge that managed to hide the northern end and the rest of the zoo from view. A pair of tiny, densely overgrown islands sat in the widest part of the pond; as a boy he'd swum out through the murky water and explored them, disappointed to find only a couple of discarded beer cans. From where he stood, he could see only a part of the southern end of the lagoon. A few yards out, a pair of young women laughed and pedaled one of the paddle boats out toward the islands.

Whelan went quickly up the sloping walk to the bridge to have a look around. In Chicago the weather was considered warm any day after February that the sun was out, and it was out today, bringing hundreds of people to the zoo. There was a line of people waiting to rent paddle boats, and the cafeteria seemed to have a decent crowd, and people strolled along the far ends of the lagoon, but none of them was Les. He scanned the crowds carefully and then allowed his gaze to move along to the eastern side of the lagoon, where there was normally the least foot traffic. He could see no one there. At the far southern end, a small tattered-looking man dozed on a park bench. A few feet from the bench, a man in a Russian-style fur hat was tossing something that looked like bread into the water and had been rewarded for his pains by a collection of several dozen ducks and a couple of white geese. Behind him and apparently hoping to be taken for ducks stood a handful of pigeons. Whelan looked again at the crowded northern loop of the pond and started walking.

He looked inside the men's room first—in his youth, a

storied place for assignations and chance meetings between lonesome men. It was empty now but still had the same time-honored public toilet smells he remembered.

There were a number of old men nursing cups of coffee in the cafeteria but Les was not among them. He approached the counter and a friendly-looking young man smiled at him.

"Yes, sir?"

"I'm looking for an older guy about six feet tall, needs a shave, wears a blue raincoat and a ratty blue fedora."

The young man scanned the room and gave Whelan a loopy smile. "I don't think I saw him."

"Okay, thanks."

As Whelan left, the young man called out, "But we get a lot of old guys in ratty hats."

"I know. I hope to be one someday."

He stood outside the cafeteria and watched people getting into paddle boats. They were smiling as they got into their little blue boats and laughing as they struggled to get the proper rhythm going, but when they got out into open water and the wind coming in off the lake hit them, they weren't grinning anymore.

Whelan scanned the area once more and shook his head. I lost him. I forgot people are seldom as dumb as they look. He turned and looked back toward Clark Street, where a bus was just pulling into a corner stop, and he was fairly sure Les had doubled back to conclude whatever business he had in mind.

"Damn," Whelan said, and went back to his car.

Nine

Well, he told himself, I've already demonstrated that I can't follow a sixty-year-old fence. Let's see what else I can put on my résumé.

He drove up Clark Street to Lawrence, then began cruising the area in ever-widening circuits, and twenty minutes later, when he was on the verge of giving it up, his luck changed.

Whelan picked up the Caprice on Clark Street and decided he needed diversion. He kept back in traffic, allowing almost a block between the two cars. The Caprice made a bulky tour of Clark for several blocks and stopped twice, once at a small grill where a trio of kids stood just outside the door and the second time at a game room just off Wilson.

At their first stop, he pulled into a parking space across from a Korean importer advertising all manner of clothes and a new approach to grammar—BEST PRICE MEN'S SHIRT, PANT, HAT, GLOVE, JACKET—and watched as Bauman and Landini got out of their car, each slipping into his own particular gait—Landini in a lazy strut like a bored bodybuilder, Bauman rolling from side to side like a pro wrestler. As they approached the three kids, Bauman looked around with a sour expression—a pro wrestler with heartburn.

He let Landini open the conversation, and Whelan enjoyed the rich interplay of meaningless hand movements as Calabria met Clark Street: Landini made his wonderfully expressive gestures and the three white kids went through their repertoire of rap singer movements and signifying, and through it all Detective Bauman shook his head and smoked his wretched little cigars. Eventually he bulled his way into the little circle, put his great pouch of a stomach in one kid's chest and did his own well-honed act, and the three kids weren't rapping anymore.

Next Whelan followed the Caprice to the game room where the two detectives disappeared inside for less than five minutes. When they emerged, Landini was angry and Bauman was rubbing his stomach and looking like a man in need of a menu. From his spot in front of a hydrant, Whelan could see Landini waving his hands and trying to exact from his immovable partner a concession of some sort and getting nowhere.

At the corner of Clark and Wilson, he pulled up alongside the Caprice and rolled down his window.

"Hey, sailor, how about a good time?"

Bauman looked straight ahead for a second, then turned and blew smoke at him. "Playing detective again, Sleuth?"

"I'm just a lonely guy cruising the streets."

Bauman jerked his thumb toward the rear of the car. "I made you a couple lights ago."

"Not bad. But I've been watching you guys strut your stuff for about a half hour. I took notes."

Landini snorted and shook his head but refused to look at him. Bauman turned slowly and stared at him. Just when Whelan was expecting a short burst of Bauman's temper, the detective laughed silently.

"Gettin' even, huh? Kinda childish, ain't it? Feel better now?"

"I feel like lunch."

From Landini he heard an irritable mutter that sounded like "thinks he's twelve years old."

"See?" Bauman said. "You pissed off Landini here. That what you wanted? I don't know, Whelan, I don't think that's such a good idea. These young cops, they got no sense of humor about theirselves."

"I remember that. I thought I was Sergeant York. They should have given me a plastic gun."

The light changed and a motorist in back of them leaned on his horn, earning for himself the finger from Landini, a gesture casual yet rich in feeling. Bauman leaned out the window and told the motorist to "Eat shit and die young." Whelan glanced in his rearview mirror and saw an Arab-looking man gripping his steering wheel in open terror.

"Come on," Whelan said to Bauman. "Follow me and we'll talk."

He pulled out in front of the Caprice and amused himself by cutting Landini off, then went on up Wilson to Broadway. He turned onto Broadway and drove on to the House of Zeus.

At the entrance to the restaurant he waited. As he slid out of the car Landini was combing his hair and muttering. He slipped the comb into a back pocket, peeled off his cashmere sweater and tossed it into the front seat. Bauman's heavy wool sport coat hung open so that his great gut could get some sun. Today's shirt was the color of canned salmon.

Landini said something and Bauman threw back his head and laughed. He patted his partner on the shoulder and grinned at Whelan.

"You really pissed him off, Shamus." To Landini he said, "You got a hard-on 'cause he made you the other day and now he's been on your tail and you didn't see 'im."

Landini's response was to look up at the marquee of the House of Zeus and grimace. "I hate this fuckin' place."

"Many a customer has expressed the same feeling," Whelan said, and pushed his way inside.

There were no arguments in progress unless one counted the unending dialogue between the two cousins. Rashid barked something over his shoulder at Gus, and Gus spat back and pointed his paring knife in his cousin's direction.

If there's a hell, Whelan thought, and these guys wind up there, I know exactly how they'll spend their days.

Half a dozen customers sat at the tables and booths and ate in an uneasy peace. A small boom box perched at the far end of the counter and rained noise on them.

Landini shook his head and made a face, and Bauman smiled at Whelan. "Have your friends kill the rap music or I take out the radio."

"Hey, Rashid."

Rashid turned slightly and flashed his thousands of teeth. "Hello, Mr. Detective. And you have brought your friends the Police."

"This one says to turn off the rap music or he'll shoot the radio."

"Good," Gus said. "Shoot it. I hate that shit anyhow. This one,"—he indicated his cousin—"wanted to be American businessman, now he wants to be American teenager."

Rashid held up his hands in mock surrender. "Okay, okay, I gonna turn him off. You don't like my nice music, okay."

"Rap is not music, Rashid. Rap is what people do when they can't sing or play an instrument."

"This is American music. American *culture*." Rashid's eyes bulged with the effort of restraining his laughter.

"I don't like these two assholes," Landini muttered. "You sure they're Greek?"

"Hey, Gus. The detective here wants to know if you're Greek."

Gholam turned and squinted at Landini. On matters of ethnicity and national prejudice, he knew no fear, saw no humor. He pointed with the knife blade at the most prominent of the restaurant's macabre murals, a blood-spattered canvas epic in which Darius the Great hacked and carved his way through the Greek army.

"That one, with his head cut off and foot of great Persian king Darius on his back, that one is Greek. He is only Greek in here." He tilted his head slightly to one side. "Maybe your family is Greek."

Landini looked like a man who has smelled bad things. He pointed to his chest. "You talking to me? *My* family? My family came from Italy." He made two syllables of it, "*It*-ly."

"If you guys can interrupt your ethnic festival, we can order lunch. I'm buying," Whelan said.

"Best news I've heard all day," Bauman said. Landini just shrugged.

They ordered and waited at the counter, then carried the little plastic red baskets back to a corner booth. Whelan had a falafel sandwich and onion rings, Bauman ordered a *gyros* and a Shalimar kabab. Landini had a Greek salad. The tomatoes looked good, the slab of feta cheese was still white, the olives were Spanish and the lettuce was going brown fast. Landini shook his head and began eating.

Bauman tore off half his *gyros* in one bite, chewed for a moment, then nodded. "Thanks, Whelan," he said through his food. Landini looked up, gave him a short nod, and resumed eating.

"You're welcome."

Landini cut his salad with a watchmaker's precision and used his fork so that each mouthful of salad had a small bite of feta cheese on top. As he ate and chewed, his gaze moved from Whelan's plate to the mountain of food in front of his partner. He watched Bauman gnawing at the *gyros* and shook his head.

Bauman paused with a piece of meat hanging from the corner of his mouth. He looked like a snacking Rottweiler.

"What you lookin' at? You got no manners, or what?"

"I'm lookin' at all the fat and cholesterol you're putting in your body, that's what I'm lookin' at. For Chrissake, you might as well eat poison."

"Look at you, Landini, you eat what the fucking turtles eat."

"Yeah? They ever have heart attacks? They die young? Fuck, no, they outlive everything."

Bauman looked at him for a moment, blinked several times, then turned to Whelan. "I got a partner that admires turtles." He looked back to Landini. "Who cares how long they live, they eat flies and shit, they're stupid. What do you care what I eat? My food bothers you, don't look."

Landini glanced at Whelan and shook his head again. "Lunch yesterday, two Polish. Dinner, tacos, *six* tacos."

Bauman laughed. "You're talkin' to the wrong guy, Landini. Whelan eats the weirdest food in the city."

"Be nice to him, Bauman. He's concerned about your diet, he likes you."

This earned a sudden stare from Landini. The young cop leaned forward so that Whelan could almost read the inscription on his gold medallion. He pointed his fork at Whelan.

"You watch your mouth, you hear?"

"Easy, friend. You commit a violent act, they're not gonna let you be a cop anymore."

"Back off," Bauman said quietly. "How come you don't like our boy Whelan? Guy buys you lunch, you can at least be nice."

Landini gave him a sullen look and said nothing.

Bauman turned back to Whelan. "Want to get down to business, Snoopy?"

"Why not? I've been out humping for you."

"Not for me. For that nice lady."

"Right. Anyhow, I came across a couple of people and I wanted to know what you know about them."

"Arright. Who?"

"A guy named Lester, for one."

"Lester," Bauman said in a dull voice.

"Old guy. Runs a little book."

"Oh, Lester Dixon, sure. I know 'im. He's proof that hoods aren't too smart. Who gave you Lester?"

"Street kid."

Bauman's eyes said he didn't think so, but he let it go.

"Lester give you anything?"

"Nothing worth the time. I thought for a while he might—somebody gave me the impression he worked with Jimmy Lee Hayes. Thought they might be partners."

Bauman ate a french fry. "He's a sleazy old guy. Not what you'd call a pillar of his community. But he wasn't Jimmy Lee's partner. Just his fence. Jimmy Lee used to run his goods through a genuine operator named René Oboza. René had a classy operation, a warehouse, fleet of trucks, his own network of places to sell the stuff. Very nice. Your top-of-the-line hood. We busted old Rene and now he's probably selling candy bars to the other guys in the joint. Jimmy Lee had to find him a new guy, and times are tough, so Lester's what he come up with. Small-time fence for a small-time thief."

"Doesn't look smart enough to be a fence."

"Who says these fuckers are smart? Lester's tried just about everything: his sheet is a comedy. Been busted for auto theft, for runnin' his book, possession of cocaine, sellin' handguns to minors…" Bauman laughed and covered his eyes with his hands. "He did everything and he was dogshit at all of it. He's a fuckup, Whelan. Anyway, he's not a fence anymore. Semi-retired now."

"What does that mean?"

"Means we put him out of business but if he got a chance he'd be out there selling what people steal. He's sixty-something and he's got a bad heart. Went straight from the slammer to a hospital. But if he started doin' situps and watching his cholesterol, there's no doubt in my mind what kinda hobbies he'd take up. Probably still moves goods now and then, just to keep his hand in." Bauman grinned. "He's got a little room up there in the Carlos Hotel, probably full of stolen cameras and hot stereos."

"Have you talked to him?"

"We've talked to everybody that knew these guys. That's a stupid question." Bauman washed his french fry down with some A & W root beer, then looked around. "I get this feeling you knew who Les was, Whelan."

"He didn't show me a business card. And now I'm a little disappointed. I thought I had come up with a new angle, somebody who worked with Jimmy Lee Hayes and wasn't dead yet."

"Not yet, you haven't."

Whelan nibbled at his food and bided his time.

"What's the green shit?" Landini peered at Whelan's Shalimar kabab with a wary look.

"It's just the sauce. It's kind of a paste with different spices in it. It's hot. Want to try?"

"Fuck, no."

"No sense of adventure," Whelan said, and took a bite. Time to try out the other name. He looked at Bauman. "How about another old guy, somebody named 'Whitey.' "

Bauman was shaking his head before Whelan was finished, and then he stopped. " 'Whitey'? Who's that?"

"Couldn't tell you. It's a name I got."

"From where?"

"A guy in a gin mill."

"I think maybe Les give you this guy, that's what I think, Whelan." He took a last bite of his sandwich and chewed slowly.

"No. But you can ask him."

"I will." Bauman watched him for a moment. "So what'd you hear about this Whitey?"

"Nothing substantial. Like I said. It's just a name I came up with. I thought you'd be able to put a person to it."

Bauman pursed his lips and pretended to think. "No. Don't ring no bells. You?" he asked Landini.

"No. And what's he care? How come you got your nose in this stuff when you're supposed to be looking for the kid? Why is that?"

"Eat your lettuce," Bauman said. "It's brown," he said, frowning at Landini's salad.

"I'm looking for anybody that can give me the kid. Anybody that knew him. And so far, I'm striking out because I think Officer Friendly here set me up looking for a kid that nobody's ever gonna find."

"You'll find him, Snoopy. I got confidence in you. You're always comin' up with something."

"You never heard of anybody named Whitey doing business with Jimmy Lee Hayes?"

"No, I don't think so," Bauman said, and gave Whelan a little smile.

"Okay," Whelan said, and smiled back.

He blew off much of the afternoon trying to pick up Lester again, making several trips to the grill on Sheridan and Irving, as well as hitting a tavern up the street. At the Carlos he went in to speak to the desk clerk.

"I'm looking for a man who lives here. Mr. Dixon."

The clerk, a young black woman in the process of winnowing through a pile of receipts, looked at Whelan for a moment with slightly narrowed eyes and then shook her head. "He's not in, sir."

"Do you know when he'll be back?" She shook her head.

"Can you give him a message for me?"

"Of course."

He handed her his business card. "Have him call me when he gets in, and tell him if I'm not in to leave a number where he can be reached. I have an answering service."

She nodded and studied his card, obviously interested. "All right, sir. I'll put your card with his other messages."

He looked at her. "Let me guess: one of his messages came from two police officers, a big heavy one with a crew cut and a young dapper guy with a medallion the size of the moon."

The woman stared at him and gave away nothing, and he helped her out. "The young one smells like he drinks his cologne." She looked away to hide her smile and when she was able to meet his eyes, he said, "You can tell them I said hello when they come back."

She allowed herself a little nod, and he left.

There was no answer when he called Sandra around five-thirty, and no way to leave a message. Another clue that he'd found a soul mate: the last remaining woman in Chicago without an answering machine. He decided to drop by her apartment later. For now, there was no way to put off another night on the street.

Bobby Hayes emerged from the tavern combing his hair. He peeked in the darkened glass of the tavern window to make sure he had his "do" just right, then slid his comb into a hip pocket just as Whelan had seen Landini do it. Whelan watched him strut his way up the street. There was a slight wobble to the strut, an uncertainty of footing where the sidewalk got a little choppy. Bobby Hayes had a load on.

Whelan gave him a two-block head start and then pulled out. At the corner of Clark and Lawrence, Hayes went into the Sugar Bowl, a twenty-four-hour grill across from the entrance to St. Boniface Cemetery. Whelan found a parking place a couple of car lengths from the restaurant and got out.

Inside the restaurant, Bobby Hayes had found himself a booth. The waitress was just setting down cutlery and a napkin and water, and Whelan decided he had time to kill. He took a short walk up the street, grabbed a cup of coffee to go from a little sandwich place, then went back to his car and waited.

Even on a full stomach, Bobby Hayes was walking no better when he came out of the restaurant: the liquor had had time to make its way through his system now. Whelan watched Hayes make his way back toward the tavern, then pulled out, drove into an alley and backed out onto Clark again and drove after Hayes. A few feet from Ed and Ronda's, Hayes crossed Clark Street and got into a rusting black Mustang. Whelan drove on past him, then pulled into a parking spot and waited till Hayes went by, pulling out after him when Hayes was half a block away. Gradually Whelan gained on the Mustang and when Hayes turned west onto Montrose, Whelan was right behind him. The Mustang had Tennessee plates and a busted taillight. Hayes drove a couple of blocks west, past Ashland, and turned up a side street, Marshfield. Whelan turned right after him and when the Mustang parked in front of a hydrant, Whelan went on past and parked a few yards away. In his rearview mirror he could see the other man clearly.

Bobby Hayes struggled out of his car like an arthritis patient, dropped his car keys and almost fell into the street retrieving them. He made it to the sidewalk and looked up at the apartment building in front of him. He dropped his keys again and seemed to have trouble locating them this time. Finally he picked them up, glanced up at the building again, and made his way into the hall. Whelan got out of his car.

By the time he reached the building, the other man had made it up the stairs. Whelan walked over to the Mustang, leaned against it, and looked up. A moment later the lights went on in a second-floor apartment and Bobby Hayes appeared, lurching past the front window.

As he drove away Whelan couldn't shake the image of Bobby Hayes: an alcoholic little man struggling to look slick, a scared man, perhaps a lonely one, striving mightily to seem on top of it all. A loser in a bright knit shirt. Whelan thought about what little he knew about the players in this one: small-time crooks, old men, runaway teenagers. People sometimes imagined crime to be about people with power and money, and there was some of that, but most of it was about people like these, most of it was about losers.

It was dark when he parked on Argyle Street and he could smell weather coming. A snow sky in May. Low and gray and dense, the cloud mass threatened to drop onto the city, and he could smell the wet in it. He wasn't sure it was cold enough for snow, but it was up there hoping to happen and the damp in the air made him shudder. Sleet, maybe, a night of sleet racketing against his windows. The winter that never ends, he thought, in the City of the Big Shoulders and the Bad Attitude.

Whelan stood shivering and gazing at the gaudy lights on Argyle Street. Up the street a couple of elderly Vietnamese women emerged from a store and scuttered along the street in high-top gym shoes, the best they'd ever be able to afford. A new Grand Prix pulled into the parking spot ahead of him and a young Vietnamese couple emerged on opposite sides. The man ran a hand across his hair and grinned as the woman clutched at the collar of her coat and said something unmistakably about the cold. Whelan watched them trot across the street and enter a Vietnamese restaurant. He looked longingly at the restaurant and then made his way up the street toward the Apollo.

The same people were at work in all the places he'd hit, the same guy with the cleaver in the Lucky Grocery Market, the same confident-looking young woman stood behind the counter of the little restaurant. Behind her, he could see the old man standing at the register. The woman hesitated, then nodded when he waved. In the Cambodian jewelry shop another intense negotiation was in progress but the tall man with the high forehead gave Whelan a long look when he passed by.

A few doors from the Apollo he found himself looking into the window of a grocery store and staring at a row of the rosy-colored ducks. He stopped and stared at them for a moment. They beckoned to him, called to him.

I need a duck.

He went inside and purchased one of the hanging ducks,

then came out with the parcel tucked under one arm. He walked, head down and wondering how one served such a duck, and he was pondering the possibilities when his foot hit a raised chunk of broken pavement and he pitched forward.

He lurched to the right to keep from falling and his momentum took him into the doorway of a gift shop, and he was almost on top of the man in the doorway before he saw him.

The man stepped back with a sharp sudden movement and took a street-fighter's pose. Whelan dropped the parcel and put out a hand against the doorway to stop his fall.

"Sorry," Whelan said, and looked the startled man in the eyes. He was tall and thin and worn at all the edges, a broom handle body in a khaki coat cut for a larger man. His hair was long and dark and dirty, and thin on top. There were purple circles under his eyes and what looked like scratches down one cheek, and his skin was the blotched red of a man who lived on the street.

Whelan felt the breath leave him and saw the wide boyish surprise in the other man's brown eyes, and then the shame and confusion in his face, and they recognized each other simultaneously. He opened his mouth to speak, and the other mouthed something that could have been "Paulie," and moved farther away.

Whelan stared. "Jesus," he heard himself say. Then he blurted "Mick?" and the man was by him in one long movement and down the street. Whelan watched the other man rush off toward the corner in a stiff-legged stride and disappear around it. Confusion held Whelan back, confusion and the overwhelming sense that he'd witnessed something he should not have seen, and when he finally made it back to the corner, the other man had disappeared into the night.

Paul Whelan took a few steps down the street, then stopped and lit a cigarette. He smoked in quick nervous puffs and then tossed the cigarette away and backtracked to the corner. There was nothing to be gained from remaining there but he stood there just the same, with the wind whipping at his face and coming in at his open collar and would have stood there all night if he thought it would do any good, for he had just seen a dead man.

Sandra smiled when she saw him. "Well, *hi,*" she said, and he knew she was glad he'd come. Then something in her face changed. "Paul? What's wrong? You look like…come on in."

She pulled him in from the hallway and half pushed him to the sofa. "Give me your coat…and I'll take your—what is this?"

He managed a smile. "It's a duck."

"What kind of a duck is this long? Oh, *God,* it's got the…" and she made a groping motion with her free hand.

"Yeah, it's got the head on, the beak, the whole deal. I thought we'd eat it. Sometime."

"A duck with the beak still on," she said, the way she might say "a hamburger with maggots on it." Then she gave him an appraising look. "Are you hurt?"

"No, no."

"You sit. I'll get you a cup of tea. Or do you want a beer?"

"No. Tea is fine. I'm chilled to the bone."

"Sit," she repeated, and then vanished into her kitchen, carrying the duck the way a person would carry a dirty diaper. A moment later the room was filled with the scent of cinnamon and clove and then she came back, carrying two mugs. There was a tea bag in each.

"Cinnamon and clove," he said, just to be saying something. "Reminds me of an old Sergio Mendes song."

" 'The Moon is like a tangerine,' " she sang. "I know that one. Don't worry: yours is English Breakfast. No herbs and spices for Paul Whelan."

"I appreciate that. But I'm cold enough that I would've drunk the one with cinnamon."

"Doesn't feel like May, does it."

"May in Chicago, sure it does."

She sipped at her tea and watched him over the rim of the mug. "Are you going to tell me what's wrong?"

"I'm all right."

She shook her head. "You are not. And…you have to tell me things like this. That's where we're at, you and I. It's got nothing at all to do with whether we're going to be seeing each other six months from now. You have to tell me things like this."

"Or you're gonna give me the gate?"

"Oh, who knows. But it'll certainly tell me a lot about us."

He sipped at his tea and nodded. "You're right. I'm just kind of shocked. If I'm right, something is happening that's going to make me wish I'd never gotten involved in this case. Also, I'm having a bad week." He pointed to the side of his head. "You can't see it now, but this morning I had a large egg right here."

"Somebody hit you?"

"It's important to make that good first impression. It was somebody good, too. I had to sit on my butt in an alley and wait for the earth to stop spinning."

"In an *alley*." She stared at him for several seconds. "An alley. I know it's what you do, but there has to be some way to avoid some of the things that happen to you."

He thought about that. "There are many ways, but I couldn't do exactly what I do now, not in the same way. And I'm not ready to start going about my job in a different way. People still come to me because I do something they can't get anywhere else."

"So who hit you?"

"No idea. I was sitting in a restaurant on Argyle Street and I got a glimpse of somebody out the corner of my eye, and for a second I thought it was this boy I'm looking for. So I went tearing out the door after him and up this alley and somebody clubbed me. I'll admit I could have handled it better. More carefully. Shit, I'm too old for people to be seeing me on my butt in alleys."

"Do you think it was him? The boy."

"No." He was half surprised to hear his answer. "I think the kid I'm after is no banger. His first instinct is to get away, to find a place to hide, and this was somebody a little harder, a little more violent."

"And tonight? You went back there, didn't you." It was a statement, not a question.

"Of course. That's where he is. The kid, I mean. I'm pretty

sure of it."

"You said you thought he was dead."

"I did. Then some street kids gave me a piece of information that made me think he might still be alive, and somebody else told me he might be up there on Argyle Street, though I can't figure out why. And I go up there and somebody takes a serious whack at me."

"And tonight? Something happened to you tonight."

"Yeah, I saw a ghost. I saw Mickey Byrne."

She worked for a moment at placing the name. "The dead man's brother, the one you grew up with."

"Right. I saw him."

"You sure it was him?"

"I was close enough to touch him. I could smell him. He smelled like wood smoke, like a guy that's been warming himself over a fire in a trash can. It was him. He was standing in a doorway maybe a hundred feet from the alley where I got hit and he looked at me and he was just as surprised as I was. I think he said my name, I think he said 'Paulie.' It's what everybody called me."

"Then what?"

"He ran from me. He acted like I was Typhoid Mary."

"And you're thinking it was him last night."

"It's a good bet."

She reflected for a moment. "You thought he was dead."

"For all that happened to him, he should have been. He was shot up over there, he came back and pretty soon he was living on the streets. I heard all kinds of things about what happened to him when he got out of the service and none of it was pleasant. I heard he was in detox, I heard he was living in alleys, I heard he'd lost his mind, I heard he had TB. Somebody told me he was dying in a VA hospital, then somebody else told me he was dead. And I saw him. And…" He fought for the words. "For a split second I was just glad to see him, I couldn't even speak. Another moment and I would have hugged him. And then I saw his eyes, and they were telling me this wasn't the same guy anymore. He wasn't glad to see me."

"Maybe he's still not…maybe he's still a very sick man."

"Oh, I'm sure of that. I just wonder if he's turned into another kind of man because of it."

"What do you mean?"

"I'm not sure how to explain it. But the guy I was looking at, the face I was looking into, was a hostile man, a stranger. If he hadn't said my name, I would have bet the rent that he didn't even recognize me."

"And you think he was the one who hit you."

He shrugged. "It's sure looking that way. I need to know why."

"Paul, it doesn't have to be connected to this other thing. People living on the streets get rough around the edges, and some of them are pretty tough. You told me that yourself."

"Well, sure. They get mugged by teenagers, rousted by cops, run off from half the places they show up. They're in physical discomfort almost every moment they're awake. They spend the winter wondering if it'll kill them and the summer looking for water and shade."

"Yes. They go through all those things. So maybe…maybe it's just the street that's happened to your friend."

"Maybe. I don't know. I guess I've always assumed there are some people who never completely change. I think there are people like that. And I thought he'd be one of them."

"Maybe he hasn't changed completely. You told me he was always a little pugnacious to begin with, always quick to anger. Sounds like somebody who might have some rough edges as an adult. To that, add his life on the street…"

Whelan nodded. "And all the other stuff: family dead when he was still young, then Vietnam."

"And he was wounded, you said."

"Yeah, shot up bad, and then very sick." Then he thought of Rory. "And by now I bet he knows about his brother."

Sandy grabbed him by the shoulder, shaking her head. "Jesus, Paul, I think this man's doing great just because he hasn't killed himself."

"I suppose that's the way I should look at it, but it's not enough. He was a good guy, Sandy. He had a great heart, he wasn't afraid of anything and he always talked like he thought good things were going to happen to him eventually. We used to sit on this other kid's porch and watch the sky, look for constellations and shooting stars and talk about how our lives were going to be twenty years later, and every one of us thought special things were going to happen. We used to make fun of Mickey just because his particular pipedreams changed all the time. He'd get this excited note in his voice and say, 'You know what I'm gonna do?' and we'd all say, 'What this time, Mick?' and everybody'd laugh. He thought he was going to be a magician, and then a writer, and a scientist, and an explorer—he'd just come out with the most outlandish notions while other guys were talking about buying a car or coaching high school basketball."

She thought for a moment. "Let me ask you something. If you were Mickey, and your life had been very hard and you found yourself living on the street in your hometown and when you least expected it, you looked up and saw one of your best friends from your childhood...Put Paul Whelan in that doorway. How would you feel?"

"Well, I know I'd be a little embarrassed, but I'd be glad," he began, and caught the appraising look in her eyes. She watched him, unblinking, not his lover for the moment but a tough street social worker who'd heard lies from far better liars than Paul Whelan. He sighed. "No. I'd want to die on the spot. I wouldn't want anyone on God's green orb to see me like that, least of all somebody I grew up with. Not somebody that liked me. I'd want to see nothing but strangers for the rest of my life."

She said nothing for a moment. He studied the pale green eyes and saw the intelligence and, right now, the satisfaction, and nodded.

She got up to take her cup to the kitchen and reached out for his. As he handed it to her, she said, "Now what?"

"What do you mean?"

"I mean, what do you do first?"

"'First'?"

"I think you know exactly what I mean."

"I have to finish this other thing. I was wrong about that

kid. I think he's still alive and somebody's going to kill him."

"Is it time to bring the police in?"

"I don't have anything to give them yet. Nothing they could use. And I think they know if the kid is out there, he's in big trouble."

"And when you're finished with this other thing, you'll go look for Mickey?"

"That's as far as I've gotten. I don't know about anything else."

"Yes, you do. I know you. You know what you want to do, and you know what you ought to do. And this time, I think they're the same thing."

"Maybe I'll find out that he's in this. His brother was."

"And maybe you won't. He's not his brother."

Whelan pondered that for a moment and then realized that part of him was not convinced. "Sandy, you didn't see his eyes. He wasn't the same guy anymore. And I'm not so sure I'll find him again: probably won't hang around, now that I've seen him."

She was shaking her head before he was finished. "Maybe you're right. I wasn't there, I don't even know him. But I think if you want to, you'll find him. You just wanted somebody to tell you it wasn't crazy. It's not: if you don't find him, you'll never know." She went to the kitchen with the cups.

When she came back, she stretched her long body on the couch and watched him for a long time, the green eyes half closed. She looked pleased with herself, and comfortable in a way that had come late to their relationship. Whelan went over and sat down on the couch beside her. He was still chilled from the street and she felt almost feverish to him. He leaned against her hip and said nothing.

"Stick around, soldier. This is the best place for you to be. It's why you came here tonight."

"I know that."

She turned slightly to rest on her back and smiled. He started to say something but she reached out and grabbed him by the arm and pulled him down on top of her, then met him halfway in a kiss.

TEN

The sun was making a claim to the street and if he ignored the bite in the air Whelan could almost convince himself it was finally spring.

It's spring in my heart, he thought, but I'll never admit it.

He stopped in the Wilson Donut Shop under the El station and it was one of those mornings when he knew half the people there—Ruth the waitress and Wiley, a chain-smoking old man he'd used for information, and Spiros slinging ham steaks and hash browns over the hot grill, and he was happy to see them all.

All men are my brothers, he said.

He got a cup of coffee and looked around. Over by a window, staring out at the street with his mournful blue eyes, was old Tom Cheney of Graybull, Wyoming. He jumped slightly when Whelan put a hand on his shoulder.

"Easy there, cowboy. I'm on your side."

The old man grinned. "Sit down and take a load off."

"How you been, Tom?"

"Gettin' by, gettin' old, gettin' ornery. How about you?" Cheney squinted slightly through the smoke of his cigarette.

"Can't complain."

"Working?"

"Always. Not that I have much to show for it."

"Never knew that to matter much to you." The old man leaned back and gave him a quizzical look. "You got a woman somewhere, Whelan?"

"What?"

"You heard me. You're not deaf yet. I said, you got a woman somewhere?"

"Is it that obvious?"

Tom Cheney laughed. "You're just setting there, grinning at everybody, grinning out the window. You're in love or you've lost your mind, one or the other. So you tell me, are you in love, or have you gone simple on us?"

"Probably both."

The old man nodded and sipped at his coffee for a second. "I knew a fella once, this was back in Sheridan, long time ago. Rodeo rider, made the whole circuit, all the way from Prescott up to Alberta, Canada. He had the nicest gal you'd ever want to see, right there in Sheridan. Pretty, too. They kept company for years and years, and everybody was waiting on them to tie that old knot, and it never happened. This fella, he wasn't real excited about the idea, and the gal, she just kept waiting.

"Finally, when this had been going on for years, the gal just up and left him. She run off and found herself a schoolteacher down in Laramie, and this old cowboy never knew what hit him. She was getting on fifty years old, and I guess he thought she'd got to where she'd always be there for him, marriage or no. He was wrong."

"Is there a point to this?"

"Oh, no, no. I just felt like telling a story, is all."

"I'll bet. If I tell you I'm not planning to let this one get away, will you cease and desist from the sermons?"

"Wasn't any sermon at all. You know how old men babble." And Tom Cheney fixed him with a look that told him he'd been instructed on the expected behavior.

He left the doughnut shop with a second cup of coffee and a promise to take Tom Cheney to the fights at the Aragon or a Cub game.

Whelan was still smiling at the world when he reached his office building. The sun was still shining and there were neither dead squirrels nor warring motorists in front. What there was in front, was a gray Caprice.

"Damn," Whelan said.

Detective Albert Bauman leaned his bulk against the car and puffed at one of his dark little cigars. Bauman was dressed for the new weather. He'd tossed the overcoat and fished a blue-

and-white plaid sport coat from the dark terrors of his closet, and under this he wore a knit shirt that would have embarrassed a peacock. He was smiling at Whelan.

This is not good, Whelan told himself.

"Top of the morning, Snoopy."

"Mine just went south. Where's your conscience?"

"He's got a personal problem with a member of the opposite sex. I left him hanging on the phone with her, mumbling into it about how they need to work things out. Sounded to me like she wasn't buying any of it."

"She probably caught him showing some other lady his collection of chest hair. You need to see me, or are you just sunbathing?"

"Yeah, we oughtta talk."

Whelan motioned for him to come in, then pushed his way into the hall. The first floor was fully lit and he could hear voices down the hall, the sounds of business being transacted, of people interacting. Whelan had lights on his floor now but there were no noises because there were never any people. Thus far, Nowicki was the only human being Whelan had ever seen going into or coming out of A-OK Novelties.

"How come they aren't lined up waiting for you, Shamus? These other guys seem to do a business." Bauman grinned, then noticed the new tenant. "What the fuck are 'novelties'?"

"I think they're the same thing as 'notions.' "

"That helps me."

Whelan put the key into the lock. "How come you waited outside? You usually just let yourself in."

"I'm trying to mend my ways. Landini thinks B-and-E is beneath the dignity of a police officer."

Inside the office, Whelan slid into his chair and Bauman pulled out the visitor's chair and dropped two hundred and twenty pounds on it. The chair sighed.

"So what's up?"

"I thought we'd talk some more about this name you give me yesterday. Whitey."

"What about it?"

"I think I figured out who you're talking about."

"You know, I thought you might. You going to give me that?"

"I thought we'd have an exchange of ideas."

"I haven't had one in weeks."

"Sure you have. Your wheels are always turning."

"What do you want?"

"First of all, where'd you get Lester?"

"Told you that. A street kid."

"Where?"

"Outside the Dunkin' Donuts at Clark and Belmont."

He watched Bauman weigh and process this information.

"Got a name for this kid?"

Yeah, I do, he thought, but you have to get your own. He reached back to his conversation with the group-home workers to come up with a name. "Sonny. I talked to a couple of girls and they pointed this kid out to me, said he used to know Tony Blanchard." Bauman's eyes seemed to take on a little glow. He nodded for Whelan to continue. "He gave me Lester's name. I was under the impression that Lester actually worked for Jimmy Lee Hayes but I guess I was wrong."

Bauman hesitated before finally saying, "Yeah, you were. The other thing, where's Lester? Nobody seems to know where he is."

"I haven't talked to him."

"Since when?"

"Yesterday morning. I tried to get him to tell me about this Whitey but he wouldn't give me anything."

"Maybe he doesn't have anything to give you."

"Sure."

Bauman ground out his little cigarillo in the ashtray, bending it into an L-shaped casualty but not quite putting it out.

"And where was this?"

"The restaurant on Irving and Sheridan where he hangs out. The Crystal something-or-other."

"And that's the last time you saw him?"

"No. I followed him later on, I thought he'd lead me

someplace interesting."

"And did he?"

"Yeah, to the Farm-in-the-Zoo."

Bauman winced. "I hate that fucking place. Smells like the place my ma used to go to buy chickens. This Polack place on Milwaukee, nobody even spoke English. You could get chickens cheap there. They were alive when you come in, and you'd point to the one you wanted, and this Polish lady would fucking assassinate the chicken and they'd pluck it. I hated it. They had rabbits there, too, but I didn't know what for. My ma told me they were for pets, but later on I found out they were for hassenpfeffer and shit like that. I can still smell that place." He shook his head at the memory, then gave Whelan a look of curiosity. "So what did old Lester do at the Farm-in-the-Zoo? Did he feed the goats, Whelan?"

"What he did was, he lost the private detective who was following him. He went in and out of the buildings and I think he doubled back to Clark Street while I was watching the pigs fight over lunch."

Bauman surprised him with a laugh. It was more a snorting sound, but it was genuine. Bauman rubbed his eyes with his thumb and forefinger and shook his head. When he looked at Whelan again, his dark gray eyes were moist. "Lester? Old Lester left you in the zoo? You sure he didn't, like, put on his Keds and break into a sprint, Whelan?"

"Have a good time, Bauman. He shook me, but I can follow a couple of guys in a gray Caprice till the cows come home."

"Not if I knew somebody might be tailing me."

Whelan half turned in the swivel chair and looked out at Lawrence Avenue. They were putting something new up on the marquee of the Aragon.

"Where do you think Lester was going?"

"No idea."

"Gonna have a little meet with somebody, you think?"

"That's what I was assuming."

"And now we can't find him. Wonder what that means."

Whelan sensed that Bauman was changing gears, and waited.

"Those kids told me this guy was looking for Tony Blanchard. Why would that be?"

Bauman's gaze came back into the room. "Ain't any big mystery about that. I think Jimmy Lee wanted to find the kid bad. I think the kid knew who was taking out Jimmy's people."

"How would the kid know that?"

"I think he saw. I think he saw one of 'em getting whacked." Bauman punctuated his statement with a nod. "What I wanna ask you, Whelan, is, have you seen this guy Whitey?"

"No. I've got a description, that's all. Old guy, big teeth, whitish blond hair that sticks up. One kid told me he looks like a skull."

Bauman seemed amused. "A skull, huh? That's nice. These kids, they got a way with words. So you haven't seen 'im yet?"

"Nope. And I'm not sure I want to. People seem to be a little nervous talking about him."

"What people?" Bauman stared at him.

"The kids that saw him. Lester—I don't think Lester liked dealing with him much."

Bauman nodded slowly, still watching him. "That all you got?"

"All I've got now." He waited a beat, then tossed out a new card. "No, I've got one other thing, you maybe already know this. Jimmy Lee Hayes's brother."

Bauman blinked slowly. "No, Whelan, I don't. Isn't that amazing. Tell me about this brother."

"Younger brother, I think he is. Name's Bobby. He's kind of a nervous type. Blondish hair, blue eyes, thin, about five nine. For all I know, he's a dead ringer for Jimmy."

"Nah. Jimmy's big, got dark hair full of grease and shit, probably thinks he looks like Elvis. So where'd you find this guy?"

"Hangs out in a saloon on Clark Street over by Chase Park. Ed and Ronda's."

"Clever name for a saloon. So how'd you come by this information?"

"Lester ran into him."

"He didn't say nothing to me." Bauman gave him the lizardon-a-rock stare.

"When did you talk to Lester?"

"I don't know. Couple weeks ago, why?"

"That's why you don't know about him. He just got into town."

Bauman nodded slowly. "Picked kind of a bad time to come for a visit, huh?"

"You could say that. Anyhow, Lester told me he ran into the brother in this tavern."

"We'll have to check out this Bobby Hayes. Thanks, Whelan."

"Got anything for me?"

Bauman raised his eyebrows. "Whaddya need me for? You seem to be doing good. Well, I gotta go protect Mr. Landini from his social life. You keep in touch, okay?"

"Absolutely." Whelan watched Bauman lift his bulk out of the chair and leave the office, the scent of Right Guard mixed with cigar smoke trailing behind him.

Okay, Whelan thought. How much did you not tell me this time?

The young woman was on duty at the Carlos again when Whelan came in.

"Is Mr. Dixon in?"

"I don't know, sir. I'll buzz him for you. Your name?"

"Whelan." She made a call on the hotel desk phone and watched Whelan as it rang. She shook her head. "He's not answering."

"Do you know whether he ever came in last night?"

"No—another girl had the desk during the night."

"All right. Well, I already gave you my card. Thanks."

He cruised. He hit Lester's haunts and made the circuit from Addison to Foster, up Sheridan and back on Clark, and the waitress at the greasy spoon, the bartender down the street, the vendor who sold Lester his green sheet, all shook their heads when Whelan asked about the old fence. As he drove back up Sheridan toward his office, he turned up Windsor and made a slow pass by the rooming house where Les had made his first stop in the cab. He pulled up in front and looked the building over, lit a cigarette and hit a radio button that earned him Maynard Ferguson playing to a wild crowd. In a first-floor window next door, a thin-faced man watched the street, his chin cupped in one hand. The windows of the rooming house were unpopulated, but in several there were the unmistakable signs of a rooming house: ketchup bottles and milk cartons and jars of mayonnaise on the window sills: cheap refrigeration. When he'd been watching the building for almost a half hour without seeing signs of life, he got out of the car, stretched, and went up the broken sidewalk.

The glass in the door was wire-reinforced but the wood was splintered along the lock, where someone had kicked it in. Whelan gave it a push and it swung open, and the smell of stale wine and body odor assailed him. He heard and felt the crunch of broken glass to go along with the smell, and felt sorry for the poor soul who had dropped his bottle.

He was turning to look at the mailboxes when he sensed rather than saw the other man in the corner of the hall. He spun around and the other man gave a startled movement backward.

"Shit," the man said. As he reached behind him, seeking the wall, the man held out a worn-looking cane, pointing it at Whelan.

"Easy," Whelan said. He held up both hands, palms out. "Take it easy."

The only sound was the man's panting. He kept his cane in front of him and his eyes on Whelan's and said nothing. His body seemed to be bent over to one side and he was missing all his front teeth on top. The man was in his sixties, perhaps older, and like most of the homeless was still dressed for winter despite the warm spell: thick red knit cap and a heavy gray woollen coat. Balls of grayish lint clung to the hat. He'd carry this load of clothes around till there was no further chance of the cold taking him off his guard.

"I'm just looking for somebody. A man named Whitey. Do you know the people in this building?"

The old man curled his lip slightly, exposing the black gap in his mouth, shook his head. After a few seconds during which he blinked many times, he began to lower the cane.

"Do you live here?"

Another shake of the head, and the look of a man who's been rousted from a thousand doorways. The cane touched the tile floor and he put weight on it.

Slowly, the man edged toward the door, never taking his eyes off Whelan. His gaze seemed to halt at Whelan's shirt and then he nodded.

"Smoke?"

Whelan patted the pack in his shirt pocket. "Yeah, sure." He fished out the pack, shook out a cigarette and held it toward the old man. The man took it and Whelan came up with a match.

"I'm looking for a man in his fifties or sixties, white hair, tinted glasses. Wears a light-colored raincoat. Seen anybody like that?"

The man tried to look interested, squinted, then shook his head. Another puff on the cigarette brought him a coughing jag. Still coughing, he moved toward the door, took one final look in Whelan's direction and was gone.

Whelan scanned the row of brass mailboxes for names. On one, MOORE had been scratched with a key or nail; RAYFIELD had been written in blue ink on first aid tape over another. The rest were blank, and several had been forced open. One mailbox appeared to have had its label peeled off recently. A building where the mail, such as it was, would be dropped in a pile on the bottom step. The smart ones would have theirs delivered somewhere else. Two names and he didn't even know the one he was looking for. Perhaps this was just a place where Les was supposed to pick up the note. He shook his head and went out. A few feet from the door he found a gangway that ran to the alley behind the building. It brought him into a barren little courtyard strewn with refuse. A man in dirty blue coveralls was attempting to pick it up but his heart wasn't in his work.

Whelan watched him take single pieces of paper and march doggedly to the dumpster, drop them in and return for more, all in slow motion. At this rate, he would have the yard cleared by century's end.

"Excuse me?"

The man looked up and dropped the cardboard container he'd just picked up. "Yes, sir?"

"Do you know the tenants in this building?"

"Nope."

"Could you tell me if you've seen a man here, with white hair and glasses, clean-shaven. Big teeth. His hair is kind of bushy."

The man shook his head. "They're all old."

"Who manages the building?"

"Mr. Blakely."

"How can I get in touch with him?"

The man pointed and Whelan turned to see a sign above the back door that read BLAKELY MANAGEMENT and gave a phone number.

"Thanks."

"Okay," the man said, and picked up the solitary piece of cardboard again.

At the office he called Blakely Management and spoke to Mr. Blakely himself. Blakely sounded like a man with things to hide: he danced and dawdled through the conversation and played dumb, and Whelan's description of Whitey did nothing to jar him out of his performance.

"Let me ask you this: have you rented rooms or apartments to anyone in the last six months?"

Blakely shuffled through what sounded like a file and grunted. "Yeah, a couple. But to younger people. Nobody old. Maybe you got the wrong building."

"Yeah, maybe. All right. Thanks."

Whelan had another look at the notes he'd taken on the three killings. He flipped through the pages of his notebook and stared at his own scribble, waiting for something to jump out, a pattern, something in the method of the killings, the time, the locations. Makowski, the first victim, had been shot at close range on a side street in Uptown, and his body dragged into a nearby vacant lot; Chick Nelson had been found dead in his truck in the parking lot at Waveland Park, two hundred yards from the lake; Rory Byrne, the last one, had been found on a tiny patch of unused land where North Avenue met the river. Makowski and Rory Byrne had apparently been killed at night, Nelson during the day. Nelson and Rory had been stabbed, their stab wounds in front.

The three places had nothing in common, at least not at first glance. Whelan tucked the notebook in his shirt pocket and left the office.

He drove first to the spot where they'd found Makowski. He parked and got out to look around. The building to the left of the lot was under rehab, a hulking structure of yellow brick, perhaps twenty units, but empty now unless squatters had set up in the back rooms.

To the right stood a smaller building, most of its windows boarded up. The newspaper accounts had not speculated on the exact spot of Makowski's murder, but no effort had been made to hide or bury the body, and Whelan was fairly sure he was standing close to where it had happened. He stepped through a gaping hole in the chain-link fence around the lot. Brownish clumps of prairie grass and weed blew in the wind and fought to keep their hold on the earth. Much of the lot was bare gray dirt, and the afternoon sun picked out the shards of glass, green and brown, where wandering drinkers tossed their bottles.

He got back into his car and drove to the lake, entering Waveland Park at Irving and cruising the narrow parkway that navigated the parking lots. The writer in the *Tribune* had been a bit more specific, mentioning that Chick Nelson's truck had been parked in full view of tennis courts and the playground. That made it the far lot, east of the courts. The dark form of the totem pole came into view. Whelan made the turn and drove into the lot, then parked. A couple of Filipino-looking women sat shuddering in the playground and watched a trio of fair-haired children clambering over the slide. The women looked miserable. A couple of nannies earning their nickels the hard way.

Behind him, the tennis courts were busy with several pairs of energetic players, including one pair of young women. Despite the cold, they wore short tennis skirts and Whelan found himself wishing he were twenty-two, with a racket. He remembered sitting on a bench no more than fifty yards from this spot and watching a series of drug transactions in progress. On that chilly fall afternoon, a smiling young man with curly blond hair spilling out from under his Sox cap had gone from car to car and done business. The cars had been parked in the farthest corners of the lot, for none of the motorists realized they were all there for the same reason.

Whelan had watched the kid climb into one vehicle after another, sit for a while, make small talk, pass the driver a small parcel or plastic bag, grab a handful of cash and slide back out the door, smiling. It had all taken less than a half hour, and when it was finished, the parking lot was empty and the young guy in the Sox cap was walking east, as though to watch the big gray waves come in to smash the rocks.

Sitting there now, he recalled the enterprising young dope dealer and realized that the killer had picked another spot where you could get away with all sorts of things in broad daylight.

He drove south on Sheffield and stayed on it through the thickening traffic that marked the Lincoln Park neighborhood, and on to the place where Sheffield disappeared in a line of railroad tracks just past North Avenue. He parked behind a warehouse and walked back to North.

Half a block west, the street became a bridge over the north branch of the Chicago River, the murky brown artery that bisected the city. North branch met south branch at the edge of the Loop to form one big brown nasty river and, in times past, had gone on to deposit their scary contents in Lake Michigan. Eventually the Army Corps of Engineers had produced a series of locks designed to reverse the flow of the river, so that it now moved away from the big lake with its bluish green water. Now, the Chicago River deposited the bad things it carried in other places. Whelan was unsure exactly where the river did this, and thought it was one of the things one didn't want to know.

But whichever direction it flowed, the Chicago River had its own folklore. Farther north, boat enthusiasts who lived alongside it built piers for their motorboats and ignored the giant rats that scrambled along its muddy banks. Factories deposited poisons in it and a few heroic souls still sat on its banks and took out catfish and bullhead. A friend of Whelan's, a city man with dreams of wilderness adventure, had once taken a canoe trip upstream on the north branch. Whelan's friend had envisioned himself basking in the sun and waving to the smiling crowds as he navigated through the various neighborhoods. Reality had proven to be something else again: the would-be canoeist was horrified by the rats and repelled by the smell. In the poorer neighborhoods the children pelted him with stones and as he got near the Loop a group of teenagers had taken turns trying to find his range with beer cans and sticks.

A few feet from where they'd found Rory Byrne there was a shrimp house. This one was Ben's. Not far from here, also along the river, was Joe's. Four blocks south and a stone's throw from the river, was another, Goose Island. It was a Chicago tradition, fish and shrimp houses along the river, and no one alive knew why. Whelan had bought fried shrimp and fish chips and smelt from all of them, and in each place had asked why fish houses were always located along the river. No one had ever been able to give him an intelligent answer, and he knew a couple of people who actually believed that some of the fish sold at these little shacks was brought out of the murk of the river. It was a terrifying thought.

The wind hit him with the fish smells and the odors of deep-fried batter, and when he passed the hut he could see three or four people lined up at the counter for their little greasy bags of fish. Whelan cut across the tiny side yard that served as a parking lot and walked to the edge.

The superstructure of an old railroad bridge, long since abandoned, formed a sort of visual frame for the place. In the daylight there was a rustic quality to the scene, a pair of railroad tracks stretching out toward the south on their way to infinity.

They were overgrown with weeds and grass, the rails coated with a thick skin of rust. A few yards down, Whelan could make out the evidence of habitation: fast-food wrappers and stale buns, a wine bottle, an orange rind. A man without a home had camped here, probably for more than one night.

Closer to hand, the ground was strewn with bottles and cans and plastic bags. Fifty feet below, the brown water of the river moved by at a fast pace. He picked his way over to the old bridge and sat on a crosspiece and had a smoke. This was where Rory had been killed. The body had been found in the morning, so he had to assume the killing had taken place at night. Whelan took another look around and envisioned this place at night. What would make someone come here at night?

"What a place to die," he said aloud.

He thought about the sites of the three killings and shook his head. Early on, he'd assumed that the victims were followed and killed where it was convenient, but now that theory was out the window. This wasn't a place where somebody came by chance, nor was the place where they'd found Chick Nelson. He didn't have a handle on the first killing, but these other men, they hadn't been pursued. They had been lured to their deaths.

Whelan tried to imagine what it would take to get him to come down to such a place. A familiar face, that's what it would take. Familiar face and a good story. For a moment he sat watching the water rush by and finished his smoke. He wondered what assumptions Bauman was working on, and asked himself, not for the first time, when people would start telling him the truth.

Marty Wills left the grill in a hurry and walked north on Sheridan. There was still a good deal of light in the sky but the day was rapidly cooling off. The boy moved in a hunched-over walk, collar up and hands thrust deep into the pockets of his khaki jacket, and Whelan wondered how the kid ever made it through a Chicago winter.

He stayed on the opposite side of the street and followed

Marty at a distance, keeping well back. Loser or not, Marty was proving not to be quite as simple as he seemed. Every few yards he looked over his shoulder, and when he paused at the corner of Sheridan and Wilson to light a cigarette, he took a long look back up the street. The boy stood there for a moment waiting for the light to change, then crossed Wilson at a trot. Whelan let him get halfway down the block and then picked up his pace. At the next corner, Marty stopped, looked around again, and then turned right.

Now there was no way to play this one safe, and Whelan broke into a run. He covered the block quickly, crossed over to the east side of the street and hid behind a parked car. The lights at the far end of the block were out and with the coming darkness, he could barely see down the street. He strained to focus on the dark figure moving rapidly away and saw the boy turn south at the next corner. Marty was doubling back.

Aw, come on, kid. No spy movies.

Whelan moved back across the street and retraced his steps to Sheridan and Wilson. He ducked inside the McDonald's and took a seat at a booth by a side window. At the next booth, an elderly woman nursed a cup of coffee and stared out at the gray street. Eventually he could make out the slender hunched-over figure of Marty Wills approaching the intersection. Twice as he watched, Marty stopped and let his gaze sweep the street behind him. When he was a few yards from the corner, the boy broke into his stiff-legged trot and Whelan realized that he was headed for the Burger King on the corner. The two dueling hamburger stands were across from one another on a diagonal line, and from his window Whelan could actually see into the front section of the Burger King. He watched Marty Wills enter and move quickly into a back section of the restaurant and it was plain that he was meeting someone.

The sense that he himself was being watched made Whelan look around. A slim black man in a tie was watching him from the counter. As Whelan looked at him, the man said something to one of the teenage counter workers.

Great. I'm about to be rousted from a McDonald's. He

got up and approached the counter and the manager moved to meet him.

"Welcome to McDonald's. May I help you, sir?"

Whelan grinned. "I was supposed to meet somebody here and now...Well, I don't want to take up your space without buying something. I'll have a cup of coffee and a piece of your famous apple pie."

Mollified, the manager nodded, said "Yes, sir," and rang up Whelan's order while his staff fell all over themselves to bring the coffee and the tentlike little cardboard package containing the pie.

Whelan took his tray back to the booth and slid into his seat. Eyes on the door across the street, he stirred the coffee and then sipped at it and shook his head. Not good, but unmistakably McDonald's coffee: he'd had it in Ohio and Michigan and Montana and Seattle and in two dozen different places here, and it always tasted exactly the same, and he wanted to know how they did it. The pie he'd bought as a prop.

He waited and watched the street and drank his coffee, and eventually the door opened and gave him what he'd been waiting for. He watched Marty Wills come out alone and look up and down the street before crossing Sheridan and heading in the general direction of his home. Whelan blew on his coffee and stared at the glass door of the Burger King and waited for Tony Blanchard, and when the door finally opened, it gave up Mickey Byrne.

"Aw, Mick."

He put the coffee down and stayed frozen to his seat as a knot formed in his stomach. For a long moment he watched the narrow back in khaki trudge up Sheridan with that stiff-legged walk, toward Argyle Street. Mickey Byrne and Marty Wills. He shook his head: the combination made others possible. Mickey Byrne and the missing boy, Mickey Byrne and Jimmy Lee Hayes. Mickey Byrne and...all of them.

He had a cigarette and finished the coffee, and when he was leaving, he stopped at the next booth and slid the little pie container toward the old woman.

She glanced at it, then up at Whelan.

"I bought it and I'm too full. I haven't touched it."

She nodded. "Thank you." One bony hand moved out and took the pie by one corner of its package. She slid it toward her and began studying the picture, and when Whelan left, she was just peeking inside.

Outside, Whelan stared up Sheridan and thought he could just barely make out the fragile shape of a boyhood friend. He realized that the best thing he could do for himself this night would be to call on Sandra McAuliffe. Instead, he went home.

Eleven

In the morning he woke fuzzy-headed and unable to lose the image of Mickey Byrne. To fight it off, he went over the places he'd seen the day before and tried to squeeze something new out of them.

Eventually he found himself thinking about his life, his daily bachelor patterns, and the possibility that he might be letting go of them soon. No matter how he looked at it, it was clear that he'd have trouble adjusting to a life with different patterns—he'd been in this one for a long time. There was, of course, the possibility that they could work something out, come to some mutually satisfying arrangement that allowed each to hang onto some vestige of independence, some illusion of complete freedom. And if they couldn't?

He got up on one elbow and found his cigarette pack on the bedside table. Two left. It occurred to him that he'd begun to smoke more, just this past month and a half, and he realized that Sandra McAuliffe was the cause.

More correctly, Paul Whelan's multiple reactions to Sandra McAuliffe were the cause.

You're running scared, Whelan, he told himself, and put the cigarettes down.

In fifteen minutes he'd shaved and run through a quick shower, then put on water for coffee. He walked to the kitchen window and threw back the yellow curtains the way his mother had done five thousand mornings in this very room. The sun sat high in the east.

"Hang in there, babe, we need you."

In a few moments there was coffee and a couple pieces of slightly burnt toast on the table, sun in the room and Stan Getz on the radio, and he had no answers for his life, but a new plan for his day.

Except for the bright sunlight he could almost have convinced himself that he'd stopped time, that he had just lost Lester moments earlier and was now standing on the bridge trying to find him in the crowd. A bigger crowd today, a sunny Friday crowd. At the north end, people were lined up for the blue paddle boats to go out onto the little lagoon, and behind him a line of small children tugged and fought against authority as authority dragged them into the Farm-in-the-Zoo, and down at the south end of the pond he saw the same two men as before, the big one feeding his birds and the other man sitting on his bench a few feet away.

Up close the big man was something out of *Lives of the Saints,* six three or six four and heavy, with close-set dark eyes and a thick red beard that covered his face up to his cheekbones. He held a plastic bag in his left hand and with his right dug into it and came out with fistfuls of crumbled bread. He tossed the bread out onto the water. Some of it made it that far, some fell at his feet, and wherever the bread landed it was appreciated: he was surrounded by wood ducks, mallards, teals and geese, half a dozen pigeons and a couple of starlings that stole in at the very edge of the circle and pecked quickly at the bread.

This urban Saint Francis didn't seem to enjoy his work: there was an intensity to him that demanded attention, an urgency in his face, in his eyes, that contrasted with the peaceful nature of his work.

"Looks like the sun is gonna stay a while," Whelan offered. The man said nothing, gave no hint of having heard. Whelan stood a few feet from him and when he was certain the man would not speak, he moved on.

The second man shot Whelan a quick look and then let his gaze drop as Whelan lowered himself onto the bench two feet from him. He was a wreck, this man, a dirty, skinny, weathered survivor of the streets. He'd made it through another northern winter but not by much, from the looks of him. Where his skin had been exposed to wind and sun, it was several shades darker than the rest of him, and there was dirt in the folds of his knuckles that was never coming out. He sat with his knees crossed and legs tucked under him, like a small boy, and kept his arms folded tight around him.

Whelan made a show of taking out a cigarette and lighting it. The man turned slightly to watch him from the corner of his eye, and Whelan held out the pack.

"Smoke?"

"Yeah," the man said in a high, unsteady voice. He poked and pawed at Whelan's cigarettes until he got one to come out, then stuck it in his mouth and puffed at Whelan's match until he had a light. "Thanks," he muttered.

Whelan nodded. The man was sporting a thin black mustache, a Clark Gable kind of mustache. Filthy clothes and rotting shoes and matted hair and dirty hands and all, and this man was still keeping one last shred of his vanity. The man met Whelan's eyes for the first time. Large dark eyes, kid's eyes, and a little boy's body language that told the world he thought he was in a harsh, hostile place.

"You're welcome. Think we're finished with snow?"

The man shrugged. "God, I hope so. Got snow in May once before, though. Big snow, too."

"I remember." Whelan looked over at the two islets. In a couple of weeks the young trees would erupt in buds but at the moment they looked as desolate, as dead, as the forest in a Gothic tale. The islets were alive, though, on this sunny morning: crows, it looked like a hundred of them, and they were moving from branch to branch and cawing to one another and making occasional visits to the ground below. Whelan remembered what his father had always believed about crows: that they were intelligent, that they spoke to one another and had the human race figured out. Whelan's friend Sergei, an elderly Russian Jew who spent his mornings in coffee shops and his evenings studying English at Truman, told him the crows in Russia could talk. Whelan had always ascribed that to the Russian need for supremacy in little matters.

He looked at the man on the bench. "I was here a couple of days ago. I was supposed to meet a man and I missed him but I think you were here. This guy is an older man, about six feet tall, walks with a stoop. Blue raincoat and a blue hat. Had a newspaper that he carried under one arm."

For a moment Whelan wasn't sure the man would answer. He cupped both hands around his cigarette and leaned forward, watching the blue paddle boats making their lazy circuits of the lagoon. Then he met Whelan's eyes and held up a finger stained from a lifetime of cigarettes.

"One guy, this was?"

"Right. He's..." Whelan caught himself. "But he might have been with another man. He might have run into another guy here."

The man on the bench nodded. "I dunno if this was the guy you're looking for but he was wearing a blue raincoat and had this blue hat like they used to wear. Don't know about a newspaper."

"There you go. What did the other guy look like?"

"He was old, too. Didn't have no hat. Glasses, white hair. He was wearing a raincoat too. He smiled a lot, he had real big teeth. Funny teeth, made him look strange."

Whelan took a puff at his cigarette and forced himself to slow down. "Looks like a skull sometimes," he said casually.

The man smiled for the first time. "He sure does. That's just what he looked like to me, a skeleton."

"Wonder how much I missed them by. You got a good look at them, did they meet here?"

The man made a little shake of his head. "No." He screwed his face up in a frown and gestured toward the water with his cigarette. "They were in one of them boats."

Whelan watched a pair of young women make the turn a few feet away from the spot where the bearded man was feeding his birds. They were laughing and panting, apparently unused to this kind of exertion in the morning.

He stared at the water and let it come together. "A boat,"

Whelan heard himself say. Then, to the other man, "So what did they do? Go cruising around the lagoon?"

The man shrugged. "That's what they do in them boats. Nothin' else to do, really. They come right by here, that's how I saw their faces so good. And then they went in there close to them little islands."

"Then what?"

"That's all I saw. I wasn't watching them. There was a bunch of kids coming in a couple of them boats, and they were all laughing. It was kinda nice to watch. I didn't pay no attention to them two old men after they made the turn by the islands."

"Well, I appreciate your help."

The man nodded and worked at the last half inch of his cigarette and stared out over the water. Whelan took another look at the man and wondered if he'd make it through any more winters.

I don't know how you got to where you are, Whelan thought, and it's none of my business. I just know you're not going to be here long.

"Here, maybe buy yourself a hamburger or something." He held out a folded ten. The man covered it with his dark hand, flashed a quick look at one corner of the bill and looked at Whelan.

"Thanks, mister. Thanks a lot."

"It's all right."

Whelan got up and stretched, then walked on past the bench. As he moved in front of the man, he touched him lightly on the shoulder. "See you around."

"Sure."

He followed the curving wall of the pond and as he drew even with the little islets, the crows renewed their raucous noise. Whelan gave them an idle glance and saw several birds descend from the upper branches to the ground, where a dozen or more crows already bunched together. The crows in the high branches called out and the ones on the ground cawed and shouldered their way in, and then Whelan stopped.

They were feeding.

He backed up a few paces till he was at the point nearest the larger of the two islets. The floor of the islet was alive, a dark roiling mass of birds, and whatever they had found was big enough to feed all of them.

"Damn," Whelan said, and knew that he had found Lester.

He made the call from the pay phone inside Café Brauer, the zoo cafeteria, and made it anonymous in case he was wrong. Then he retreated to the high ground, to the raised driveway that overlooked the pond. Behind him stood the massive monument to Grant, a columned granite superstructure topped by an equestrian statue of Grant gazing out upon the zoo. Generations of teenagers had met in the dark under the stone canopy, where presumably the bronze general couldn't see them, to drink, make out, spray-paint the walls and do anything else that came to their fevered minds.

Directly below him were the islands. Whelan had a cigarette and waited, and eventually things began to happen. From a tunnel to the south, a squad car appeared and rolled up the broad park sidewalk till it perched at the lip of the pond. Two cops got out and stared at the larger islet for a long moment, occasionally speaking. One of them shook his head and walked back to the car while the other moved toward the Bird Man. Whelan was pleased to see that the bearded fellow had little more to say to the cop than he'd had to Whelan. A few shakes of the head was about all the cop got. Whelan watched him walk back to his partner.

A few minutes later another squad car came around the curve of the pond, from the direction of the zoo itself, and the four cops had a conference. As they talked and gestured toward the islet, the crows continued to move from tree to ground and back again, keeping up their strident chatter, oblivious to their growing audience.

Eventually a new player came onto the scene and Whelan knew the cops had taken it all seriously. The Fire Department Rescue Squad showed up, and after a short talk with the street cops, two fire department divers in wet suits lowered themselves into the cold water. They weren't going to be doing any scuba diving: the water was only chest high, but the wet suits were coming in handy. The four cops watched the divers wading out toward the islets and Whelan remembered something an old sergeant had once told him: "A cop gets punched, a cop gets shot at, a cop gets called a lot of names, but a cop don't get wet."

All at once the crows flew up in a dark cackling cloud and then the divers were on the islet. A moment later one of them shouted back to the police. The birds' cacophony hid part of what he said, but Whelan heard enough. He heard the diver say "We've got a body."

He waited in General Grant's company for twenty minutes as the operation wound itself up. When the body had already been brought off the islet, a gray Caprice pulled up behind the first of the two squad cars. The south end of the pond was already a crowded place, what with three squad cars and a wagon, plus two Fire Department vehicles and a Park District car, and a small crowd of onlookers had materialized. Whelan watched the little audience split as a familiar figure, a thickset gentleman in a loud plaid jacket and a peacock blue shirt, bulled his way through.

Whelan gave Bauman time to talk to the uniforms who had been first to respond, then to the divers. He saw Bauman bend over the covered corpse and pull back the covering, then stoop closer. One of the cops shook his head. Whelan lit up another cigarette and decided it was time to go down and meet the guests.

The little squadron of cars was already breaking up when Whelan got down to the pond. He sat on a bench on the far side of the pond for a few minutes, hidden from view by the islet itself, then, when only the Caprice and one squad car were left, got up and walked toward them.

Landini saw him first and mouthed an obscenity. Bauman was puffing on one of his little cigars and turned, looked at Whelan, then back at the island. He said nothing till Whelan was a few feet away, then squinted at him.

"Well, now here's a fucking bolt out of the blue. We get a call about a stiff on this island and who shows up as soon as we get the guy off but Paul Whelan the famed investigator."

"Yeah," Landini said, "I wonder why that is."

Whelan ignored him. He met Bauman's eyes. "Lester?"

"Part of 'im. The birds were hungry, Whelan. But it was Lester, yeah."

Landini moved closer to Whelan. "I still want him to tell us how come we get this call, and all of a sudden he shows up."

"He didn't just show up." Bauman sniffed. "You called it in." He stuck a finger in Whelan's chest.

"Yeah."

"Anonymous tip, they told me."

"What would you have done? I couldn't be sure I was right, but I could tell there was something out there and I was pretty sure it was something dead."

"How come you didn't go home and get your mask and fins and find out."

"How was he killed?"

"The fuck do I know? This is not exactly a pristine corpse here. The M.E. can tell us how he was killed, that's what he gets paid for."

"He touched it," Landini said to no one in particular.

Bauman indicated Landini with a nod. "*It.* He calls a stiff 'it.' Yeah, I touched 'im. I touch 'em all. You seen me touch a dozen stiffs. Whelan's seen it too. It's something I do."

Landini looked away in exasperation. "He fucking touches dead bodies, don't know what the fuck kinda disease and shit they might have, he touches 'em."

"Somebody should always touch a dead man," Bauman said quietly. He took a puff on his little cigar and then shot it into the pond, near a duck. The duck fluttered away and landed again a few feet from the cigar. "Looks like that thing that Joe Danno's got hanging from the ceiling."

"No," Whelan said. "That one you're annoying is a mallard. The dead one at the Bucket is a merganser."

Bauman shook his head. "This really pisses me off."

"I'm not real happy about it either."

"What do you care? You're lookin' for the kid."

"I told you before, I'm looking for anybody that can tell me about the kid."

Bauman's look made his feelings clear. "Lester? Lester couldn't find his dick with both hands. What was he gonna tell you about this kid?"

"I don't know. And now we'll never know."

Bauman stared at him for a moment and then looked back at the water. "This fucking makes my day."

Whelan looked at Landini. "And you know what kind of a day that means *you're* gonna have."

"I need you to tell me that?"

"Later, guys."

When he'd gone a dozen paces or so, Whelan heard Bauman clear his throat.

"I'll be talkin' to you, Snoopy. We got to compare notes."

Whelan waved and kept on walking.

Sam Carlos was humming and setting out strawberries in pint baskets, and Whelan knew why he was humming: at the top of each little plastic basket was a layer of perfect strawberries, a layer thinner than baby hair, and below that layer, a wet clotting mass of berries in various stages of decomposition. Sam's hand-lettered sign said the strawberries were a buck and a half a pint.

Sam was driving a new Buick these days, and Whelan was fairly sure he'd paid cash. Sam noticed him and waved, a happy American businessman.

Whelan was opening his door when the one across the hall opened. He turned and saw Nowicki peering out at him.

"Hi."

"Uh, yeah, hi, you had a whaddyacallem, a client."

"Oh yeah? Did he leave a message?"

Nowicki shook his head. He seemed to be uncomfortable with his information.

"Did he say who he was?"

"Said he was a friend of yours."

"No name?"

"Nope." Nowicki looked up and down the empty hall. "He tried the door."

"They all do."

"No, I mean he was tryin' to get in. You know, like he was breaking in."

Whelan stared at him for a moment. Nowicki licked his lips. "He said you usually leave it open."

"He did, huh? What did this old friend look like?"

"Big, maybe your height but bigger built. Dark hair, kinda slicked back." Nowicki ran his hand over his own disappearing hair and looked at the palm, as though afraid more had come off.

"Slicked back? Not a crew cut?"

"No, not that cop."

Whelan found himself smiling. "You've met the cop?"

"No, no," Nowicki said. "Never met him, but…I mean, hell, anybody'd make that guy for a cop. No, this was a different guy, this wasn't no cop. Hillbilly."

"What?"

Nowicki shrugged. "Hillbilly, he was. You know, a stump-jumper. Had a southern accent. You don't know him, huh?"

Whelan shook his head and said nothing.

"I thought you oughtta know. I like to mind my own business, you know, but, I mean, if you saw somebody tryin' to get in my joint here, I'd wanta know that."

"Right. Well, thanks."

"It's okay. He said he'd be back. Said he'd see you later."

Whelan nodded and then closed the door behind him. He crossed to his desk and set down his coffee and sank into the chair. A familiar churning had returned to his stomach, and the office seemed unusually chilly.

At any given time in a neighborhood like Uptown there would be some small-time thief trying to burgle an office. I've got a burglar, he told himself, but he knew better.

TWELVE

Roy's Garage was on Broadway, a short block from Argyle Street, and a relic of bygone days, like armor and flintlock pistols. Flanked by newer, taller office buildings, it hugged the ground and clung to its space, and made Whelan think of a sapling fighting for sun among the big trees. The garage was a boxy white building with the shiny, porcelainlike front of a fifties' gas station, which was probably what it had been. Roy still had a pair of gas pumps, both promising a brand of gasoline that Whelan had never heard of. A small sign on each pump said the gasoline contained 15 percent alcohol.

No one came into the office when Whelan entered, and no one would have stopped him from grabbing the contents of the register and all the Snickers bars on the counter display. He went through the back door of the office and walked into the garage itself. Two men, one in his sixties, the other barely out of puberty, were staring in obvious concern at a faded yellow Olds 88. The car's engine was idling and the noises emitted were not good noises; they bespoke a car about to meet the ghost of Mr. Olds himself.

The only other vehicle in the garage was a motorcycle, and it didn't look any better than the dying Olds. Whelan cleared his throat but the two mechanics didn't hear him over the car's death rattle. He moved a few paces closer and got the attention of the older man. He had gray hair in need of cutting, and a flat nose that appeared to have been broken at some time. The man's stained blue coverall said ROY but then so did the young man's.

"Sounds like mine," Whelan said, nodding toward the Olds.

"Bring 'er in, we can take care of 'er." He looked at the Olds. "We'll be through with this one in a little bit," he said but it didn't sound as though he believed it. The young man looked at him for a moment, then back at the Olds, and shook his head.

"You Roy?"

"The owner, yeah. His name's Roy too. He's my nephew."

Whelan shook his hand and said "Paul Whelan," then handed Roy his business card. The old mechanic squinted at the card and picked at his chin with his free hand. He looked like a man reading bad news.

"I'm looking for Tony Blanchard. I understand he used to work here."

"Yeah. But he don't work here now. I ain't seen him in a long time. Maybe a year."

"Now I was under the impression that he was still working here in the summer."

Roy looked puzzled, then nodded. "Wait, wait, you're right. He was here in the summer."

"And he did some work for Jimmy Lee Hayes." Roy began to protest and Whelan held up one hand. "And then the kid quit and started running errands for Hayes. Who you knew pretty well."

Roy didn't like the choice of words. He frowned and shook his head and looked for support or suggestions from his nephew. The boy looked at his uncle and then at Whelan, showing wide pale gray eyes as vacant as Roy's grease pit. Only the sound of his breathing showed that the boy was a sentient being. If fixing the Olds required any kind of thought from this apprentice mechanic, the owner might as well buy a bus pass.

"I've talked to the police, Roy. I know Detective Bauman, and we talked about you: I know you let Jimmy Lee use this place for a while."

"I got nothin' to do with any of that. Jimmy Lee used to come here and meet his friends…"

"And do business. Selling things that didn't belong to them."

Roy surprised him with a hostile look. It changed his entire face, made him appear capable of something more than the futility in his grease pit.

"What you want from me, mister?"

"I want the boy. I want to know anything anybody on earth knows about that boy and I don't much care what I do to get it."

"You don't think the cops was here, asking all this same crap? I told them everything I know about Jimmy and that whole bunch."

"I doubt it."

Roy folded his arms across his fleshy middle. "Yeah? What you think you can get that they can't?"

"They don't have the time I've got, Roy. I'm getting paid, I can sit on this one forever."

Roy snorted but broke off eye contact. The vacant-faced lad had moved a respectful distance from Roy and stood watching them. "I ain't seen Jimmy nor none of them, and that's the gospel truth."

"Got any idea where Jimmy might be?" Roy shook his head. "And Tony?"

"No, uh-uh. None of 'em."

Whelan tossed in a quick shot. "How about Mickey?"

"Don't know no Mickey."

"Sure? Tall, skinny guy, wears an Army coat?" Roy shook his head but refused to meet Whelan's eyes. "You knew the other ones, though. Chick and Matt, and what's-his-name, Rory…" Roy made a faint nod of concession, "…and Whitey." Something changed in the old mechanic's attitude, a wariness came into his face.

"Who?"

"Whitey."

"Naw, him I don't know."

"You knew Lester, right?"

"That old lyin' bookie, yeah. Owes me some money." Roy tried to grin, a good old boy reminiscing, one old scoundrel telling tales about another.

"Well, I wouldn't count on collecting. He's dead now, too."

Roy blinked and shuffled his feet. His face had lost color, and now Whelan could see the burst capillaries from a life of hard drinking.

"That whole bunch, Roy, they're almost all dead now."

Whelan watched Roy and waited.

The older man looked at the kid, found no help there and faced Whelan again. "How'd he get killed?"

"I don't know how. But I know who. At least, I've got a pretty good idea. And I think you do, too. Thanks for your time." Whelan walked back out toward the office. Over his shoulder he called out, "You've got my card, Roy. Give me a call if you think of anything."

And good luck with the Oldsmobile, he thought.

Dark clouds hung over the House of Zeus: the line was long and not moving and the ice machine was down and the crowd looked ready to call for blood, so Whelan took a quick ride over near the ballpark. Things were hopping in Lakeview, and the great whitewashed basin of Wrigley Field was the magnet. The Cubs were trying to shake off the effects of their disastrous East Coast road trip. They were back in the Friendly Confines and talking tough and making dire predictions for the rest of the league and the Wrigley Field faithful were buying the whole routine. Everyone but the sportswriters was apparently willing to overlook the fact that Cub pitchers had been tagged for eleven home runs in eight games. In Philadelphia they'd given up twenty-six runs in a three-day bloodbath and Mike Schmidt had given the entire pitching staff nightmares enough to last a lifetime.

Now there was a little less vigor to the Cub bluster, though the manager still claimed that his squad was "just missing one or two pieces of the puzzle." The pilgrims were marching east all through Lakeview, young people carrying their beers and making a show of street drinking, families, old people. The neighborhood would be full of cars with Indiana and Iowa license plates, full of people whose idea of a vacation was to drive into Chicago to see a 13 to 12 game in Wrigley Field. And if there was a game, and the weather was decent, it meant John the Hot Dog Man would be out.

Whelan found him at Southport and Waveland. His little

red three-wheeled cart was parked on the sidewalk and his customers were already lining up. Whelan had five people ahead of him and didn't mind the wait. When customer number five had walked away gnawing at a Polish, John turned to wipe down his work surface and said "Yes?"

"I want two thousand hot dogs and one Polish."

John turned and smiled. Selling hot dogs was apparently thirsty work: his glasses were slightly steamed and perspiration rolled down his face from beneath his cap.

"Long time, Paulos. I thought you were dead."

"No, just real hungry. Business seems good."

"Oh, not bad. What you gonna have?"

"A hot dog and a Polish, and I need a Dr Pepper."

"Everything?"

"Of course. Peppers, too." Whelan looked over the little red-and-white car. For almost a generation, John had been the neighborhood hot dog man, pedaling his little cart into the area and appearing at various corners before ballgames, then moving to other locations during the evenings. On a hot summer night you could always find him somewhere on Southport, steam coming from half a dozen little stainless steel bins and people lined up for his dogs. Then one fateful night, a drunk had run him down as he crossed Addison, sending the cart and its contents shooting off in all directions and John to the hospital. John had sued the drunk for his hospital costs and the loss of his beloved cart. The upshot was a new motorized cart, state-of-the-art if there was one for hot dog vendors, and John hadn't stopped smiling yet. He worked the neighborhood from April to November, then went to Greece for two months. Life was good if you could sell enough hot dogs.

John slathered mustard onto the dog and the Polish, scooped onions, relish and tomatoes on top, added cucumbers and cucumber salt, then tossed on a couple of sport peppers. Whelan handed him three bucks.

"Thank you, sir."

"I've always wondered, John—you eat a lot of hot dogs?"

John curled his lip. "I don't like 'em. No good for you."

• • •

He had eaten the hot dog in three bites and was about to assault the Polish when there was a knock, and a premonition told him who it was.

"Come on in."

Bauman stepped in and closed the door behind him. Then he opened it again and peered into the hall. A moment later, he shut it again. He indicated the hall with a nod.

"This guy, the one that sells novelties, he think he's some kinda operative? Or do you pay him a buck to watch your door."

"He's just a nervous guy."

Bauman started to smile. "Makes you wonder what he's really selling, don't it?"

"Probably better I shouldn't know."

Bauman moved slowly across the room, then dropped his bulk onto the guest chair, and Whelan heard the wood groan. He studied his visitor and decided there was something about Bauman's mood he didn't like. Amusement, that was it: Bauman looked amused.

"Your mood has improved since this morning."

Bauman moved his shoulders slightly in a shrug. "So what's for lunch there, Snoopy?"

"A Polish."

"From where?"

"The hot dog man on Southport."

Bauman leaned forward in interest. "I could eat about five of those." He sat back and busied himself opening a new pack of the little cigars, and Whelan watched him.

"So what brings you here when we spoke, oh, less than three hours ago? Got something to tell me about old Les?"

Bauman cleared his throat with a low rumble. "Leonard George McCarty. Junior."

"What's that? Lester's real name?"

"No, not Les. Whitey. That's your guy Whitey's real name. Leonard George McCarty, Junior, only like all these great thinkers he's got other names he's used."

"So you're already familiar with this gentleman."

Bauman nodded. "Oh, yeah, down at Six, we're all familiar with Leonard George McCarty. He's another one of these Southern Gentlemen. He's got what you'd call a colorful sheet. Here and in Nashville, where he had, uh, thriving business interests. Now there's a lot about this guy Leonard George McCarty that's, you know, interesting. For one, he and old Jimmy Lee Hayes, they were half brothers." Bauman paused to play with his little cigar and looked innocently at Whelan. Whelan thought over the various responses possible, and elected to bite into the Polish.

"Kinfolk, as they say down there. Told you old Jimmy Lee come from a family of hoods."

Bauman relaxed and Whelan knew it was time to play audience.

"So tell me about him."

Bauman shrugged. "Near as we can make out, this guy was Jimmy Lee's mentor, kind of. He was a couple years older than Jimmy, and I guess you could say he's the guy taught Jimmy Lee how to be a scuzzball. But he was a bad guy and they had to put him in the shitter to contemplate his evil ways. So, here I'm looking for Jimmy Lee Hayes and my good friend Paul Whelan the Sleuth, he's looking for a runaway, uh, youth, and he comes up with this name. How do you figure that?"

"You didn't know he was out?"

A glimmer came into Bauman's eyes, as though he'd thought of something amusing. "Who keeps track of these lowlifes?"

"Would you recognize him?"

Bauman scratched at his neck and made a little sideways nod. "Well, yeah, I guess I would. This goes back a few years but, yeah, I suppose I'd recognize him if I saw him. Only thing is, I'm not gonna."

"Why?"

The amusement came back in the gray eyes, and the familiar malice was there along with it. "That's another, you know, interesting thing. 'Cause my guy Leonard George McCarty's in a Nashville cemetery. Died of a heart attack in prison. He never *got* out."

"When did he die?"

"What difference does it make? July, I think. Yeah, July."

Whelan watched him for a moment and Bauman looked out the office window. "Then who's *this* guy?"

"Fuck if I know," Bauman muttered, and Whelan watched him.

The setting sun brought them out. They were gathering in front of the arcade on Belmont and the music clubs, converging on the Dunkin' Donuts. He parked across from the lot on Clark Street, spread the *Sun-Times* across the steering column and began paging through it. From time to time he looked up, hoping for a glimpse of the two girls, even hoping that his luck was running and a long-haired boy with a tattoo would show up.

The darkness was growing and he was about to get out and get himself a cup of coffee when something changed in his field of vision. Something very still had moved.

Whelan looked up, shot a quick glance in the rearview mirror, then scanned the kids across the street in the parking lot. For a moment he could see nothing unusual, and focused again on the nearest group of kids. Then a gray shape separated itself from a light pole half a block away and Whelan looked up. The dusk blurred his vision at the edges, and this man ahead was a creature of the dusk, a pale figure in a nondescript raincoat, moving slowly away. Whelan squinted to get a look at him.

The man in the raincoat craned slightly to peer over the traffic on Clark and Whelan followed his gaze to the kids in the parking lot across the street. The man stopped and stood motionless for a moment and then, just as Whelan realized who he was, the man in the raincoat turned, as though spoken to. He seemed to find Whelan immediately and then he was moving away. As he turned, he shot one last glance back at Whelan and even at that distance Whelan would have sworn the man had met his eyes, consciously, a challenge. Then the pale man turned and Whelan saw him hurrying across the parking lot of the

Senior Citizens building on the corner.

Whelan tumbled out of the car and ran after him. At the entrance to the parking lot he stopped and surveyed the cars. No one moved across it, no car pulled out. A few feet away, an elderly man wearing layers of flannel shirts sat on a bench, one knotted hand on the worn handle of a cane.

"Excuse me, sir. Did you see a man in a raincoat run into the parking lot here?"

The man squinted at Whelan, looked him up and down before deciding it was all right to speak to him. "Think so. He wasn't runnin', though. Just walkin' fast."

"Did you see where he went?"

The man turned with great difficulty and pointed off into the darkness with his cane. "That alley there."

"Thanks."

At the mouth of the alley he stood and watched and told himself he'd lost the man already. Then he lit up a cigarette and tried to find the bright side: he told himself that at least on this one night, the man called Whitey would be deprived of his night's watch over the kids on the corner. Then he remembered the look in the old man's eyes.

He knew me, Whelan told himself. He knew me.

He waited in the darkness at the mouth of the alley and finished his smoke, and had to admit that there was at least a chance that the man who called himself Whitey wasn't there to watch the kids at all.

He parked a few doors down from his house and on the far side of the street—the big old apartment buildings that anchored the block at both ends had been rehabbed and were starting to eat up the parking space, and more than once he'd had to park on the next block. He got out of his car and moved diagonally across Malden, thinking about the man in the raincoat, and in his mind's eye he saw the man staring at him, noted the high cheekbones and the long face, the strange tuft of blondish hair that stood up like a used brush, and he was thinking again about the rooming house when he heard the car behind him.

He turned and instantly knew he'd turned too late. The driver laid rubber, closing the twenty-yard gap between them in a heartbeat. He had time only to register impressions: big man, slick dark hair, sideburns. The car was easier: he knew the car. He fought the impulse to run and began to spin to his left, and he'd just begun to leave his feet when the dark car reached him. He felt the side of the hood strike his hip, and then the car was by him in a dark rush and he was falling heavily onto the pavement. He rolled backward into a parked car and felt the hard projection of a fender in the small of his back, then rolled over to regain his feet. He staggered and fell back against the parked car, looking down the street after the dark car. At the corner it made a sudden jerky turn, taking the corner with two wheels up on the curb, left another layer of tire on the street and tore off with a screech.

For several moments he stood motionless, making an inventory of his injuries. His hip ached where the car had struck him, and he could tell he'd made a three-point landing because pain spoke to him from a knee, an elbow and a shoulder. He moved what would move, flexed what would flex, and decided nothing was broken.

Across the street he saw a shade go up and could make out the stubby form of his neighbor, the dignified, easily offended Mr. Barsano. In a few seconds, Mr. Barsano would be contacting the police and the FBI and perhaps NATO. At the moment NATO seemed like a good idea. Whelan leaned against the parked car and took in deep breaths, not certain that his heart would last the night. When he thought he'd collected himself, he made it across the street and up the sidewalk to his house. The shade was down again in Perry Barsano's house but Whelan could see a fat finger holding the shade away at one side. He fought the impulse to wave.

Inside, he crossed the room in darkness and found his easy chair. He lit up a cigarette and took a puff, and reflected on what he knew: he knew the car, of course, a dark Mustang with bad springs. It was the driver that puzzled him: not the neat, wiry form of Bobby Hayes but another type altogether, a different package. This man who had tried to kill him with a car was a big man, much bigger than Bobby Hayes, a big man with black hair, slick black hair, and this was the second time he'd tried to get a piece of Paul Whelan.

I know you, Whelan told himself. I know you.

THIRTEEN

In the morning, he made coffee, then called the answering service and was surprised to hear Shelley's voice.

"What are you doing answering phones on a Saturday?"

"I switched with the new girl. She had a wedding to go to. So if you call me on Monday, you'll get Lydia."

"Lydia, huh?" He shuddered and Shelley laughed. "I thought you meant that other one, the one that cracks her gum."

"Eileen. She quit."

Whelan had spoken only twice to Lydia but had managed to learn that she believed she was psychic, that she had lived dozens of lives before, most notably at the court of Catherine the Great, that she believed her first husband had been reincarnated as her pet cockatiel and that she kept the ashes of her late parents in an oleo cup in the refrigerator.

"Sorry to hear that."

"What's up with *you* on a Saturday, Mr. Paul Whelan?"

"I've got some things to do and I have a feeling people will be trying to get in touch with me. If they do, tell them I'll stop in the office sometime late this morning."

"Will do."

At nine-thirty he drove the few blocks west and south to the apartment building on Marshfield. The black Mustang was nowhere in sight but Whelan rang the bell marked "Hayes" inside the tiny hallway. The other bells bore names in blue plastic but Bobby Hayes's was handwritten on a piece of white paper, giving it just the transient touch it needed. As Whelan expected, there was no answer.

Ed and Ronda's was open, of course, had probably been open for hours. A true shot-and-beer joint was open before the birds sang. Years before, in his days as a beat cop, Whelan had stopped into Kelly's Pub over by De Paul, looking for a man charged with assault in another bar. It was seven in the morning on a Tuesday or Wednesday, and Whelan and Jerry Kozel had pounded first on the locked door, then gone round by the horseshoe pit to come in the back way. The day bartender wasn't due till nine and the place was officially closed, but inside Kelly's they were rocking and rolling. Four off-duty firefighters, a secretary from Daley's office, two old men from the rooming house up the street, a retired cop from Town Hall, three college kids slumming, the mail carrier and a banker on a bender. Over it all, Willie the porter was presiding, a little West Virginia man with a withered leg. The firemen were watching *Rocky and Bullwinkle* and the three college kids had the jukebox shaking, and outside the world went about its business, but time had stopped in Kelly's.

In keeping with custom, the front door was locked, and Whelan went around to the side and found a way in. Ed and Ronda drew a quieter crowd than Kelly did, in fact several of Ed and Ronda's customers appeared to have died in the night. A big man in a T-shirt was sprawled over a table off to one side, and a woman at the far end of the bar was nursing a coma. Another woman was behind the bar, a thin woman whom Whelan had seen once before, coming down the back stairs. The woman wasn't sure she liked Whelan's looks. She leaned on the bar surface with both hands and let her body language announce the fact that she owned it.

"Morning," Whelan said.

"We're not open," she said and her dark eyes said she hadn't seen anything to be afraid of in years.

"Good, then we have time to talk," he said, and flipped a card on the bar. "You must be Ronda."

"We already got one of these," she said, picking the card up and then dropping it.

"I've been passing them out all over town. Gave one to

Ed, one to Bobby Hayes. If you want, give that one to Jimmy Lee Hayes."

She met his gaze and a mirage of a smile appeared at the corners of her mouth. He decided in her day she'd been pretty, and wondered whether running the tavern or life with Ed had put the lines in her face. "Who?"

"Jimmy Lee Hayes. Bob's big brother."

She placed the card in front of him. "Don't know the man."

"I like this place. Nobody knows anybody. Jack the Ripper could drink here and be sure of his privacy."

Ronda's look said she could handle Jack the Ripper and Whelan and anybody else fate sent her way on a bad day.

"Well, maybe you could have Bobby give me a call when he comes in. Tell him I need to talk to him about his brother. I have something he'll want. If he doesn't call me, I'll just have to come back."

Ronda said nothing, but folded her arms across her chest. She met his eyes for a moment, then picked up his card, glanced at it once again, then dropped it. Whelan walked casually toward the door, admitting to himself that it had been a grandstand play, but sometimes a little grandstanding was good for the soul.

Outside, he heard bird noises, an angry robin. It seemed to him that robins were always angry—perhaps that was why there were so many of them. He stopped for a moment to locate the bird. The trees here and across the street in the park were in the midst of their early May transformation, a remarkable change that always seemed to take about one week—less for the cottonwoods, which appeared to bud overnight. He found the robin in the middle of a barren-looking catalpa tree that hadn't quite caught the spring fever with its neighbors. High in an oak across the street, blackbirds were eyeing him and calling out to one another. Whelan thought of Lester the fence and shuddered. Alfred Hitchcock understood the birds.

Somewhere on the first floor someone was yelling into the phone in Korean but he knew in seconds that he was the only living thing on the second, and the realization did not bring happiness. The lights were out in A-OK Novelties: apparently Nowicki gave himself weekends off from whatever larceny he was involved in.

Whelan paused at the top of the stairs and listened. The air in the hall was stale and unmoving, and he was fairly certain he was the first person to enter the hall today. He went inside his office and opened the window, then popped the lid on his coffee. For several minutes he stood blowing on the coffee and watching the steam sail off the top and out onto Lawrence.

Four men dead. A man everyone believed dead was trying to catch up with Paul Whelan. A dead man was trying to take him out.

For what? He lit a cigarette and blew smoke out onto Lawrence. Not the boy, he didn't think it was over the boy. It was more complicated than that.

Something I might find out, or something I already found and just don't see.

The phone made him jump and he caught it before the second ring.

"Hi, baby."

"Hello, Shelley. Nobody else seems to be glad to talk to me today."

"That's because you've been sticking your nose in their business."

"Which happens to be my business."

"Nice profession."

"My mother wanted me to be a priest."

"They all do. They think they can keep you out of trouble that way. You had two calls."

"Who?"

"One could've been a wrong number. He hung up."

"You know it was a 'he'?"

"Yeah, he kinda grunted when I answered, like he was irritated. The other one was your friend, Mr. Charm School."

"Bauman? Early for Bauman."

"Said he had information."

"All right. Thanks, Shel."

"Take care now, baby."

"I really try."

"Sure you do," she said, and laughed in his ear.

To kill time, he went through the motions of cleaning his desk and sorting the top drawers of his file cabinets. After forty minutes, he gave it up and went out for a fresh cup of coffee. When he came back, the phone was ringing.

So that's all I have to do, he thought.

He answered on the third ring and his caller hesitated. In the background he could hear music, it sounded like Dottie West.

"Whelan?"

"Hello, Bob. Stop in for a little pick-me-up?"

"I just come in to say 'hey' to a buddy of mine and I get this message. Says to call you. So here I am, son."

"I'm glad you called. We've got a complicated situation here."

"What's complicated about it?"

"We've got a problem, you and I. You see, somebody almost ran me down last night and it was your car, Bob."

"I was here at Ronda's all night. You can ask anybody here." Whelan could almost hear him winking at the woman behind the bar. He wondered when the place stopped being "Ed and Ronda's."

"I'll bet I could. But I didn't say you were driving, I said it was your car."

"My car? My car was settin' right out…"

"And it gets better: you know the driver."

"I do, huh?" The smile was gone from Bobby Hayes's voice.

"Yeah, I believe you do. Big man, black hair, wears it slicked back kind of the way you do, sideburns. But a big guy. Denim jacket, it looked like."

"Don't sound like nobody I know."

"I don't have the time, Bob. Somebody tried to run me down and I got a good look at the plates *and* the driver. Now, I don't know why anybody'd want to run me down, especially somebody I'm not interested in at all. But I did get the plates, Bob, so I've got the owner of the vehicle by the balls, if you catch my drift."

Bobby Hayes breathed into the phone. "Don't nobody really know what you are interested in. Can't nobody figure you out."

"You guys are a bunch of bad listeners, Bob. I've been telling everybody from day one, I want this kid. Tony Blanchard, nobody else, not you, not your 'deceased' brother. Anything that was going on with your brother's people or this Whitey character, that's none of my business as long as I find the kid. I don't find the kid, I keep asking questions and then I'm about at that point where I think I involve the police. 'Cause, you see, Bob, I get paid if I find the kid. Cash money."

"They's lots of ways to make money."

"Maybe so, but right now I've got my teeth into one. You help me out with my problem, I won't make any more for you."

Bobby Hayes laughed. It wasn't much of a laugh, a little wobbly, unsure of its footing. "What kind of trouble could you make for me?"

"Things change, Bob. I've got a little more to bring to the table than I did the first time we talked. I know a lot."

"Oh, yeah?"

"What I don't know, is where the kid is. That's where you can help."

"I don't know nothing about him."

"Sorry to hear that. Well, you spread the word among your, ah, principals and let me know. Maybe we can set something up."

"What for? There ain't nothing to talk about."

"Have it your way, Bob," he said, and hung up, wondering if he'd regret it. He thought for a moment and decided he'd be grateful if he were still around to regret things.

He sat sipping his coffee and eventually the phone rang again.

"Hello, Snoopy," his caller said. "What do you want now?"

"What do you mean, 'what do I want'? I was returning your call."

"Just jerking your chain. Actually, I called to share information with you."

"I'm deeply moved."

"Don't mention it. We got the word on old Lester. The M.E.'s report."

"And?"

"Lester's still dead." Bauman chuckled. "Okay, we got time of death, sometime Wednesday morning. Method of death, puncture to the heart, thin blade. Surprise, huh?"

"What else?"

"One of the birds was dead, too." Bauman snorted. "I guess old Lester was poisonous." He laughed and then Whelan heard him inhaling one of his little cigars, and waited.

"So what you got for me, Whelan? Anything?"

For a moment he had no idea how much, if anything, he was willing to give up. Then he heard himself say "I told you about the brother, right?"

"Yeah, yeah, old news."

"Okay, I've got something more lively for you. Somebody tried to kill me last night. Tried to run me down in the street in front of my house. My feelings were really hurt."

"Get a look at the car? See the plates?"

"It was dark and it happened pretty fast. Dark car. Black, maybe blue."

"Right, maybe brown, too, right? Maybe purple, maybe burnt fucking umber."

"Hey, how about if I run you down in the dark and see how good your color perception is?"

"What about his tags? See his plates?"

"No." Whelan paused a moment, heard Bauman expelling breath and bad attitude. "But I saw the driver."

"And?"

"It was a guy I've never seen before. A big white guy with dark hair, slicked back, I could see the sheen off his hair. And sideburns, long sideburns."

"Coulda been Elvis," Bauman said. Then, in a different tone, "How big?"

"Hard to say, he wouldn't let me measure him. But better than six feet and built heavy. I think he was wearing a denim jacket." He waited a moment, then asked, "Sound like anybody?"

"Yeah, Elvis," Bauman said, but he was thinking.

"Okay, well, I've got another little thing for you. I think I've got a place for you to check out."

"What kinda place?"

"A place where you might find Bobby Hayes. Maybe even his deceased brother, who knows? It's on Marshfield up by—"

"Montrose. Forty-three-something Marshfield, right? Yeah, we know about that place, Whelan. And we know Jimmy Lee Hayes isn't in there. We've got the place under surveillance, we seen the brother come and go a few times, even saw *you* checking it out. You see? Your Police Department is on top of it, Whelan."

"Have you brought Bobby Hayes in for questioning?"

"What do you think? Of course we've brought him in for questioning. And he went right into his hillbilly-in-the-big-city shtick."

"I've seen it: he claims not to know anything, doesn't know the kid, doesn't know any of the deceased members of his brother's play group, hasn't seen his brother."

"I know all of that, Whelan. Try to make a better use of your time, okay? What else you got?"

"We've tapped me out."

"All right. Nice talking to you, Whelan."

"How come you're in such a good mood?"

"It's a nice sunny day and I'm talking to my friend Whelan, and we got dead birds in this case, and I got a partner who's a really amusing guy. Know what he came in wearing today?"

"A gold lamé shirt?"

"Better than that. A hickey. He came in with a hickey on his neck, way up where you can see it. Does great things for his professional image. You know: 'Sir, we got to ask you some questions, so please ignore this big purple thing on my neck.' " Bauman cackled into the phone and Whelan waited for him to collect himself. "See, Whelan? It's a great world if you keep your sense of humor."

"I see that."

"Later, Whelan."

• • •

Late in the afternoon he was standing in the window with his eighth cup of coffee, watching them put together a new message for the big marquee of the Aragon Ballroom and feeling that he'd wasted a day. The men outside the Aragon seemed to be having trouble with the name, a famous bandleader from Mexico. The man's name seemed to be either Lupe Reyes Guerra or Lupe Guerra Reyes, and for a time they seemed to have trouble locating enough "e's." They were just finishing when the phone rang one more time, the call he'd been waiting for, though he couldn't have said who he wanted to hear on the other end.

"Whelan?" Bobby Hayes breathed heavily into the phone, sounding as though he'd just run the hundred.

"Yeah. What's up, Bob?"

"Well, you wanted information about that kid." In the background Johnny Cash was wailing about Folsom Prison, and Whelan heard the clink of ice dropped into a glass.

"Right. Got something I can use?"

"We got to talk."

"I thought that's what we're doing now."

"Yeah but...there's somebody else you need to talk to, then you'll have the whole story."

"Have him call me. I'll wait here. I'll wait here forever, Bob."

"He ain't gonna call you. He needs to know if you're gonna make trouble for 'im. Got to see you face to face."

Whelan laughed. "He's already seen me face to face."

"I don't know what you're talking about. He can come to your office."

"No, thanks."

Bobby Hayes was silent for a moment, then said, "How 'bout Ronda's?"

Whelan thought for a moment. Counting Ronda, there would be at least three hostile people there. "Nope."

Bobby Hayes made a little growl of exasperation and Whelan heard him slap the bar or the side of the phone booth. "You know Roy's?"

"The garage? Sure."

"There."

Whelan was about to laugh when he had an idea. "Meet you halfway, Bob. I'll be at the garage, but I'm not going inside."

"What? So how you expect…"

"Take a deep breath, Bob. I'll pull into Roy's driveway. I'll get out of my car and stand right next to it, and you fellas can come out and talk to me right out in the open. Get some fresh air and watch the cars go by and look for odd license plates and everything."

For a moment Bobby Hayes said nothing and Whelan wondered if the suggestion had left him speechless. "Now wait a minute…" he began.

"What's the matter?"

"Can't do it like that."

"Why not?"

"Not…out in the open."

"Bob, put your thinking cap on. If you were me, would you go alone into a garage to meet with a guy you think tried to kill you?"

"Nobody's gon' do nothin' to you."

"Right. I feel reassured. Sorry, Bob. We do it my way."

"This ain't gon' work."

"It's all you've got, so it better work. Call me back and let me know what you decide. I've got to go."

"All right, wait. Wait. Lemme think." Bobby Hayes breathed into the phone for a five-count, then said, "Okay, but you be alone."

"I'm not bringing anybody else into this. It's mine. And so is the money I'll be making." Right, he thought, all five hundred dollars of it.

"All right. Nine o'clock at Roy's."

"Is Roy going to be there?"

"Shee-it, we don't need that. What kinda car you drive, son?"

Whelan laughed. "Bob, you're probably the only guy that doesn't know that. Ask Jimmy." He hung up. For a moment he felt a tight little surge of satisfaction that he was forcing it all out. Then he thought about what he had just agreed to do, and his complacency died young.

In the next couple of hours he drove back to the rooming house on Windsor and cruised the block several times, then drove back up to Argyle Street. He made three circuits of the neighborhood, drove up and down alleys and parked for half an hour at a time on the main drag and watched the foot traffic. Then he went home to kill the rest of the time he had on his hands.

As he entered his house, he glanced at his phone. If he had an answering machine, he knew, there would be several messages on it, most particularly a call or two from Sandra McAuliffe. They wouldn't necessarily be pleasant messages. He thought about the many moments in the past two days when it would have been no trouble at all to call her. It occurred to him that he was close to blowing a relationship, and he wondered if, at an unconscious level, it was intentional.

What the hell am I doing?

For an hour he sat in his armchair and listened to old jazz records, Miles Davis and Jimmy Smith. When it was nearly seven o'clock he toyed with the idea of going out for something to eat, then gave up the idea of food almost immediately. Another idea soon took hold: Larry's Dog 'n Chicken Shack should be closing up soon.

Night was claiming the city and he could see Marty and the Korean woman stacking stools on the counter and sweeping the outer area. Behind the counter, the Korean man cleaned the grill. At a few minutes before eight, the Korean couple unlocked the front door and Marty emerged.

This time Marty Wills got into a car, a Pontiac shed of its original paint and clad now in nothing more than a dark primer. Whelan hadn't seen the car before but knew the driver. Danny Wills stared straight ahead as his brother climbed in, then pulled out into traffic and went north on Sheridan. The unpainted Pontiac weaved almost into oncoming traffic to get around a bus and Whelan was content to use the bus as a shield. At the corner of Sheridan and Argyle, the Pontiac stopped and Marty Wills got out, cast a quick look at his brother, and moved quickly up Argyle. He was carrying a white paper bag.

Whelan turned onto Argyle and parked, got out, and began following Marty, keeping to the north side of the street. Marty Wills was almost a block ahead. From time to time the boy shot quick glances over his shoulder, and at one point he froze as a car moved slowly by. A squad car rolled up from the opposite direction and the boy went rubber-limbed into his normal strut, the sullen teenager afraid of nothing.

Marty walked past the places where Whelan had first made inquiries about Tony Blanchard: past the grocery stores and the little Vietnamese restaurant and the markets. In the window of the restaurant, Whelan thought he could make out the elderly Vietnamese man watching the street from his window.

When he was across the street from the Apollo restaurant, Marty Wills dropped the white paper bag into a trash can and kept on walking, casually now. It struck Whelan that the trash can was approximately where he'd glimpsed the shadowy figure that he'd pursued. Whelan ducked into a doorway and watched. When Marty reached the El tracks, he stopped, leaned against the wall of the El platform and lit a cigarette. A moment later, a slim figure in denim appeared, moving quickly through the foot traffic. His sandy hair was pulled back in a pony tail, and though he was too far away for Whelan to see the scar, he knew this one. Like the other boy, he was a study in nonchalance, moving casually toward the trash can, hands in pockets and a little bounce to his step. Under one arm he had what looked to be a newspaper. When he reached the trash can, he stood beside it for a moment and scanned the traffic as though waiting for a ride. Then he dropped the paper into the basket, retrieved the white paper bag and backed up a few feet. As he turned to retrace his steps, he cast a quick glance inside the bag. Then he looked up and scanned the street till he met the gaze of Marty Wills. He nodded once and smiled, and Whelan was surprised to see the sallow face of Marty Wills transformed by a wide grin. Then both boys melted into the background, one across the street and into the Argyle Street El station, the other back up Argyle. Whelan followed from across the street and saw what he expected to see: at the corner of Kenmore and Argyle the boy turned and slipped into the alley, the same alley where Whelan had been jumped.

For several minutes Whelan remained in a doorway. He lit a cigarette and watched the street. One by one, he scanned the stores and businesses across Argyle and then his gaze rested on the little restaurant. The kids were gone, the old Vietnamese was no longer in his window, and Whelan finally put it together. He nodded to himself. Nice job, old fella.

He made his way back to his car. He waited several minutes, then pulled out and made a long, slow circuit of Argyle Street and the side streets and alleys, but now he saw no one but the natives and the tourists. As he slowed down to a crawl at an alley, he noticed a young Vietnamese man staring at him and realized he was becoming obvious. Time to pull out.

The image of Mickey Byrne in the doorway came back to him and he refused to think about it.

Not now, he told himself. I didn't bring him into this, I don't think I can get him out.

A station wagon full of kids cut him off. Whelan hit the horn. The driver, an enormously fat man, took both hands off the wheel and waved as though helpless. Whelan passed, took a look inside the car. The man shot him an irritated look and muttered something. Behind the driver, half a dozen chubby faces frowned Whelan's way.

Whelan tried to focus on the road and fought the images trying to gnaw their way into his consciousness. Gradually he gave it up, and saw the two boys, fifty yards apart, grinning at one another like teammates in an alley baseball game. A couple of street kids with no idea how this all might end.

No: they knew. They both knew, they understood as well as Whelan himself did. The thought forced him to admit several things to himself: the first was that Marty Wills had a bit more heart to him than Whelan had thought him capable of. The second idea was more complicated, and he wasn't comfortable with it, for it meant breaking a personal rule. He still had no real idea why all these people sought Tony Blanchard, and he'd been hired by a well-meaning client—with a healthy shove from the Chicago Police—to find him. And now he'd found him. He could tell Mrs. Pritchett the boy was alive and let her keep her five hundred dollars. There was no law that said he had to finish something. And he no longer wanted to finish this one.

On his way back to his house, he told himself there was one piece of good news in all this: he no longer had to keep his appointment at Roy's Garage.

Fourteen

Whelan sliced an onion and arranged the pieces atop a pair of chicken breasts. He was about to douse the whole thing in some of Joe Danno's homemade barbecue sauce when the phone rang, and he found himself hoping it was Sandra McAuliffe.

"Whattya doing home, Sleuth? No date?"

"I was hoping you'd be a female caller."

"No such luck."

"Yeah, well, that's the kind of day I've had."

"Is that right? Well, I know a guy who's had a worse day. Know where I am?"

"No. Should I?" And the answer began to form itself in his mind.

"I'm up here at Roy's Garage, Whelan. Roy ain't here. Somebody else is, though. Know who?"

"No."

"This guy Bobby Hayes. And know what? He's dead."

Whelan felt his stomach tighten. He was barely listening when Bauman added, "Why don't you climb into that sleek machine of yours and motor on over."

"Why? You have something I should see?"

"I don't know, maybe, maybe not. But I know you won't mind coming down to look things over with me."

"I was getting ready to eat."

"I'll buy you a hamburger or something. Come on down, Whelan."

Whelan was about to try one more protest when Bauman hung up. Looks like I'm going to the garage anyway, he told himself.

• • •

Whelan could smell rain in the air and by the time he made the swing on Broadway that took him to Roy's, he could smell trouble in it, as well. This was probably as busy as Roy's Garage would ever get: it was overrun with cars and people, most of them representatives of the Chicago Police. Four squad cars and three unmarked, a wagon that they wouldn't need and an ambulance they'd need even less, and an evidence technician's car. Blue shirts and plainclothes: one wore a flannel shirt and jeans with holes in the knees, and Whelan saw a young black female officer in a suede jacket with fringe. He spotted Landini in animated conversation with two uniformed officers, demonstrating his baseball swing and presumably giving them a fashion lesson at the same time. Here, Whelan thought, was masculine splendor: beige sport coat over a pale yellow shirt, open at the throat to reveal tonight's choice of chains, medallions, and bangles. Chocolate brown slacks over cowboy boots.

Off to one side he spotted Bauman talking with a couple of middle-aged sergeants: he recognized one as Michael Shea, an old friend of Bauman's. They were standing next to a black Mustang with Tennessee plates. Bauman looked up as Whelan pulled into Roy's driveway.

Whelan walked slowly toward the three cops. From the corner of his eye he saw Landini watching him. He met the young cop's gaze and nodded, and Landini returned it with as little effort as possible.

Bauman was gesturing with a fat hand that held one of the evil cigars and the two white-shirted sergeants were laughing. Bauman grinned, took a long drag on the cigar and then blew smoke in Whelan's direction.

"Okay, here's my guy the private operative. You guys know Whelan here?"

The taller of the two sergeants shook his head.

"Oh, I know him," Michael Shea nodded and gave him an interested look. "I've been in his house for coffee," he said brightly.

Whelan smiled. "That's right. Interesting night."

Shea looked at the other sergeant. "Mr. Whelan was involved in a disturbance with several individuals who were exercising their right to burn a cross on somebody's lawn. I show up, I see this big guy down on the ground, still holding a baseball bat and Mr. Whelan here is wrecking the windshield of a guy's car, he's using an ax like he's Arky the Arkansas Woodchopper, and there's this cross burning on a guy's lawn, and these two other mopes start running as soon as they see us. You needed a scorecard to figure out who were the bad guys." Shea smiled. "Good coffee, though."

"Glad you liked it."

"That guy still live there, the colored guy with the white wife?"

"Yes."

Shea shrugged. "What do I know? My wife says I'm a dinosaur, I got no new ideas."

Bauman pointed at the other cop. "This is George Nugent. George, Paul Whelan. Used to work out of Eighteen."

The sergeant nodded. "How you doin'."

Whelan returned the nod.

"C'mere, Whelan." Bauman moved around the car to the passenger side and peered down. He motioned Whelan over, then backed away and let him have a look.

Bobby Hayes sat flat on the concrete, head back against the door of the car, eyes fixed on something in the distance. The front of his shirt and jacket were wet and dark. Bobby Hayes had not bled overmuch but Whelan was conscious of the smell. He turned to Bauman. "Stabbed?"

Bauman nodded. "More than once. I got a feeling the first one hit the bull's-eye, though. Not much blood."

Whelan looked down at the dead man and visualized him leaning casually against the car as his killer approached. A killer whom he knew. He saw Hayes slide down against the car, coming to rest on the pavement.

"So whaddya think?" Bauman watched him.

"I don't know. Why did you bring me down here? Let me

guess, he had my card in his wallet."

"Well, it's like this..."

"Bauman, I pass that card around all over town, I order two hundred a month. If somebody walks in front of the number thirty-six bus and you find my card in his wallet, you going to call me?"

"I won't but somebody will. No, we found something more interesting, Whelan. He had your card, sure, but he also had this cocktail napkin with your phone number on it, your home phone number and your address. Now what do you think aboutthat?"

"He never called me at home. He called me at the office."

"When? Today, maybe?"

"Yeah. He was trying to set up a meeting."

"A 'meet' huh? You been watchin' old movies again, Whelan? Where was this 'meet' gonna happen?"

Whelan pointed inside the garage. "In there."

"You'd be a dumb fucker to do that." Bauman glanced at the dead man. "You'd be dead, too. So why did he want to meet with you?"

"I don't think he believed I was looking for the kid. He thought I wanted his brother."

"His brother, huh? You know something about Jimmy Lee Hayes that you're not sharing?"

"You know what I know."

Bauman smiled and there was a look of amusement in his close-set eyes. "So what do you think about this?" He indicated Bobby Hayes with a nod.

"You already asked me that." Whelan looked at the body again and shrugged. "I didn't see him tonight. I talked to him late this afternoon."

"You had a meeting, you said. Looks to me like he was waitin' on you."

"I wasn't coming."

"He thought you were."

"Maybe. But he wasn't alone. I think the guy sitting here," Whelan pointed to the driver's seat, "killed him and walked."

Bauman jerked a thumb in the direction of the garage.

"Tried to break in there, too."

Whelan frowned. "Wonder why." Bauman was watching him. "Anybody see anything?"

"Vietnamese lady walking down the street, scared shitless, we're not gonna get anything from her. Old street guy."

"One of your old regulars?"

"Nah, they come and they go. Don't know this one. Says his name's Willie, stays in the alley here behind the garage. Skinny old guy with no teeth."

"What did he see?"

"Says he saw a guy running away from this car." Bauman was watching him. "Said it was a big guy, white guy. Black hair, kinda greasy, long sideburns. Clean shaven. Blue jeans, jean jacket. Sounds familiar to me. How about you?"

"Could be." He watched Bauman's eyes. The detective scanned the traffic and then his gaze seemed to come to rest on the restaurants at the corner of Broadway and Argyle.

"You ever been up there, Whelan? Argyle Street? Wait, sure you have. Stupid question for Paul Whelan, huh? You been in all these places probably."

"That one on the corner, Mekong. I've been there. It was good."

Bauman nodded absently, still staring in the direction of the restaurant, and Whelan remembered their conversation one night in which Bauman mentioned his improbable relationship with a Vietnamese woman. Bauman had mentioned that she was Vietnamese but of Chinese ancestry and worked in a restaurant on Michigan Avenue, and had never said anything about her again. Then Bauman gave him a sly look and Whelan wondered if a gray Caprice had been taking a more than passing interest in his movements.

"What do you want from me?"

"I just wanna know that you didn't talk to nobody else today about this 'meeting.' You're sure you didn't talk to anybody else about it?"

"Like who?"

"You talked to Bobby Hayes and nobody else, right?"

"That's right."

"Okay. You know why I really brought you down here?"

"I'm listening."

"Wanted you to see this guy. You're dickin' around with stuff that don't concern you. I think you started lookin' for the kid and decided it was all part of the same shit, so you think it's all your case. I got the call tonight, and I had this feeling that I was gonna go to this garage and maybe find my old friend Paul Whelan."

Bauman stared at him and Whelan looked away. "And if you keep fucking around with this stuff, I think you're gonna end up like this guy. *Capisce?*"

"Yeah, I *capisce*. You'll be happy to know I'm just about at the point where I give it up."

Bauman gave him an interested look. "Is that right? That don't sound like you, Whelan. I thought you never let 'em go till they're done."

"Yeah? Well, I think I'm letting this one go. It's starting to turn my stomach."

Bauman pointed the cigar at him. "It was Lester. You didn't like that, did you? You were lookin' kinda green at the lagoon there."

"Not as green as you and your partner."

"What're you gonna tell that nice lady?"

"I'm gonna let you tell her what really probably happened to the kid."

"Oh, I don't think you are," Bauman said, but Whelan was already turning away. "Don't leave town, Snoopy," he said, but cracked up in the middle of it.

Whelan waved without turning. Once inside his car he turned on his radio and lit a cigarette and rolled down his windows. As he pulled away from Roy's Garage he told himself once more that you could throw a stone from Argyle Street and hit Roy's. Maybe he couldn't walk on this one, not just yet. He puffed at his cigarette and admitted that he'd been telling Bauman the truth: the whole thing *was* beginning to turn his stomach.

• • •

The note was taped to the glass pane in the front door, up about eye level, where only a drunk could miss it—a visually impaired drunk at that, for the note had been written on Day-Glo orange paper. Whelan knew who it was from before he even read it. He opened it slowly, expecting a long, detailed accounting of his failings. Instead, he found two lines from an angry pen, plus a postcard.

> Dear Mr. Whelan,
>
> Please use the enclosed postcard to notify us if you are alive. Remember, the post office will not deliver mail without proper postage.
>
> Yours,
>
> S. McAuliffe

He went inside and stared at his phone for a moment, then decided he didn't have nerve enough to call just yet. He went into the kitchen and looked into the refrigerator. The uncooked chicken looked like old scar tissue. Instead, he pulled a beer from the refrigerator, took it into the living room. He glanced at the phone again and turned on his TV.

The TV was willing to give him bad movies, two talk shows and roller derby. A few feet away, the phone lurked.

He shook his head. My phone sends out signals audible only to small dogs and Paul Whelan.

He turned his attention to the television. The better of the two movies was about a talking cat. He sighed and got up.

She answered on the fourth ring. "Hello?"

"Hi. It's Paul…"

"Well, it is, isn't it. And you're not even dead, as one might have thought."

"I'm sorry."

"That's a start."

"It has nothing to do with you."

"That is not completely true."

"Yeah, it is. I'm not hiding out from you. I'm not trying to figure out how to escape. I just…I'm involved in some things that…It's just hard for me to think about us going to the movies on Saturday night until I resolve this."

"Your work is serious and getting involved with me is—what, frivolous?"

"No, nothing like that."

"I went out with a cop once who would go off and get pie-eyed and then tell me I couldn't possibly understand him and his manly work, with my little office job."

"It's nothing like that. It's simpler. They call it depression. I'm depressed. I'm also worried and I don't know if I'd be any company at all."

"What do you think relationships are for?"

"I'd be the last to know."

"Don't you ever feel like talking about these things?"

"Afterwards. Not when they're happening. It never occurs to me, never would. For the better part of my life I've had no one that I could talk to at times like this. I just have no experience in it, so it doesn't come naturally to me. My first inclination when trouble comes is to block everything else out till the trouble is somehow dealt with. Till I've done what I was supposed to do."

"And you're in trouble now?"

"Some."

"Physical danger?"

"Hard to say."

"Are you safe in your house?"

He thought about the address in Bobby Hayes's wallet, about the attempt on his life out on his street, and hesitated before he answered. "Well, of course I'm safe here."

"I heard that pause. Come on over."

"No. Like I said, I'd be dogshit company. I'll call you tomorrow—if you're going to be home."

"Call me tomorrow? For…what, exactly?"

"I don't know. Breakfast? Maybe we can go out someplace."

She hesitated. "I don't like this."

"It has nothing to do with you," he repeated, and believed it.

She sighed. "Be careful, Paul."

"I will," he said, and was about to add something when she hung up. He stood there for several moments with the phone in his hand, trying to interpret her sign-off and tone of voice, and wondering if he'd just managed to put the finishing touches on the best thing to come his way in years.

Sleep was slow in coming. He lay on his back and thought of what he'd seen in the last two days and decided that there was a way of finishing this one after all. The decision brought no great satisfaction but the more he examined it, the more he realized that it was the right one.

In the morning he called her. He could hear music in the background, and she sounded cheerful.

"Do you want to go out for breakfast?"

"No, I don't think I do. But I'm glad to hear your voice. I'm glad you're all right. I had visions of you hopping in your car and going somewhere you don't belong and getting hurt."

"I just thought...Do you want to do anything?"

"I don't know. I know I don't want to have breakfast and make small talk for an hour and then get dropped off."

"I thought we might spend the day together."

"Just when I start to write you off, you show rare glimmers of good sense. Come on over."

In the end, they spent much of the day walking up and down the lakefront and settled for lunch from a hot dog stand at the North Avenue Beach. He felt relaxed for the first time in more than a week and realized she was aware of it.

When they returned to her house he busied himself with her admirable collection of take-out menus, an assortment that almost but not quite rivaled his. He was turning a Chinese menu over when he realized she was standing in front of him. She wore a thick white chenille robe and was gazing at him with a little half smile.

"Put the menu down," she said. He let it drop and as she

lowered herself onto his lap, she allowed the robe to fall. He put his hands to her skin and was about to say something when she put her mouth on his.

He was able to finish perusing the menu an hour later. Dinner still seemed like a good idea but had lost some of its urgency. Whelan could now envision going another hour without dinner, but Sandra was in the shower. She was singing and her voice, he noted, had not improved with excitement.

She was still singing when she emerged. She had her hands in the deep pockets of her robe and a flush had appeared on her cheeks.

He dropped the menu and crossed the room to her. She leaned against the living room wall and let him push against her. His hands found their way inside the robe, and he kissed her.

"My own freshly showered woman," he said.

She kissed him again and pushed him away. "*Could* be your own—if you played your cards right." She took a couple steps away. "And you couldn't do any better. I don't care how many women you know." She was smiling but there was a challenge in her green eyes.

"That was never in question, Sandra."

She shrugged. "I just wanted to say it. Now order me dinner."

Whelan ordered enough Chinese food for six, and when they'd made it through pot stickers and moo shu pork and shrimp in garlic sauce and Peking chicken, they spent an hour sipping coffee and reading the Sunday papers.

At ten, he decided to leave.

"I'll call you tomorrow. In the afternoon."

"Okay." She got up and walked to the door with him. At the door she put her arms around his neck and pushed her body against him. "You could stay, you know."

"I was thinking about it but…I think I'm going out to check on a few things before I actually call it a day."

She drew back, as though he'd said something offensive.

"Easy, there. I'm just going to be looking around, trying to figure a few things out. I'll stay in the car. Mostly."

She shook her head. "I guess I should feel flattered that you pay so much attention to me when we're together, because you are the most obsessive, the most *preoccupied* man I've ever known. Be careful."

"I will. I'm just going to try and get this thing over with."

"When do you think that will happen?"

"Tomorrow," he said with a great deal more confidence than he felt, and he could see she wasn't buying it either.

Argyle Street was busy and the people coming out of the restaurants with their steamed-up windows looked happy, happy and a little chilled, hunching shoulders against the wind and grabbing at their collars. Most of them were Vietnamese and would have told him it was a cold night. Whelan drove with his window down and let the crisp lake wind fill his old car. He made the pass by the little restaurant where he hoped all of this would end soon, and a few moments later swung by the garage on Broadway where a man had been found dead within hours of talking to Paul Whelan.

At Wilson and Broadway he stopped for the light and idly scanned the people crossing the six-way intersection: black people and white people, a couple of short, stumpy old Russian men, a pair of skinny black teenagers, a Latino woman with a small child, an African looking woman pushing a laundry cart, a Vietnamese couple watching their neighbors with wary looks.

You ought to be looking wary. Go on home, folks, there's a killer on the street.

Fifteen

The flat-faced man was working the bar at Ed and Ronda's and he gave Whelan a careful nod, then looked around for his cigarettes.

I make you nervous, Whelan thought. It's the company you've been keeping.

"Hello, Ed."

Another nod.

"You heard about Bob Hayes?"

Ed lit up a cigarette and blew a little cloud of smoke into the air. "Heard they found him up by a garage. Somebody cut 'im."

"What else did you hear?"

"That's all I know."

"You knew him pretty well, didn't you?"

Ed pursed his lips and shook his head. "Nope. He drank here a few times, liked to talk. That's all. Couldn't tell you a thing about him."

"How about Jimmy? You knew Jim, I think Bob told me that."

This new tack seemed to catch Ed in midthought, paralyzing him. Whelan could see Ed's poor mind working on a way out. The barman fought to keep his eyes from meeting Whelan's.

Finally he consented to the faintest nod. "Knew him to see him, wasn't anything more than that. He come in for a drink, that's all. Not regulars, neither of 'em."

Whelan nodded. "How about a Coke?" He put a few singles on the bar and fished out a cigarette, going through all the motions of a man settling himself in for a long afternoon in a friendly tavern.

Ed watched him with a forlorn look in his close-set

eyes. Whelan had known many men like Ed, men of modest intelligence and less intuition, who could no more hide their feelings than change their height. Whelan could read Ed's look with no difficulty: old Ed was merely wishing Whelan would vaporize, have a heart attack, choke on an ice cube. Old Ed wished him dead.

Whelan played with his matches and cigarettes while Ed slapped ice into a glass and held it under the soda gun. He set down the Coke and said "seventy-five."

"Thanks. Listen, you're from the South, right?"

"No."

"I could've sworn you were…"

"Ronda's from the South."

"Oh, right. She heard about Bobby Hayes?"

He shrugged. "She heard what I heard."

"How'd she take that?"

The little brown eyes showed some spark. "He wasn't nothin' to her."

"Of course not, that's not what I meant, Ed. I just meant, you know, women get all bent out of shape about these things."

Ed shrugged and looked up and down his bar. "She got a little shook up."

"Bobby Hayes called me a couple hours before he was killed. He called from here. This would be Saturday afternoon."

Ed's confidence made a modest comeback. "I wasn't working. Can't tell you a thing." He even smiled now.

"Then I'll need to talk to Ronda."

"What's she gonna tell you?"

"Well, Ed, you never know that until you ask. Where can I reach her?"

The quick sullen look that Ed gave him said a lie was on its way and Whelan was grinning before the bartender even spoke.

"I don't know where she is."

"Come on, Ed. How hard can it be to keep track of your wife?"

Ed looked around for his cigarettes, found them next to the register, then fumbled in his shirt pocket for a book of matches.

"She's at home. No, I think she's on her way here," he muttered.

"On her way?" Something in Ed's answer didn't make sense but he let it go. Ed was watching the back door.

"Yeah. She'll be here, I don't know. Maybe half an hour."

Whelan took a sip of his syrupy Coke, put it down and nodded. "I'll be back later. Thanks."

Ed was silent as Whelan left, but Whelan could feel the other man's eyes in the small of his back.

He got into his car and started it up, then drove around the block. When he'd made one leisurely circuit, he drove up the alley and pulled up next to a garage covered with graffiti. Windows down to allow in the cool air from the lake, he hit a couple buttons and found Ella Fitzgerald doing "Mack the Knife," the live version where Ella forgets the words and decides to make up a few verses of her own. Ella was singing her apologies for annihilating the song when Whelan saw the red Chevy come up the alley and pull into the little parking lot behind the tavern. A moment later, Ronda got out and closed the door, then walked toward the tavern.

From a distance, Ronda still had a young woman's walk and he had to admit that in a tough, leathery way she was good-looking for her age. He got out of his car and called out her name. She turned, squinted in the sun and went tense when she recognized him.

"Afternoon. I wonder if I could ask you a couple more questions."

He watched her face and, tough as she was, it gave up a lot more than she'd have wanted to. Whelan saw the little look of fear, then the quick glance over her shoulder at the tavern. Then she was regrouping, an alley cat caught on the back stairs.

"What kinda questions? I got to get inside. I'm working."

"I know. You heard about Bobby Hayes?"

She nodded and the flinty look in her eyes wavered a little.

"He was waiting to see me that night. Did you know that?"

"Mister, he didn't tell me how he spent his Saturday nights. I don't know nothin' about what all he did when he left my place."

"You were working when he called me."

"How would you know that if you weren't…"

"Ed," he said happily.

From six feet away he could hear her teeth grinding, and the tightness in her posture told him Ed was going to have a long afternoon.

"You remember him making a couple of calls? Come on, Ronda, I heard him smack the bar when I said something he didn't like."

She shrugged her narrow shoulders. "I was busy. I don't stop and listen every time somebody uses the phone."

"Didn't sound busy. I could hear the jukebox. Johnny Cash was singing and nobody in your place was talking. Maybe you had a full house and they were just being respectful to Mr. Cash. Who was he with, Ronda?"

"Wasn't with nobody I recall."

"Big guy, dark hair, kind of slicked back. Long sideburns. Name's Jimmy Lee."

She shook her head and put on a casual expression but she was chewing on the inside of her cheek.

"I think you know who I mean. In fact, Ronda, I think you know a whole lot about all of this. More than I do, that's for damn sure. I think you know all about Whitey, and I think you know a lot about Jimmy Lee Hayes, who tried to kill me the other night, which sure puts us on different footing than I thought we were on."

She blinked, met his eyes to see if the last part were true, then looked away. "You're talking to the wrong gal. I run a tavern and you got a problem with some people that drank in it, that's all."

"Maybe so. I actually hope that's all true. Because the guy out there who killed Bobby Hayes is a bad guy, Ronda, and there's no telling who he'll kill next. I'm just going to make sure he doesn't kill the kid I've been looking for. I'll be seeing you later, ma'am."

He stepped out of Ronda's path and watched her as she made her hasty way into the bar. She turned at the back door, shot him a quick look from the corner of her eye and went in.

• • •

In his days as a beat cop, he remembered conversations about how much of his life a cop spends sitting: in the squad car, over coffee and doughnuts, on the bar stool. Now that he was on his own, it hadn't gotten all that much better: he walked as many places as possible, but when it came to surveillance or the numbing boredom of waiting out a suspect's next move, he found himself frittering away great chunks of the day, whole irretrievable pieces of his life.

He was sitting in his car and watching an evening go up in smoke, and the waiting was torment because he'd decided on a long-shot course of action and had no idea where it would take him. He sighed and sipped at the coffee, long since gone cold and not much good when it was fresh, and watched the activity inside the little Korean snack shop.

When Marty began slipping on his Army coat, Whelan said "Here we go," and got out of his car. The Korean locked the door behind Marty, and Whelan gave the kid a couple of seconds, then came out of the next doorway and grabbed his elbow.

"Come on, Marty."

Marty gave a sudden yank but Whelan was ready and slipped around behind him, grabbed the kid's other elbow and the fight was over.

"What the fuck is this shit?"

"Take it easy and I'll tell you in the car."

"Car? What the *fuck*, what car?"

"Quit swearing at me, Marty, or I'll pop you one."

He half led, half pulled the kid to his car. "We're just going to talk," he said, and when some of the stiffness left Marty's bony shoulders, shoved him into the front seat of his car. "And you can't outrun me, not on your best day." Marty swore again but the resignation in his face told Whelan he'd bought that one, too.

Grinning to himself, he walked around the front and got in. As he went through the labors of starting the car, he looked over at Marty. The boy listened to the erratic sounds coming from under the hood and curled his lip.

"Your car is dogshit, man. Oughtta put a fucking bullet in your engine block and sell the rest for parts."

"Funny, an expert on cars wasting himself in a corn dog stand. You're keeping your light under a bushel."

The Jet continued to make grinding sounds and the sullen teenager muttered to himself, something that sounded like "torch the whole fucking thing" and Whelan allowed himself a quiet chuckle, grateful for the distraction. Then Whelan pulled out into northbound traffic on Sheridan.

"Just relax. This won't take long. At least, I have hopes."

"Where we going?" Marty asked, and his sudden wide-eyed look said he had at least a general idea already.

"Argyle Street. We're going to Argyle Street."

"No fuckin' way," Marty said, and turned suddenly toward the door. Whelan grabbed the soft part of his arm. There wasn't a lot to it, but enough to hold onto, enough to pinch.

"Sit down. I know where he is, Marty. I followed you Saturday." He took his eyes off the road and met the boy's gaze. Marty stared at him open-mouthed, gone speechless with guilt.

"Shit."

"I would have found him anyway."

The boy made a long groan through clenched teeth and whacked his head against the window.

"Cut it out, Marty."

The boy half turned toward the door and scrunched his thin frame up into something like a fetal position.

"You didn't do anything wrong."

After a while, Marty uncoiled and stared at the street. "So what do you want me for?"

"I want this to go smoothly. I don't want trouble for anybody, not him, not me, and not…not anybody. You get me in, that's all."

"No. No way, man. I don't give a fuck—"

"Ease up, kid, take a deep breath. You get me in, or I come back with the cops, and that makes trouble for somebody, if not for all of us. Just get me in. I'm not going to do anything to him."

"What do you want with 'im, then?"

"Maybe nothing," Whelan said, and meant it. "Maybe he stays where he is."

The boy cursed again, this time under his breath, and looked straight ahead. In moments, they were on Argyle Street, and Whelan drove past the little Vietnamese restaurant and this time didn't look in. He turned the corner and parked at the mouth of the alley, fought the urge to have a quick smoke, and then looked at Marty.

"Show time," Whelan said, and got out of the car. He was around to the passenger side before Marty opened the door.

Marty slumped back into character, rolled his eyes, let his shoulders go slack, and crawled out of the car like a man asked to clean toilets. He swung the door closed and then thrust both hands in his jeans.

Whelan patted him on the shoulder. "Let's get it done, Marty." He took a deep breath, grinned at Marty and hoped the boy couldn't sense his fear. He stayed a couple paces back as Marty, head down, plodded into the alley. Marty's worn-out running shoes scraped casually against the alley pavement.

Forget it, kid, Whelan thought. They won't hear it over the beating of my heart.

Three or four doors down the alley they stopped at a small brick garage with a red steel dumpster beside it. The dumpster was filled to overflowing, and Whelan saw boxes and cans marked with Vietnamese characters.

Marty stopped and gave Whelan a sullen look.

"Lead the way, Marty." The boy made a little shrug and walked up the gangway and through the yard. He stopped at the back door and looked down.

"Is this it?"

"Whaddya think?"

I think I want to get it all over with, he thought. "Go ahead in, then."

Marty nodded and opened the wooden door. Inside, Whelan found himself on a small concrete staircase leading down into a basement. From somewhere above he heard the sounds of several women speaking in Vietnamese and occasionally the harsh, nasal voice of an older man. The old man was apparently a laugh riot: he sang out something and the women filled the air with a burst of high-pitched laughter. The old man yelled something and one of the women sounded near to losing it.

Down the stairs, Marty stopped again and stared at the door into the basement. Whelan moved down quietly till he was directly behind the boy. He could smell the sweat in the kid's musty cotton jacket, and he could almost feel the fear, and he felt sorry for him but this was the way it had to be done.

"Go in, Marty, or knock, but do it."

Marty knocked twice, then turned the doorknob and pushed it in. Whelan felt the cool damp air pushing out into the stairwell, and he had just taken the first step into the basement when Marty turned and slammed the door against him and began screaming for whoever was inside to run. The door caught Whelan across the forehead but he took most of it on his shoulder, and then he pushed back.

"Get out," the boy was screaming, "I'll kill the fucker," and a slender shape was attempting to boost himself out a side window. Marty spread his legs and took a martial arts pose.

"Come on, you fucker," Marty said. He was panting and red-faced, and Whelan just went straight at him and took him out with a shoulder in the chest. He felt a fist graze his ear and then Marty was falling in front of him. Whelan crossed the basement in three long strides and grabbed the escaping boy around the legs and pulled. They fell back onto the concrete floor and Whelan landed on his left elbow. Pain shot up through his arm all the way to the shoulder. The boy began flailing and squirming to get away, and he was yelling in Whelan's ear. Whelan felt the kid's bony fingers clawing for his eyes. He put a hand on the kid's face and pushed, coiling back, and gradually rolled himself over so that he was on top of the boy.

He sat up and tried to catch his breath and was about to tell the kid that the fight was over when he caught movement from the corner of his eye, something coming at him, and he raised his arm. The object struck him on the forearm and near the shoulder and Whelan fell backward and off the boy.

He rolled across the floor and to his feet like a boxer after a flash knockdown, and when he came up he had both fists cocked. The right arm throbbed and didn't seem to want to stay up but he tried not to show it. Behind him, Marty Wills scuttered out of the way and Tony Blanchard scrambled over to him.

Whelan stood and faced the old Vietnamese man. He didn't seem so old or so small now, and the hands Whelan had seen wielding a broom as though it were a great weight now held an ax handle. The old man shouted something in Vietnamese and Whelan could hear the panicked voices of the women upstairs, but there was no trace of panic in the old man's pale brown eyes. No panic in his face or posture either, but a different message there: this was a fighting man, a man who'd seen violence and deep trouble and hadn't found any reason to run from it, and Whelan wasn't getting past him.

The old man advanced and when Whelan began to circle, sidestepped to cut him off. The ax handle changed hands and the old man had gone righty to lefty, a seventy-year-old with Marvin Hagler moves. He feinted with the ax handle and forced Whelan to take a step backward, and now Whelan was trying to see where the two boys were.

The old man swung the wood and Whelan took it on the forearm, where it found the spot that it had already softened. Whelan shot out a jab and the old man moved his head, not as fast as he wanted to but enough so that the punch merely grazed him. He poked out casually with the ax handle and it caught Whelan a stinging blow just under the chin, and Whelan was wondering if he was outclassed.

Whelan moved to his right and the old man came straight in, shouting in Vietnamese, and Whelan was trying to say something to keep him off, and he could hear Marty yelling behind him. The basement room seemed to be filled with shouting people, and he felt hot and short of breath. He was bracing himself for the old man's next assault when he caught movement from his left and a tall khaki figure flew at him. The flying tackle took him off his feet and he landed with the other man on top of him. He punched at the new assailant and they began to roll, the other man digging his fingers into Whelan's jacket for leverage. Whelan grabbed a handful of the man's hair from behind and tugged, and then the other man was scrambling off him.

Whelan stumbled to his feet and faced Mickey Byrne. Ax handle raised, the old man took a step toward Whelan and Mickey moved to cut him off.

"No, no!" He held up a hand and the old man stopped, his gaze going from Mickey to Whelan. Mickey Byrne stepped between them and stared around the room, his gaze finally coming to rest on Whelan. He was panting and there were blotches of unhealthy color in his face and a red mark on his cheekbone where Whelan had caught him with a punch, and his hair clung wet and matted to his skull.

"Get outta here, Paulie, or you'll get killed. Just walk, man." Mickey Byrne bent over, hands on his knees, and panted.

"Wait, Mick." His breath came in gasps and his own voice sounded unsteady. "Talk to me."

"No, get out. There ain't shit to talk about, just get out. You come back, you're dead. There's shit going down here you don't know about."

Whelan studied the other man's ravaged face. Mickey Byrne smelled of cigarettes and old cotton, his clothes bagged on him like castoffs. He'd been twenty pounds heavier as a boy than he was now at thirty-six.

"I know enough," Whelan said.

Mickey shook his head. "No, man. You don't know what's goin' down. You're gonna get yourself killed. You come back here and I won't be able to save your ass again."

"You sure you want to?"

Mickey Byrne blinked several times, incredulous. His mouth opened but nothing came out and his eyes reddened. "What do you think I just did?" He looked over his shoulder at the old Vietnamese man, who stood in a half crouch, waiting for any sign that he was needed again.

Behind them, Whelan could feel the eyes of the two boys

on them. A rustling noise and then a quick whisper told him someone watched from the stairs and he wondered, just for a shiver in time, if he'd make it out of this one.

Mickey Byrne followed Whelan's gaze to the back stairway. "That's just the women from upstairs. The restaurant." He looked at the old man and nodded, said something short in Vietnamese.

A boy's voice said "Mick?" and Mickey Byrne nodded, wheezing, and said, "It's cool."

Some of the tension left the old man's body but not much. Whelan reached inside his shirt for his cigarettes. He shook one out and held the pack out to Mickey. Mick nodded, still laboring to get wind into his lungs, and pulled one out. Whelan lit up and held out the match, then waited as Mick Byrne puffed. Both men began coughing at almost the same moment.

Whelan shook his head and tried to think of something to say but was more aware of all the damage he'd sustained.

"I've been in this room less than a minute and I hurt in about eight places."

"Shouldn't've come here," Mick Byrne muttered, his hand moving to touch the bruise on his cheekbone. Whelan noticed that Mick's knuckles were red, and one of them was bleeding.

"Now what?" Whelan asked.

"You shouldn't have come here, man."

"Maybe so, but here I am."

He looked at the Vietnamese man, who remained unblinking and ready a little more than an arm's length away. The man regarded him with pale brown eyes, intelligent eyes. Not the eyes of a porter but of someone far different. Eventually the old man's gaze moved from Whelan to Mickey Byrne, and Whelan could see that the old man still needed convincing.

"Does he speak English?"

A glimmer of humor appeared in the brown eyes and answered Whelan's question.

"A lot better than you speak Vietnamese, Paulie."

"I never learned it. You did, though."

"I learned a little in-country, some back here."

Whelan wanted to ask where but other things needed to be

said. “I wasn’t going to do anything to hurt the kid, Mick.”

Mickey Byrne shook his head. “Anybody finds out where he is, anybody comes here after him, is gonna get him hurt. Now we got to find him another place.”

“No. You should finish this up. You should help me end it.”

“No, man, I don’t even know why you got into this.”

“Long story.” He took a puff of his cigarette and looked at each of the men in the room. In the doorway he could see the faces of two women, one of them the owner of the restaurant. Her breezy self-confidence seemed to have left her. Whelan studied Tony Blanchard. The boy looked bewildered.

He looked at the Vietnamese man again and said to Mick, “I’d sure feel better if he’d drop the ax handle.” The old man stepped back and lowered the ax handle but his expression left no doubt whether he’d be willing to reconsider.

Whelan studied Mickey Byrne for a moment. Mick’s face was set in anger and stubbornness and for a moment Whelan felt they’d both stepped twenty-five years into the past.

“I don’t know why you’re here, Paulie.”

“I was hired. It’s what I do. I’m a private detective, people hire me to look into things—usually to find somebody. And that’s what I’ve been doing.” He looked at the boy still sitting on the concrete floor. “Mrs. Pritchett. She hired me to find you. If you knew what I’d gone through to find you, you might trust me. Now we’ve got something in common. Somebody wants to kill both of us.”

“He didn’t know nothing about that.”

“I understand. He thought I was the guy following him.”

“Guys.” Mickey Byrne held up two fingers. “There’s two of ’em.”

Whelan pondered this, looked to the boy for confirmation. “You ever gonna talk, Tony?”

For a moment the boy stared as if he hadn’t heard. Then he glanced at Mick. “He’s right,” the boy said. “There’s two of ’em.”

“Wait, wait,” Whelan said. “I need to sit. I hurt.” He lowered himself gingerly onto the floor. The concrete was cold against his hand. After a moment’s hesitation, Mick crouched down in a stoop. Whelan looked at the boy. "Whitey and who else?"

"I don't know. I never saw the other guy up close. He wears a baseball cap, though."

"Why do they want you, Tony?"

" 'Cause I saw the old man waste a guy." The boy shrugged, as though this had just been a nasty piece of luck, and then Whelan remembered this was a boy who hadn't had much in a long time.

"Who was the man you saw killed?"

"Chick Nelson."

"I think the other guy is Jimmy Lee, Tony. Looking for you."

The boy frowned and gave Whelan a disbelieving look. "Jimmy's dead."

"Nope."

The boy stared at him. New possibilities took root, and his face lost what little color it had left. "Man, why would Jimmy be after me?"

"I don't know. I don't know the 'why' of most of this." He looked at Mickey. "I don't know why you're in this."

"Rory." Mick stared at him and color rose in his face. He seemed to be daring Whelan to question his motives.

"Okay."

"This asshole killed Rory and those other ones, the guy Tony saw him kill."

"I think he killed at least two others. He killed Les, the old fence." The boy blinked and Whelan hit him with the rest. "And they found Bobby Hayes dead on Saturday. You know Bobby?"

The boy made a nervous nod and his eyes went a little glassy. There was something pitiful about the little comet tattoo on his arm, a child's attempt at bravado. Whelan nodded toward the basement door. "They found him about two blocks from here, at about eight o'clock Saturday night. He was that close. That's why we have to finish this."

"He won't talk to cops, Paul. He talks to cops, people'll find him. He won't be safe."

Whelan stared at Mick for a moment. "You think he's safe *here*?"

"Yeah."

"*I* made it in, for Chrissake."

Mick looked at the old man and then back at Whelan. "You think you would have made it out?"

"I can help you with this, Mick. I know people, I know the cop who's investigating these other murders. He's all right. You want this kid to live out the year, we have to take the other guy off the street."

"We're takin' care of business right here, Paul. Get out of here, man, this has got nothing to do with you now." He indicated the boy with a nod. "You found him, you can tell that lady he's all right. I'll make sure he calls her when this is over. Now get out of here, Paulie, you don't belong here."

"You don't belong here, either, Mick."

Mickey gave him an oddly complacent look. "Yeah, I do. This is exactly where I belong. Now get out, man."

Whelan struggled to his feet. The shoulder hurt where he'd taken a blow with the ax handle, and he wondered if he was bleeding under his shirt. "All right." He moved toward the door, then paused. "What are you going to do now?"

"We're gonna get him out of here, for one. I'll think about the rest later."

"Hope you know what you're doing, Mick. Hope you *all* know what's out there. This guy kills people in broad daylight and disappears."

"He can change how he looks," Tony said in a small voice.

"He can what?"

Tony nodded earnestly. "He can change himself. With, like disguises. Sometimes he looks like some kinda foreigner, like a tourist, you know? He wears disguises."

Whelan sighed. "That's great. Have you seen him, Mick?"

Mickey Byrne nodded. "I don't know, I think so. He looked like a street guy. Just like an old guy that lives in alleys. Like me." Mick pinched the butt of his cigarette and took another drag and refused to make eye contact. Whelan left.

Outside, he took the chill night air into his lungs in great gulps. He wanted a drink and a hot bath to nurse his many injuries, and a place far away from Argyle Street. He drove up to Broadway and hung the left and drove on to Lawrence. He was waiting for the light to change when a group of young people emerged from the Green Mill laughing. They all looked to be in their twenties, a mixed group that included a couple of good-looking women and a black kid in a beret and a tall white guy with blond hair in a ponytail. A few feet from the cluster of handsome healthy young people, an old man dug through the trash basket on the corner and came up with a half-wrapped sandwich. Whelan watched the old man and then he was remembering another old man, one in a doorway not far from this corner, a skinny, toothless old man in a blue cap. That one had looked dazed and scared and now that Whelan thought about it, was probably neither. He thought about Bauman's "informant" up at Roy's garage and shook his head. His heart was beginning to pound and he felt hot. A motorist behind him leaned on the horn to tell him the light had changed and Whelan gunned the Olds and moved through the intersection. He turned up Racine and as soon as he could, made a swing back up to Broadway.

You old shit, he thought.

As he drove, he imagined himself calling Bauman. *"Hey, Bauman, about this old guy Willie? There ain't no Willie, old buddy."*

SIXTEEN

Lights were on in the rooming house, lights in one front window on the first floor and two on the second. Whelan shook his head. In a logical world, he'd be able to narrow his attention to three rooms. But in a logical world, Paul Whelan would be out somewhere with a certain green-eyed social worker instead of sitting in his car about to bring in a killer.

As he got out of the car he told himself he was a trained ex-cop and a passable boxer, he could take an old man with a knife, and then a little voice told him that was probably what Makowski and Nelson and Rory Byrne and even Bobby Hayes had all thought. He stopped at the curb. Makowski. Not Makowski: he had been shot. All these others, even Les, had been stabbed. Whelan wondered what had made the killer use a .22 for that one.

No old man met him in the hall this time. Whelan yanked at the inner door and found it locked. He worried at the door with a credit card but realized he'd need tools for a lock like this one. He went around to the back.

The rooming house owner was obviously a cost-conscious sort of guy: the back of the building had no light, no rear gate. Whelan stood at the bottom of the staircase and peered up into the blackness, listening and waiting for his eyes to accustom themselves to the absence of light. After perhaps thirty seconds, he began to ascend the stairs. He took them slowly, pausing every three or four paces to listen. Halfway up, a man yelled, somewhere up the street, and took the breath out of him. At the first landing he stopped. A small window in the back door appeared as an orange square of light and gave him visibility of several feet. He moved to the window and looked in. Inside he had a clear view of the long narrow hall running between the rooms, a quiet, empty hall. He turned the doorknob and it opened. With the slowest of movements he pulled at the door and then he heard the noise.

It was directly above him, on the second-floor landing, a soft muffled sound, and then it was still. With slow, delicate movements he let the door close, turned the knob to its original position and then stood for a ten-count. Then, moving as carefully as he could, Whelan crept to the foot of the next flight of stairs. He peered up the stairs to where the orange light from the door faded and was swallowed by the darkness above, and then began his slow climb. Half a dozen steps up, the staircase began to turn, a tight curve that made the climb harder and concealed the top of the stairway.

He heard the movement again, faint but unmistakable.

I'm better at this than you are, he told himself, and then took the next four steps in a noisy rush. His foot missed the edge of the third step and he began to fall toward the outside railing and two feet away a gray thing with a long thin tail jumped and tore off into the darkness.

"Shit," he said and lurched against the railing. He could hear the rat scuttering away in the brickwork.

Whelan leaned against the railing and panted. For a moment he allowed himself to relax, watching the staircase ahead and listening for any other surprises the old building might have.

Then he saw the leg.

He saw immediately that it would not move, not under its own steam, but waited till his breathing was close to normal again. Then he moved up a couple of steps to where the staircase made its turn toward the third-floor landing and faced the dead man.

The man he knew as Whitey gaped at him through eyes made huge by the stress of his death. The dead man's mouth was open and his tongue dark and thick, and the outsize dentures that had been his entry to his various personas had come loose during his final moment of violence, so that they threatened to slip from his mouth and gave the lower half of his face a twisted look. The nose was gashed, the one eyelid swollen and purple, and Whelan saw other places that would probably have swollen grotesquely if the man hadn't been killed so soon afterward. Whelan shook his head: he'd seen faces in death, many of them, in a number of places, but he'd never seen one quite so terrible. It occurred to him that Whitey might have been pleased with the overall effect, if not the method used to achieve it.

Whelan moved up a couple of steps until the third-floor landing was at eye level. He scanned the porches on both sides and then retraced his steps and turned his attention back to the dead man.

He leaned over and touched the forehead: the skin was cool but not cold. Taking the pulse was a formality but he did it anyway and found what he'd expected.

The cause of death, cause of the blood-darkened face and protruding eyes and gaping mouth, had been strangulation. Strangulation by a pair of large hands, big hands that had left their dark imprint on the old man's throat.

Whelan stepped back, hands on his hips, and studied the dead man. On his final foray onto the streets Whitey had been in the guise of a gentleman going out for his paper. He wore a gray cardigan sweater and a corduroy touring cap. The cap had fallen from his whitish hair and the paper sprawled under him.

Whitey's left arm had been bent back under the body, and just on a hunch Whelan pulled it out, prepared to look Bauman right in his beady eyes and say he'd disturbed nothing. In his final moment Whitey had been quick enough to get the knife out one more time, and he'd found his mark. The blade, worn thin from years of obsessive honing, was wet with blood. Whelan stood back and examined the stairs and lower landing. Dark splashes marked the wooden slats near the body, and a short trail of droplets showed the killer's retreat. Backing up, Whelan studied the trail and saw where his own feet had smeared part of it. A steady line of dark wet spots led from the back of the rooming house to the curb outside, and Whelan could almost see him getting into a car.

How bad did he hurt you? Whelan wondered. Bad enough

to slow you down, I'm hoping.

Whelan got into his car and went through the reassuring little ritual of a cigarette. He sat for a moment with his elbow resting on the open window and went over the courses of action open to him. Probably a good time, no, an outstanding time, to pull out of this one. He'd found the boy, and the spectral figure of Whitey had been removed from events.

No. A man who had tried to kill him once was still out there. Whelan was still unsure what convoluted thought processes had sent this man after him but it wasn't likely that it was over yet.

Nighthawks called out overhead, elegant, predatory birds perfectly adapted to life in the big dirty crowded city: they lived on rooftops, came out when the cool night air rid itself of some of the exhaust fumes and lit out after the teeming clouds of things that flew over Chicago.

Whelan watched one circle overhead and thought about the other people involved in this one, and the questions that he hadn't had the chance to ask yet. Well, he was going to be in it for a while yet. Then an image came to him that took on new significance. In his mind's eye he saw Ronda coming down the back stairs of her tavern, and the tension in her body told him things now that he hadn't thought of. His conversation with Ed had confused him and he now understood why.

He parked across the street from the tavern and sat with his radio on low: trumpet noises, early Miles Davis, but he wasn't listening. It was on for the company, not the entertainment. From his angle he could see that there was no car parked behind the tavern. The lights were on, the place was open: there should have been a little red Chevy there but he now understood why it was gone. He gave himself five minutes to watch the windows on the second floor and when he saw no sign of life, he got out of the car.

He paused at the front door and decided to go around back. The rear door was a single piece of sheet metal with a handle, with little round indentations where a dissatisfied customer had apparently emptied a small-caliber gun into it. Whelan shook his head: firing into sheet metal at close range demonstrated, if not the marginal intelligence of the shooter, then some kind of death wish. He pushed open the door.

Ronda was leaning next to the register smoking a cigarette and gazing down toward the middle of the bar, where a pair of noisy middle-aged drunks snarled at one another. As Whelan came in, he could hear the drunks more clearly: the argument was ostensibly a debate about Mays and Mantle but was probably about a half dozen other things. Ronda watched the two men as though she'd seen this performance a hundred times and it never got any better.

A man watching TV turned to look at him but Ronda didn't notice him until he moved to the bar and pulled out a stool. Then she paused with her cigarette halfway to her mouth and blinked. The hopeful look that came and went in half a second told him she'd been expecting someone else. The look gave Whelan a little edge, told him the someone hadn't shown yet, and he felt himself relax. Ronda recovered her stage presence and puffed at her cigarette and blew smoke in his direction, as if smoke could send him away forever.

Whelan set his cigarettes and money on the bar the way it was done in a neighborhood place where you assumed your neighbor wouldn't steal from you. Now he was a customer, and now Ronda had to move down to see him. She took a sip from a drink sitting next to the register and then pushed herself away from the back bar.

But it apparently didn't mean she had to speak to him. She set her smoke down in an ashtray a couple of stools from him and lifted her chin toward him.

"Evening," he said.

"Coke?" she asked and made it sound beneath her.

"No. Not this time. This time I need a shot of Walker's DeLuxe. And a short beer."

The tired blue eyes lingered on his for a moment. She tried to keep the rest of her face impassive, but it was a lost cause.

Without looking, she reached behind her, walked her

fingers across bottles and came up with the Walker's. The other hand found a shot glass and she placed the glass on the bar and poured in front of him, as they had always done in the old days. Then she went to the tapper and pulled a beer into one of the tapered short glasses and brought it back to him.

"Dollar twenty-five," she said in a stiff voice and when Whelan nodded toward his money, she took a pair of singles from his pile.

She came back and laid the change on his pile of bills. She had broken off eye contact and was about to turn away when he spoke. "I just came from a place where I nearly tripped over a dead body."

She reached quickly for her cigarette and the rest of her went stiff, and for a heartbeat he felt sorry for her.

"Oh, yeah?" she said, and squinted at him through her own smoke. He nodded and sipped at the whiskey, then took a mouthful of the beer.

"This was someone I'd already seen."

She folded her arms and made her thin self smaller and waited for the rest.

"It was an older man who called himself Whitey. Somebody had strangled him, after beating him half to death first. Seemed to me that whoever did it really meant to do a complete job."

She uncoiled slightly and took a puff of her cigarette. Down the bar, the two debaters had worked up a thirst and one of them was tapping an empty beer bottle on the bar. She shot the man a poisonous look and he seemed to shrink down into his bar stool.

"Just need a couple beers down here, hon," the man said, and tried on a smile.

"Don't call me 'hon' and don't bang your bottle on the bar or I'll tell you what you can do with it." She spoke while moving down the bar toward them. The two men suddenly found great interest in the change they had on the bar and didn't look up again till she'd set up two more beers and taken out the money.

Ronda sauntered back and took her time fishing another smoke out of a small red leather cigarette case. When she'd lit up, she allowed her gaze to fall on Whelan.

"You're ready for trouble and I don't think I came here to give you any. From what I know, this Whitey was a bad man, the kind we put away for a long time. That part's none of my business. But I noticed when I went around back that your car's not here."

"Ed took it." She picked up the watery-looking drink and took a sip.

"Ed's got his own car." Ronda looked away. "I think somebody borrowed your car and took care of some old business that I don't pretend to understand."

"What do you want from me?"

"I want to know what this was about."

She gave a lopsided shrug, one bony shoulder at a time.

"Don't know what 'this' you're talkin' about."

"I think you and Jimmy Lee Hayes have a special friendship. And I think this man named Whitey was trying to kill him, I think Whitey killed several of the people around Jimmy and was probably pretty close to finding Jimmy. And I think, without any hard evidence, that old Jimbo took your car tonight and killed this man. That's what I think."

She blew smoke out and sipped at her drink. "You know so much, why you botherin' with me?"

Whelan finished the rest of his whiskey, took a sip of the wretched tap beer and leaned back. He pointed up toward the painted tin ceiling. "I want to know why."

She gazed at him calmly and said, "Have to ask somebody else, hon."

"I plan to. Gonna keep asking. That's how I am, as you probably figured by now. I just thought I ought to tell you, when I leave here, I'll be talking to the guys over at Area Six to let them in on some of this. I expect you'll be seeing them soon."

"Don't make me no nevermind. Got nothing to do with me."

"Just your car. And the fact that you've been hiding him." She gave him a smirk and he added, "upstairs."

"That's just a storeroom," she said quickly.

"He was in no position to be choosy." She forced nonchalance and said nothing. "I called the homicide in already and gave them your car, and when they find it, it'll be a little messy. Whitey cut him. Going to be hard to explain the blood."

She gave him a sardonic smile. "So maybe he's dead, too."

"If I were you—"

"You aren't me, mister, so don't be talking that stupid shit to me. You don't know a damn thing about me." She moved over to the bar and put her face close to his. "If you did, you'd know you can't scare me. Can't scare me, can't con me."

She leaned against the back bar again and took a puff of her cigarette. "You know what I hate about men? You're all so damn stupid, and every last mother's son of you think you're smart. Those two down there, *they* think they're smart, for Chrissake." She gave the two debaters a look rich in loathing and shook her head. "The fat one? He thinks the Communists are putting poison in the grass, so's the cows'll give poison milk and bad meat."

"The world's full of stupid people that think they're smart."

"And most of 'em is men," she said through a cloud of cigarette smoke. Her voice came out harsh and coarse. She took in another lungful and looked away.

"Did you meet Jimmy Lee up here?"

"No. We knew each other years and years, I knew 'im in Knoxville. He knew my brother, I knew all his people down there. We even went out a couple times back then. Wasn't nothing to it."

"You came up here with Ed?"

She gave a little snort of laughter. "No, honey. Ed's just… he's just a mistake I made along the way. Second husband, second mistake. Wasn't for my tavern, bought with my own damn money, Ed would be out on the street, where he belongs. That's one worthless man."

"What were you going to do if all this ever blew over?"

She didn't answer immediately. For a few seconds she busied herself by mixing a highball, a strong one: dark brown, easy on the ice. She took a sip, raised her thin eyebrows and nodded.

"I thought I was going to divorce Ed and leave with Jimmy Lee. That was the original plan. Months ago, that was. Then this other trouble come up, the old man come up and pretty soon Jimmy was in trouble. You can tell a lot about people when they're in trouble. And it didn't take me no time at all to see that this big, good-lookin' man was full of shit and dumb as a milk cow. And if I thought he was gonna be around for me after all this was over, that made me dumber than him. And then I got a new idea. More I thought on it, the better I liked this one: I'm gonna sell the damn tavern and give Ed a couple thousand dollars and divorce papers, and then I'm goin' out west, no Ed, no Jimmy Lee Hayes. Got a sister in Oregon."

"Did he tell you what he was going to do tonight?"

"No. Just said he was goin' out. I told you already, none of this has anything to do with me. I didn't know he was gonna kill anybody. He kept telling me the old man was hiding from 'im, but he knew all along where he was. Jimmy got that place for him. Just took 'im a long time to get enough spine to go after 'im."

For a moment she held Whelan's gaze and he decided he believed her. "Got any idea where he is right now?"

"Who knows? Maybe dead, like I said. Maybe in a hospital." She seemed to be struck by a new idea and she laughed. "Knowing old Jimmy Lee for a lyin' sack of shit, it wouldn't surprise me at all if he was headin' for the south right now in my little car. *Still* thinkin' he's smart." She shook her head.

"What was it all about, Ronda?"

"Old poison. All it was, old poison. And if the old man cut him and killed him, I'd say it was just old business takin' care of itself after years and years. Forty years, must be. That's all it was." She gave him a shrewd look and allowed herself a smile that was obviously at his expense. "Still don't understand, do you?"

He started to shake his head and then caught himself. Forty years. "Old poison," Ronda called it. "The Old Man," they kept calling him. Ronda was right: he was stupid.

Jimmy Lee Hayes had killed his father.

He looked up and saw her amused look. "Just like the fairy tales, huh? An evil stepfather."

Ronda pointed a thin finger at him and nodded. "There's hope for you yet, son. See you around," she said and then moved away silently down the bar. As she did, she touched the dark, smooth wood of the bar exactly the way Whelan had once seen a man touch a car he was about to sell.

He left a couple of singles on the bar, nodded once to Ronda, and went out the front door.

He used a pay phone to call in the homicide. He described the location of the body and told the 911 operator that he thought the killer had been driving a red Chevy compact, but that he hadn't gotten the plates. He declined to leave his name.

Monday night: the Bucket was closed. Whelan looked for Bauman at the Alley Cat, but Ralph the bartender said he hadn't seen Bauman. His tone said he felt fortunate. Okay, Whelan thought. I've done my part.

He got into his car and sat for a moment. It was after ten and he'd been aching since Argyle Street. The aches were now showing signs of stiffening and he could feel a headache coming on. Sandra McAuliffe's apartment beckoned, but he'd just seen a dead man and he'd been in a fight with a boyhood friend, and if ever a Monday needed to be put to bed, this was the one. He started the car and drove home.

Seventeen

All was normal in the Subway Donut Shop: Spiros had six breakfasts going on the grill and Ruth the waitress was nose to nose with a customer who had crossed her. A thin man in a sweater with a tom sleeve was staring at the day-old-doughnuts counter and a dozen smokers had turned the air gray.

Whelan waved for Ruth's attention. She raised one finger for him to wait, finished reading off the errant customer, and turned to Whelan.

"You eatin' or just takin' up space today?"

"Just coffee, Ruth."

She nodded, filled a brown ceramic mug and slid it to him. He paid her, tipped her thirty cents and found a seat at the window, where he could watch the street entertainment. Just outside, a sleepy-eyed man with matted hair was talking to invisible companions. A Vietnamese family, all six of them in new gym shoes, gave him a wide berth as they passed by.

He lit up a cigarette and blew smoke at the window, and then a new cloud of smoke, rancid smoke that smelled like old tires and dead beasts, overtook his and scattered it. He didn't have to look up.

"Morning there, Snoopy," said a familiar voice, a voice with the rumble of a cement truck on bad pavement.

"Have a seat," Whelan said, but Bauman had already dropped his bulk onto a stool.

"I called your house, called your office. You got hours like the Park District."

"My hours are civilized. You just get up too early. So now that we've made small talk, what's up?" But he was fairly sure he already knew.

"Just wanted to, you know, apprise you of, uh, recent developments."

"Such as."

"Homicide up here on Windsor. Guy strangled to death. Looked like somebody used one of those little mallets on him, you know? The ones they use to tenderize meat?"

Whelan nodded and sipped his coffee.

"You heard about it? Anyhow, I think you knew this guy."

"Who was he?"

Bauman smiled. "The old guy, the one you asked me about: Whitey."

Whelan gave him a long look. Bauman's eyes were positively dancing. "Was he wearing a name tag, or did he identify himself?"

"He wasn't makin' a whole lot of small talk. That's just who I think he was. And you don't look surprised, so I'm thinking you called it in. Doin' a lot of that lately."

"So what if I did?"

"You didn't give your name."

"I got caught up in the excitement of the moment."

"What're you getting pissed off for? These are normal questions I'm asking."

"I was further into it than I ever wanted to be. So I didn't want to spend the night answering questions from strange cops."

Bauman ran a hand over his chin. "You find that kid?" he asked, looking out at the street.

"Yeah, I did."

"And…what?"

"And nothing. I found him, I'm going to tell Mrs. Pritchett he's still alive and the guy that was looking for him is dead."

"Where's the kid, Whelan?"

"Not on the street. He was staying with some people who were covering for him but by now he's long gone."

"What if he whacked this guy?"

"You saw the corpse. You think a hundred-twenty-pound teenager did all that?"

"Nope, I don't. But that's got nothin' to do with it. Bet if I want to, I can make you give the kid up."

"You could if I still knew, but I don't. Just leave me alone, Bauman. You got a homicide, it's got nothing to do with me."

"Okay. You gonna confirm it was this guy you called Whitey?"

"Yeah. It was him."

"And you think this is the one that took out all these other guys."

"I think so," he said.

"Take me a while but I think I'll have a name to go with the stiff pretty soon. If we put in a Code One…"

"Save it. You can't put a Code One on every stiff you find. Save it for a big deal. I'll give you a name to put on him."

"Okay," Bauman said.

"Leonard George McCarty."

"Nah," Bauman was saying, and now he looked irritated. "Leonard George McCarty is…"

"Senior," Whelan said. He met Bauman's gaze and repeated "Senior. Leonard George McCarty, Senior. The father of the one that died in prison. And the stepfather of Jimmy Lee Hayes." He felt the words come as though of their own volition, and it left him with a surprising sense of relief. "Jimmy Lee's daddy."

Bauman stared unblinking and then said, "Give."

"You told me once that Jimmy Lee Hayes studied at the knee of his daddy, kind of a robber chieftain. Learned from his stepbrother, too."

"The old man's retired, he's probably dead."

"Oh, he's dead now but he didn't go gracefully. His kid died in prison." Whelan paused. He could see Bauman putting it all together and wasn't even sure the rest was necessary, but he went on with it.

"From the fine character portrait you gave me a while back, Jimmy Lee would inform on anyone for a price, and I've got a hunch he had some negative feelings for his stepbrother. Somebody gave up the stepbrother, Whitey, and I'm thinking it was Jimmy Lee. When the brother died in prison, the old man decided to visit the scenic North for a little payback. I think he pretended to be joining Jimmy's bunch and then you started finding people in vacant lots and trucks."

"What else you got?"

"Not much. I talked to Jimmy Lee Hayes's woman. She runs that tavern. They hated each other, Jimmy Lee and the old man. And they finally got a piece of each other."

"So you think Jimmy Lee Hayes killed our stiff."

"Yeah, I do."

Bauman nodded. "And where do you think we oughtta look for him, Whelan?"

"Beats the hell out of me, but I'd check out Ed and Ronda's tavern on Clark Street, and I guess I'd hit a couple of hospitals to see if they treated any knife wounds last night. Looked to me like the old man cut Jimmy Lee."

"That's very good thinking, Whelan," Bauman said too sincerely. "Very neat package, there. So if we find Jimmy Lee, we got the whole thing." Bauman put an elbow on the counter and rested his round face on one hand. Whelan was conscious of the odors, of smoke on his clothes, last night's liquor, Right Guard fighting a losing fight. He looked in Bauman's eyes and didn't like what he saw coming.

"You got that look, that nice contented look, Whelan. You know you did a nice piece of work and you're finished, all the pieces fit so it's over for you." Whelan finished his coffee and waited. "Help me out. See, I'm not finished with it yet. If he isn't in a hospital takin' care of his 'owee' and he's not havin' piña coladas with this broad, where else would you look?"

"I'd look for a little red Chevy with a big guy driving it."

Bauman milked his moment, waited for a five-count and then said, "We found it, Whelan. We found that little car. If we'da found it earlier, we could've given the driver a ticket, 'cause he was driving on an expired license. Now he's caught up with his license. He's expired, too. The driver was Mr. James Lee Hayes, Whelan, you're right about that. But Jimmy Lee Hayes is dead."

"Cause of death?" he forced himself to ask.

Bauman knocked two inches of ash from his cigarillo and took a puff. He filled the air with more of his rancid smoke and wiggled his eyebrows.

"Gunshot, Whelan. A bullet in the head. Looks like..."

A .22, Whelan said to himself.

"...a twenty-two. I could be wrong."

Whelan shrugged and turned away so that Bauman couldn't see the wind go out of him. He felt a fistlike pressure in the middle of his chest and wondered if he looked as confused as he felt.

"Nothin' else to give me, Whelan? No ideas?"

"The woman," he forced himself to say. "The woman," but he didn't believe it.

Faces watched him get out of his car, a pair of faces. The Vietnamese woman folded her arms around her and looked worried, the old man drew up next to her, no ax handle this time, but the look in his eye said he didn't think he needed one. Whelan took a deep breath and went in.

They met him at the door, the woman moving back a step but the old man giving no ground. Whelan closed the door behind him and leaned against it.

"Open later," the woman said.

"We need to talk," Whelan said, looking at the old man. "Maybe you and I, maybe the three of us, I don't care. But somebody's going to talk to me or I'll stay here forever." He stared at the old man and willed himself not to blink, but a little voice told him the old man could smell fear like an attack dog.

"Where's Mickey?"

The woman opened her mouth but the man said something to her in Vietnamese. Then he looked at Whelan. "Not here," the man said. "He is not here." His English was heavily accented, nasal, his voice youthful sounding.

"Then I can talk to you."

"No."

"Sir, I'll talk to you or this lady or Mick. I'll even talk to the boy. If I don't talk to somebody here, I'll talk to my friend Detective Albert Bauman and the shit will hit the fan, if you will pardon my lapse into street talk." A trace of doubt came into the old man's eyes and Whelan gave it a push. "Where's the boy?"

"He is not here," the old man said with a stiff shake of his head.

"Then you have to tell me where he is. I need to talk to him. I thought he was out of danger and now I'm not so sure."

"He is in safe place."

The world is full of liars, Whelan thought, and the ones that live by it are good at it. You're not, old man. He studied the look in the man's dark, deep-set eyes and shook his head.

"I think the safe place is here. I think he's still here. And maybe he's safe here but I have to talk to him." The old man said no with a slight jerk of his head and Whelan held his ground. He was wondering which of them would blink first when he heard the shuffling sound, shoes on creaking wood, that told him someone was on the stairway leading to the basement. He could just make out the dark shape of the doorway beyond the kitchen entrance. The old man stiffened and fought the impulse to turn around. I'd creep up the stairs to listen, too, Whelan thought.

He indicated the doorway. "Have him come out. I need to say something to him." He indicated the unseen boy in the doorway, the old man, and himself. "The three of us, here at this table."

Whelan pulled out the nearest chair and dropped himself into it. He took out his cigarettes and hooked a finger over the rim of an ashtray, pulling it toward him. He shook out a smoke, lit it and took a puff, then put it in the ashtray. For several seconds the old man stared at him. Then he said something in Vietnamese to the woman, who nodded, shot a look of worry in Whelan's direction and went back toward the stairs. When she came back she had a hand on the boy's shoulder.

The old man nodded to him and said "Okay," and then indicated a chair. Tony Blanchard shuffled forward like a felon meeting the hangman, eyes down, arms hanging limp at his sides, and Whelan realized there was probably no one in the adult world that he trusted completely. Not even this Vietnamese hardcase who had protected him so forcefully. Without lifting his gaze once, Tony lowered himself to a chair, perching on the very edge, as though prepared for flight. The old man eyed Whelan as he slipped into the third chair and the woman retreated to the kitchen.

"Tony? I have some news for you. Will you look at me?"

The boy shrugged—Marty's shrug, these kids all had the same gestures—and met Whelan's eyes. The facial expression said alley fighter but the body language told another story, an animal mute with terror. Back stiff, eyes wide, breath coming through his mouth.

Whelan sighed. "Tony, take it easy. The first part is good news, sort of. Are you listening to me?" The boy nodded, blinking. "Whitey," Whelan said carefully, "Whitey is dead."

The breathing became audible. "For real?"

"For real. I saw the body. I checked for a pulse. He's dead."

"That's cool," he said tonelessly but color flooded his face and his eyes seemed to take on life, as though he'd had a sudden transfusion. He looked at the old man for reassurance, found none, and looked back at Whelan.

"Jimmy Lee Hayes killed him. Tony, you know why, don't you?"

The boy looked past him and said nothing.

"He's dead, Tony. He can't do anything to you now." Whelan waited for a moment and then tried again. "Did you know about them? That Whitey was his father?"

After several seconds, the boy nodded. He scratched at the top of the table with a fingernail. "Not his real father. Stepfather or something."

"Right. He told you?"

"No. I heard him talking to Bob and I put it all together. Jimmy dropped a dime on somebody that was family…"

"His half brother."

"That was it. He dropped a dime on this dude and, like, the guy got sent up. Then the guy died in prison and the old man, he comes up lookin' to kick some ass. Pretends he's come to join up with Jimmy but he's really lookin' for payback." Tony paused for a moment to see if Whelan was following, and added, "Big-time.

Big-time payback."

"Well, if that's what he wanted, that's what he got. Directly or indirectly. All these guys you ran with, they're dead."

"I didn't run with 'em. I, like, did shit for Jimmy and some of these other dudes. I made good bread, too."

Whelan stole a look at the old man. He was watching the boy with an odd look in his eye, and Whelan wondered if the old man understood half of what passed for English with Tony.

"Which brings me to the rest of it." The boy cocked his head and waited. "Jimmy Lee Hayes is dead."

"Who…oh, the old man and him, they got each other?"

"Nothing so tidy. No. Somebody else got him. Somebody shot him—it's too early for a ballistics report but I'm thinking it was the same gun that killed Makowski."

He watched and the boy's eyes told him he was putting this together, saw that it might have something to do with him. Tony's gaze flitted around the room and his confusion was obvious.

"Yeah, I know. It's hard to come up with sense out of all of this. I'd like to think this last part has nothing to do with you, that it means you're safe but if that's true…" He looked at his cigarette burning itself down in the little tin ashtray. If it is true, he thought, it means the killer is someone I don't want it to be.

"Tony, where's Mickey?"

"I don't know. He went out. He goes out a lot."

"Have any idea where?"

"Different places, I don't know. The cemetery sometimes."

Whelan winced inwardly. I bet he does. "Did he go out last night, after I left here?"

After a short hesitation, the boy nodded. "Yeah, for a little while."

"How little?"

"I don't know, man, how should I know—"

"Jesus, you sound like Marty. Was he gone more than a half hour?"

The boy looked at the old man, whose face told him nothing. Then he nodded. "I guess."

"He found out where Whitey was staying, didn't he?"

"I don't know. I never heard him say."

A chair scraped on the tile floor and Whelan turned toward the old man. He had moved closer to the table, closer to Whelan, and there was an urgency in his eyes that had not been there before.

"He hurt no one. Mickey. He hurt no one." The old man peered at him as though to see if his words had any effect. "You know this man, he hurt no one. You go from here, you leave now. You make trouble for him..."

"Take it easy, I'm just—"

"No."

No, Whelan thought, you're not the guy to take it easy. He slid his chair back and stood. The man got to his feet slowly and flexed stiff knees. Across the table, Tony Blanchard blinked at Whelan and looked on the verge of panic.

"He ain't in trouble, is he? Mick? Is Mick gonna be okay with this stuff?"

"I don't know."

"Shit. I didn't want to make no trouble for him. This is all on account of me." He looked down at the table and his eyes grew moist.

"No, I think it's on somebody else's account, Tony. You just had your own trouble."

"I caused all of this. Oh, shit, I wish I was back at Archer House. They told me. Told me I'd be in deep shit if I didn't get out."

"Your counselors?"

He nodded. "Jack did. Mr. Mollan. He told me the same shit he told Sonny Portis. He was right about Sonny and he was right about me. You know about Sonny?"

Whelan blinked and said nothing for a moment, confused and trying to force it all to make sense. "Yeah, I do. Sonny was your friend?"

"Yeah, he was okay but he got himself in deep and tried to get out by, you know, talkin' to the cops and shit like that."

"Did it ever occur to you that Jimmy killed him?"

The boy nodded. "Couple times, I wondered about that but

then other shit started comin' down, you know?"

Whelan studied the boy for a second thought about Sonny Portis and what he'd been told before, and finally formed the question to sort it all out. "Did Jack Mollan tell you he tried to talk Sonny off the street?"

Tony shook his head. "Sonny told me." He looked off into the distance, shoulders slumped. He had a hunch to his back that made him look small and frail, this boy who had taken Whelan into so much trouble.

Whelan shook his head: Jack Mollan and Sonny. A pattern began to form in Whelan's mind and he nodded slowly. "The guy in the baseball cap, the one that was down here looking for you—when did you see him for the first time?"

"I don't know. Last week, maybe."

Whelan nodded again. This one might turn out yet. "Thanks for talking to me, Tony. Maybe it's not as bad as it seems. I know you have no way of figuring out whether you can trust me but I might have an idea about, you know, a place for you to stay." The boy nodded absently but said nothing, and Whelan decided to let it drop for the moment.

He turned to the old man. "Maybe we have no trouble after all. But I still need Mick to come see me. My office or my house, it doesn't matter. He can call if he doesn't trust me."

The man made a slight nod. Whelan indicated the restaurant with a wave.

"This is *your* place, isn't it?"

"My daughter's restaurant. She is good businessman, she is good cook too. I am soldier, no businessman."

Soldier. Right.

"Thanks." He walked to the door and paused with his hand on the brass handle. "It was you that hit me in the alley."

For the first time, a glint of humor came into the old man's eyes. His cheeks and forehead seemed to darken and Whelan was sure the old man was fighting a grin.

"Yes, I hit. You chase boy."

My mistake, Whelan thought, and went out to make a phone call and one final visit to put it all to rest.

• • •

Greg Purcell opened the door to Archer House and stood for a moment in the attitude of a man expecting no visitors. The midday sun glinted white off his glasses and gave his face a blank, unfinished look.

"Yes? Oh, Hi, Mr.…Whelan, right?"

"Right."

"Something on Tony?"

After a moment's hesitation, Whelan nodded. "Uh, yeah. I did find him."

Purcell misread the pause. "Bad news?"

"No, no, not about that at least. He's fine. What happens to him next is anybody's guess but he's still alive."

"Great," Purcell said and stepped back. "Come on in."

Whelan entered the hallway and stood at the entrance to the tiny living room. He was about to speak when Purcell beat him to it.

"Jack's not here. He went out to get a sandwich."

"Should I wait?"

"Oughtta be back any minute."

"Well, then I'll wait."

A boy yelled out from the back of the house and Purcell excused himself, shaking his head and moving with the slow, weary steps of an older man. Whelan picked up an old issue of *Sports Illustrated* and leafed through it. A few minutes later he heard the door open.

Jack Mollan entered the room wearing a Cincinnati Reds cap and carrying a white paper bag about to give way to wet grease stains along the bottom. He raised his eyebrows when he noticed Whelan.

Whelan put the magazine down and got to his feet and nodded, wondering how to begin. Then he saw the look of comprehension that came into Mollan's eyes and realized he didn't have to say a thing.

Mollan took off his cap and scratched at the back of his head. "You're here to see me, right?"

"Yes."

Mollan nodded and then seemed to notice that he was about to lose the bottom of his bag. He laid it on a magazine atop a side table and turned to face Whelan.

"So you know."

"I'm in the dark about a lot of it, but I think I do, yes."

"And you expect me to talk about it?"

"I don't expect anything. I just know what you did."

"Think anybody cares? A couple of scumbags are history…"

"More than a couple," Whelan said, prodding. He held up his fingers and ran off the list. "Makowski, Nelson, Rory Byrne, Bobby Hayes, Whitey, an old fence named Les, and Mr. Jimmy Lee Hayes."

Halfway through the list Mollan was shaking his head. He kept shaking it after Whelan had finished. "No, those don't have anything to do with me. Except two. Just two."

"The first one and the last one. I know."

Mollan nodded again. "How? I mean, not that I sat up at night and tried to create the perfect crime but…how'd you figure it out?"

"Couple things. I found Tony."

Mollan gave him an appraising look. "Nice work."

"A guy showed up on Argyle Street right after I did. As a matter of fact, right after I talked to you. I asked you if you remembered Tony hanging out with anybody there. And then this guy shows up looking for him. A guy in a cap," and he nodded toward the Reds cap Mollan's fingers were worrying.

"Doesn't prove it was me. Even if it was…so what?"

"And then there was something else he said. He said you told him something and it was the same advice you gave Sonny Portis. You told me you never knew Sonny, that he was gone from Archer before you got here."

"That part was true. He was gone before I took the job." Mollan looked off into space and then studied Whelan for a moment. "Tony's okay?"

"Yes. Should I be glad you never found him?"

"No. I wasn't going to hurt him. Just ask him where these animals were."

"I need to know the 'why' of this."

"Because they were scumbags, like I said. That's why."

"The world's full of them. Far as I know, you've only gotten rid of two."

"Those were just the ones I caught up with. I don't know what happened to these other ones, didn't have nothing to do with me. I was just glad about how it turned out. The papers seemed to think it was some kind of infighting so I figured I'd just hang back and catch the survivors. Any of 'em left?" He feigned a look of curiosity.

"No, you're finished. They're all gone. But I need to know why you started this."

"You got a long nose. Maybe that's why you're good at what you do. But you got that look in your eye like you know why."

"I think it was about Sonny Portis rather than Tony. I'm not sure how it all played out but I've got an idea. I'm guessing that Jimmy Lee Hayes or one of his people killed Sonny, that they suspected him of informing. They killed him and you decided to kill them."

Mollan made a little sideways nod and said, "Not bad. Yeah, I knew Sonny. I knew him in another place."

"Another group home?"

Mollan laughed a mirthless laugh. "Oh, yeah. Another group home, one that I ran. But this one was in Ohio. He was placed with a family, they couldn't handle his personality—he was a good kid but he had a temper and this family, I guess it wasn't their fault. They weren't prepared for a kid like him, they wanted somebody, you know…"

"A kid out of their dreams," Whelan finished.

"Yeah, that's what they wanted. Anyhow, it just didn't work out for him. Next thing we knew, he was in a state agency, then on the streets and then he disappeared. Later on we heard he was in Chicago, had an uncle or somebody here."

"And you came here looking for him?"

"More or less. I mean, I came here to get situated again.

Things didn't work for me back there, I didn't have…I got divorced. I wanted to go someplace new. And I didn't have a family, no wife, no, you know, responsibilities, so…I guess I started trying to track him down. Eventually I ran into him on the street up by Clark and Diversey. He looked like he was living in the sewers, for Chrissake, weighed about seventy-five pounds. I thought it would break my heart. He didn't want to talk to me and I couldn't blame him. I'm fairly sure he was turning tricks up there."

"Was he the first kid from your home to be back on the streets?"

Jack Mollan gave Whelan a look of disgust. "No, he wasn't, and don't patronize me, Whelan. You're a smart guy, and maybe I've got some things to work out, but I'm not an idiot."

"I've never thought you were. I'm just trying to understand—"

"He was special. He was a good kid, a kid with a sense of humor and a lot of individuality; there's never any logic to why one kid's got a life and another one doesn't, but this was a good kid. Anybody'd be proud to have a kid like this. Shoulda been proud, anyway," he said, and Whelan could read his thoughts.

"He was special. We're not supposed to be, you know, we're not supposed to get involved but…He was my favorite kid. My favorite. He reminded me of me, when I was growing up. He came from…he had the same kinda background I had. Same kind of family." Jack Mollan's voice began to break and show stress, and Whelan found himself looking away, unable any longer to meet Mollan's eyes.

For a minute or two there was silence and when Mollan spoke again it was in a softer, more controlled voice. "I tried to get him into a program, found out he'd just been in this one. I saw him on the street one other time and he looked better, he was cleaned up a little and had decent clothes on. He told me he was doing odd jobs for a guy at a garage."

"Roy's."

"Yeah. And I asked around and found out that Roy's was where this Jimmy Lee Hayes and his people ran a small-time chop shop and got rid of stolen goods, shit like that. So I knew how he was making his money. I talked to a couple cops I know over at Town Hall and Area Six and they told me what a scuzz this guy was. And I watched him. I sat outside that garage and found out who he was, what he looked like, who his, you know, his people were. And all along, Whelan, I had a bad feeling about it.

"I tracked Sonny down a couple of times after that and tried to talk him out of it, told him he was in with real shit people, but I wasn't reaching him. He had money in his pocket and new clothes and the bullshit that seems to make a difference to a teenager and he thought this guy Jimmy Lee Hayes was hot shit. I was just a counselor."

Mollan ran his fingers through his hair. "Eventually I think they got into stuff that scared him."

"Jimmy Lee graduated," Whelan said. "He was moving into drugs and more lucrative commerce."

"Yeah. And Sonny started talking to a couple cops. Next thing I knew, he was dead in an alley." He raised his eyebrows and looked Whelan head-on. "And I knew who killed him, and I couldn't see straight, I wanted that big asshole so bad. A lot of things make me angry, Whelan. A lot of things, maybe more than other people. Always been that way. And this...this was it. So I went out looking for this guy. Took me a while, but I found him."

"You should have left it alone. Hayes wasn't a real smart man, the cops would have had him eventually."

"Then he'd still be alive," Mollan said in a dead voice.

"With his record, he would have been in for life. No matter what people say, prison's no substitute for freedom. Jimmy Lee would have been inside forever."

Mollan lowered himself onto a chair and sat perched at the edge, as though he'd just stopped in for a moment. He put his hands together and head down. For a long moment Whelan could think of nothing to say. He wanted to take Mollan by the shirtfront and put his face to the other man's face and tell him what a fool he was, what a waste he'd made of his life. But this was no time to add cruelty to another man's pain. Whelan thought about what Mollan had told him about his life: God only knew what other emotional baggage Jack Mollan had been carrying with him. An angry man doing angry things.

In the end he gave it up. He got to his feet and moved toward the door. Mollan looked up at him, a question in his eyes.

"I'm sorry about Sonny."

"Yeah, thanks. You going to the cops, or have you already been?"

"I made a call. The rest is up to you. I'm out of it. I wish you luck, though. And don't do anything stupid."

Mollan made a little shrug, said "Thanks," and looked off into the back of the house, seeing things only he knew. Whelan took a final look at him, a harsh man with a heart full of pain, and went outside.

The gray Caprice was waiting a discreet three car lengths away. Whelan walked slowly up the street and stopped at the driver's side window. Bauman was tapping his fingers impatiently on the outside of the door and squinting at him. To his right, Landini sat, hickey and all, arms folded across his chest and staring up the street in what could only be described as a sulk.

"He in there?" Bauman asked.

"Yes. He won't give you any trouble."

"Talk to me."

"No, I'm all talked out. He'll talk to you, just take it easy."

"Fuck this shit," Landini said, looking out his window. "We spend half the day talkin' to this hillbilly broad at the saloon and now we're gonna jaw with this guy..."

Whelan felt something pop. He leaned closer. "Hey, why don't you grow up, or rethink your career choice?"

Landini jerked around in his seat. "You wanta say something to me?"

"I just did. You're baggage, you're a teenager playing cop. You think this is some kind of game and you're some kind of hard shit, you ride around in a car all day giving people your badass impression. Look at you, you smell like Sophia Loren and you've got a hickey halfway up the side of your head. What are you, fourteen?"

Landini was halfway out of the car, face dark red, an odd little pulse visible in his temple.

"You want a piece of me, asshole?"

"Grown men don't fight in the street like animals. Police officers don't fight in the street. You want to show me how bad you are, find a gym with a ring. A ring and two pairs of sixteen-ounce gloves, that's all we'll need. I think they've got a ring at Hamlin Park, right over by Area Six. You set it up, bring all your friends, and give me a call."

Bauman blinked at Whelan, then looked at his partner. "You, get back in the fuckin' car, act your age." Then he leaned out his window. "And what the hell is with you? You got parts coming loose or what?"

Whelan watched Landini. "I'm having a bad day."

"So what? Landini here's havin' a bad life. This thing on his neck won't come off. I think the broadie sucked all his blood out."

"Hey, you—" Landini began and then found Bauman's finger in his face.

"No, *you,*" Bauman growled. "You let it go. This isn't the fucking schoolyard. This is a homicide case, there's people dead and I wanta sort it out and I don't much care if you do it with me, but you ain't getting out of my car and doin' your Muhammad Ali. You get outta *my* car, you need a new partner. You got that?"

The younger cop kept his eyes on Whelan for a five-count, then got back in the car. Bauman lit up one of his little cigars and gave Whelan an appraising look.

"So, you need a tranquilizer? You need to get laid, you need more fiber in your diet, what? What's with you?"

"I'm all right."

"Couldn't prove it by me." Bauman puffed at the little cigar and filled the air with gray smoke and the smell of burning tires. Then he sniffed and rubbed his nose and Whelan waited.

"That kid they took out about a year ago, that was one of these kids from this joint, right?"

"Yeah."

Whelan watched Bauman's wheels turning. The detective kept his eyes on Whelan but said nothing. Then he nodded.

"Talk back then was, Jimmy Lee whacked that kid. No evidence, though. Nothing to hold him on, even. These fucking street kids, Whelan, they're fair game for every kind of shit in the world." Bauman shook his head, then opened the door and hoisted his big frame out of the car. He waited for Landini to emerge, then hitched up his pants, unaware that as soon as he let go of his waistband, the pants sagged down beneath the sheer bulk of his stomach. A few feet away, Rick Landini tucked his tapered shirt in over his washboard stomach and refused to look at either of them.

Bauman looked down the street at Archer House. "A guy like that." He shook his head. "Now look at all this shit."

"Yeah. Hey, Landini, I'm sorry. I lost it for a second."

Landini fixed him with hard stare, then nodded. "My fault. I was outta line."

"No, I was just—"

Bauman scowled. "So now you gonna fight about whose fault it was? Come on, I want to get this over with." And with that, he strode heavily down the street. A beat later, Landini nodded to Whelan and followed him.

Whelan crossed the street and got into his car. For a moment he listened to the quiet of the street. When the detectives had been inside for a minute and there were no signs of a problem, he started his car.

Eighteen

Whelan sat for almost a half hour in his office with the shades down and the light off, sipping at a cup of coffee. There were moments when the frayed ends of things, the weight of final truths, were more than he thought he was willing to endure for the price of his freedom. If you looked for people in trouble, you sometimes took on their troubles. If you worked for people near desperation, you ran the risk of taking part in their desperation.

Now, sitting in the darkened office, he told himself this one could have been worse: the boy, Tony, could have been dead, and he would have had to break that news to Mrs. Pritchett. And there was one other way this one could have been worse. But it was bad enough: a boy who'd had no life at all was dead, an unhappy man had turned killer and ruined his life. An old friend was living on the streets.

The phone rang.

"Paul Whelan."

"Well, don't pay the ransom. He escaped!" Shelley laughed into the phone.

"Hi, Shel. Yeah, I was out."

"You sound like death, baby. What did they do to you out there?"

"People keep letting me find out things I don't want to know. Think it's time for me to take a vacation to someplace where they don't have electricity."

"No, you don't need a vacation, you need somebody to warm your bed up for you. What happened to—"

"You know what I like about you, Shel? The utter professionalism with which you approach your work."

"That social worker," she said, ignoring him. "Sandra what's her name?"

"MacAuliffe. Sandra MacAuliffe."

"Yeah. What about her? She sounded nice."

"She is. I think I'm screwing that up, Shel."

"What's the point of being a man if you can't screw something up, huh?"

He found himself laughing quietly at her.

"Listen, babe, I hate to interrupt your depression but you had a call. Strange one."

"How strange? I'm not really in the mood."

"Said to tell you Stan Laurel called. Do you know who that is?"

"Yeah. Yeah, I do."

"He sounded nervous."

"If you had his life, you'd be nervous, too."

"Is that his real name?"

"No, just an old joke from a long, long time ago when we thought everything was funny."

"He said he'd see you at the office."

"I thought he might come here."

"Is this guy dangerous?"

"Not to me."

"You gonna be all right?"

"Probably. I've been worse. Thanks, Shel."

"Take care, baby."

Stan Laurel. That went back almost thirty years, to a time when half their conversations centered on what they were going to be someday and the other half recounted what they saw on television. The Mick Byrne of that time, with his long, sad face and surprising ability as a mimic, could do a fine Stan Laurel, and Paul Whelan could offer a passable Oliver Hardy. The two boys in that little skit thought the world was going to be an easier place than it had turned out to be.

It occurred to him that Mick had left the cryptic message to tell him something: to tell him there was no trouble between them.

Ten minutes later the knock came.

"Come on in, it's open. It's always open."

The door swung a tentative six inches and a head poked in, a head rapidly losing the hair on top. He could just make out the man's eyes.

"Paulie?"

"Come on in, Mick."

"I called first…"

"I know. She told me."

"I think she thinks I'm some kinda weirdo."

"No. She thinks *I'm* some kinda weirdo. Come on in and sit down."

Mick Byrne closed the door behind him and crossed the room with his stiff-legged walk.

Whelan indicated the leg with a nod. "That recent? Or a souvenir from Nam?"

"Nam. Most of my kneecap is over there." He looked around the office. "How come it's so dark here? Were you getting ready to leave, Paul?"

"No. I was working myself into a catatonic state." Whelan got up and opened the shades and both windows onto Lawrence.

"Nice view," Mick said.

"I always wanted an office with the Aragon Ballroom in the background." He waited for Mick to sit. "I can offer you a cup of water from my top-of-the-line water cooler. I just had that installed."

"No thanks." Mick eyed the cooler. "There been days, though, when I woulda jumped through hoops for a cup of water. You never think what a big deal a cold glass of water is till you're out on the street and it's ninety-five and you can't have one." Mickey stared at the cooler for a moment. Then he looked back at Whelan. "I'm really sorry about last night."

"It's all right. I wasn't…I didn't know what was going on, and now I do. You were trying to protect the kid, I was trying to find him. It's okay, Mick. And I think you saved my bacon with the old man. He's bad, isn't he?"

Mickey nodded slowly. "Oh, yeah. People look at him and see an old guy pushing a broom but they don't know."

"How are you, Mick?"

"I'm alive and that's gotta count for something." Mickey rubbed his palms against his knees. "I don't know where to begin."

"Start with you, maybe. I thought you were dead."

"A lot of people thought I was dead. I let 'em think that. Seemed pretty simple to me: I figured I'd be dead soon enough. Can I smoke here?"

"You can if you give me one. I'm out."

Mickey Byrne slid a pinched pack of cigarettes across the desk. They each lit up and Whelan waited, discreetly watching Mick. His cheeks showed red webbing of broken blood vessels, his lips appeared to be chapped and his light brown hair was a tangle.

"Anyhow, I was real sick and I was drinking and getting sicker. I was in pretty bad shape when I got back, Paulie."

"I don't know anybody that was improved by Nam."

"Yeah, but I was really messed up. My head, Paulie…And I was drinking all the time. That's why I didn't come back here to stay. I came back to see Rory a couple times but I didn't let anybody know. I didn't want people to see me. For a while I thought I was going to be all right. I was in Seattle for a little while, then I moved. I had a little place—"

"Where was this? Portland?"

"Yeah. I had a little furnished place. Then I lost that and I got a room but it was just a matter of time before I was on the street. People were sending me letters, and I just stopped answering them. I think I stopped opening them."

"I sent you one," Whelan said.

"You did?" He looked surprised and gratified. "Thanks, Paul."

"I heard you were in the hospital."

Mickey leaned forward with a white-knuckle grip on the seat of the chair. "I was in a bunch of 'em, all kinds. You know, I was in a mental hospital for a while, too."

"No," Whelan said. "I didn't know that."

"When I wasn't in a hospital I was living on the street, more or less. If I had a few bucks I got a flop for the night but… you know how it is, Paulie, it's the same here." He indicated Lawrence Avenue with a nod toward the window. "That was real bad. You try to stay drunk enough so's you're not, you know, aware of how fucked up your life is but you can't get enough money to be wasted all the time. And then…man, it's so bad."

"How'd you get out of it?"

Mickey gave him a surprised look, then smiled and showed smoker's teeth. "What makes you think I am?"

"You are. You're not drinking anymore. I can tell, I know about that. I watched your hands when you took out the cigarette and when you lit up, you don't shake at all. You've got better hands than I do. Your eyes are clear and your color's coming back. You made it out, Mick."

Mickey made a little jerky nod of his head as though fighting his own eagerness. "Maybe. Maybe. I ran into a guy while I was on the street, outreach worker at a shelter, a former boozer. He caught me when I was half sober and talked to me about a program. One day a couple weeks later I kinda crawled into this place and they took me in. Eight weeks later I was earning my keep again. After four months I had a room of my own and some clothes and, you know, odds and ends that you need to live. And I was sober. I couldn't find a fulltime job but I put a couple part-time things together: I worked a couple days a week with a house painter and I worked in the kitchen of a restaurant—you know, a place that's open like twenty hours a day, soda fountain, a Greek runs it. Just like here."

Whelan laughed. "They're everywhere, Mick."

Mickey nodded. "I started washing dishes and then I got to cook once in a while when the head Greek was busy." He gave Whelan an apologetic look. "I'm a cook, Paulie. And I found out I liked it. So I was feeling okay about things. Then Rory got killed." He looked past Whelan and took a long, tired sigh, and it was a while before he spoke again. "When I came back to visit him, Paul, he was in with these fucking people already. I told him they were trouble but he insisted he was okay, said he wasn't into any kind of shit, he just did a few things here and there for them. Had money in his pocket, thought he was hot shit. I don't even know how he met any of them or really what he did with them. I just know he got in with the wrong people and they killed him. I don't know what he did, even, that they killed him."

"Nothing. The guy he worked for got somebody sent up, and this old killer came looking for him, and Rory was caught in the middle of it. I'm sorry about him, Mick."

"He was never smart, Paulie. Never really figured out what to do with himself. But he was good people." Mickey's eyes moistened and he looked away with a jerky motion. He sat half turned in the chair with his skinny legs crossed and looked to Whelan like a little lost boy. When he'd taken a couple of hungry puffs at his cigarette he turned back to face Whelan. "He said most of this was cars, what they did. Is that what you heard?"

Whelan thought for a moment. Sometimes the details did no good at all, partial truth was good enough. He nodded. "Yeah, they had a chop shop for a while and operated out of a garage. It was small time, Mick."

"That's how it seemed to me."

"I'm really sorry, Mick. Tell me about the kid, Tony."

He shrugged. "It happened by accident. Last time I came back to see Rory, he had the kid with him, the kid was just staying there for a few weeks, he didn't have a place and Rory didn't like being alone. Rory took him in, I guess. He's a good kid. Anyhow, when I found out about Rory I came back. I stayed with Minh."

"That's his name, the old guy that cleaned my clock?"

Mickey grinned. "Yeah, Dao Minh Tri. Major Tri of the Army of the Republic of Vietnam, and if they'd all been like him, Paulie, they wouldn't have needed us. I knew I was welcome at Minh's."

"Why? You know him in-country? You met him there?"

"Better than that. I knew his kid. His son was a lieutenant and I saved his ass in a firefight. Minh thinks I'm the greatest thing since rice. The kid has a little restaurant in Seattle. When I was living there he threw a little work my way and he gave me the old man's address here, said to see him if I ever came to town and needed anything. Well, that's what I did. Didn't mean to get Minh involved in anything but he was going to the wall with me if it came down to that.

"Anyhow, I started asking around and looking around for these people and I ran into the kid. He'd been staying with that other kid, Marty, and people started getting killed, so he went under. I took him back to Minh's place with me. For the last month, we've been one big happy Vietnamese family, me, the kid, Minh and his wife, his daughter and her husband and two kids. Everybody in five rooms." Mick laughed, a boy's high-pitched laugh that Whelan hadn't heard in many years.

"They probably think their place is too big."

Mickey nodded but his attention seemed to be on something else. "They said you needed to see me, Paul. What did you want to talk about?"

"At the time, I wasn't sure. Now I just want to tell you it's over."

"That guy Whitey? I don't want just him, Paulie, I want—"

"Jimmy Lee. He's dead, Mick, they're all dead."

"Who killed *him,* this Jimmy Lee asshole?"

"Another guy he pissed off. He made lots of enemies, Mick, and now he's dead." He watched as his friend turned this over in his mind, allowed him a moment, then asked, "What were you going to do, Mick?"

"I was gonna make that fucker pay."

"How?"

"Who knows," he said, and Whelan didn't push it.

"I've had a bad morning. Bad couple of days, actually. I even missed lunch, which is almost unheard of for me. Come on, we'll go eat—I've got a restaurant for you, Mick, that'll change all your ideas about food service, ambience, hygiene, you name it. You can give me your professional opinion."

Mick shifted in his chair. "I'm a little short."

"Come on, I get nervous when I eat alone."

Whelan pushed open the door to the House of Zeus just as a skinny gray-haired man launched a basket of fries at Rashid's head. The Iranian ducked and the fries went sailing through the air like potato shrapnel. Rashid laughed delightedly and then feigned injury. He cupped one hand over his eye and yelled.

"Oh, oh, I have eye injury from french fry. Where is lawyer?"

The gray-haired man turned and stalked out, muttering to himself. Still grinning, Rashid bent down and began picking fries off the floor. When the basket was filled again, he dumped it into the bin where the new fries sat under a heat lamp. He paused when he saw Whelan. He flashed all his many teeth and called out "Hello, Mister Detective Whelan." To Mick, he added, "Hello, Detective Whelan's friend."

"Hello, Rashid. How's your eye?"

"Oh, okay, no problem."

Whelan turned to Mick, who was watching him with an expectant look. "Welcome to the House of Zeus. What would you like?"

"Anything but fries," Mick said.

As they ate—Mick had let Whelan order, and the little table was covered with half a dozen baskets, more than any two people could eat but a generous sampling of the sublime and the bizarre—Whelan tossed questions out and let Mick field them as he chose. He wanted to hear it all, wanted to know where this man had spent all the wasted years and how it had been for him but he knew better than to force it out. There were things no one need know about another person, things a person should never have to divulge, private shame and missteps that need never see the light once a person had learned to deal with them, and he restrained his impulses to pry and prod.

When Mick fell silent Whelan got them each a cup of Rashid's acrid coffee. For a few moments they listened to a running argument in Farsi and English between Rashid and Gus about a case of frozen beef that had apparently been left out overnight. At one point, Gus punctuated an opinion by grabbing a knife and Rashid took the heavy fire extinguisher off the wall.

Mick watched them and shook his head. "You eat here all

the time?"

"Nobody could eat here all the time."

"I feel like I'm in Oz or someplace." Mickey lit a smoke and smiled at Whelan. "All afternoon I been spilling my guts and I don't know a thing about Paul Whelan. So what's the story, Paulie?"

"You know what I do for a living and where I go for lunch. What else do you want?"

"I also know you're the same old Paul Whelan and that's good. But how come you're not married? Seems like you'd do okay married."

"I'm kind of stubborn. Slow to change."

"That thing with Liz, lasted all those years—that didn't work out?"

"Nope."

"And now? You got somebody you're seeing?"

"Yeah, I do. Nice lady, too. At present, I think I'm testing her patience."

"On purpose?"

"No. I think I'm nervous about her."

"Don't screw it up, Paulie."

"Right."

Mickey leaned back. "I oughtta go, Paul. I actually want to get back to Portland. I got a life there. It's nothing fancy but there's people there who know what I'm like now that I'm not drinking…"

"You get away from people for a while, you forget that they find a lot of reasons to like you."

Mick looked embarrassed. "Yeah, I guess so. And I keep thinking how I'd like to run into some of the folks that saw me when I was goin' under, I want 'em to see me now that I…you know, now that I've got it together again."

"I'm glad I finally got to sit down with you, Mick. And I'm also glad…" and Whelan found that he didn't know how to say any more.

"That I'm not living out of garbage cans? Yeah, me too."

"No. That you're okay. Listen," he said, and then Mick

stopped him with an upraised palm.

"No, man, you're not going to give me money, are you? You gonna insult me now? Don't do that, Paulie."

"You'd do it to me. I'd be a little pissed, too, maybe, but it wouldn't surprise me."

"Fine, so you offered and that's enough. I don't need handouts now. I need to get back home and get back to work in my kitchen."

"All right, Mick."

Outside, the day was giving hints of high summer to come. They stood shuffling from one foot to the other and puffing at cigarettes and then Mick tossed his into the street.

"What about the kid, Mick?"

"He can come with me. Or he can stay with Marty and his brother. They're pretty tight, and Marty—he's a good kid, Paul, he's a lot more, you know, solid than he seems."

"Yeah, he is. I underestimated him. But living with them…I mean, if that's what Tony wants…but Marty's brother's a loser, Mick. Tell you what, if he'll do it, I'd like a chance to talk to him alone. See if he'll go for that. If not, have him get in touch with Mrs. Pritchett and I'll sit down with the two of them. I think I can put him in touch with people down south, his mother's people."

"Indian people? Yeah?"

"Choctaw people, his mother's tribe. It'll be his choice but he needs to know all his options. And whether he'll talk to me or not, he ought to call Mrs. Pritchett. I figure the lady who hired me and got me into all this has a right to see him one more time."

"Must be a nice lady," Mick said.

After another moment of silence, Whelan said, "I'm glad it never got down to you doing something crazy, Mick."

"Yeah, I guess."

"What were you gonna do?"

Mickey shrugged and looked embarrassed. "I don't know. Maybe break his arms for him. Maybe club him some night when he was coming out of a saloon, I don't know."

"You don't have a gun, or anything like that."

"No, man, I never had nothing to do with guns." A look of amusement came into Mickey Byrne's eyes and a slow grin appeared. "You didn't know about that, though, right? How could you? No, Paulie, I never had a gun over there and I don't have one over here. I told anybody who'd listen that I wasn't gonna shoot anything. I let 'em make me a medic."

"A medic."

"Yeah, a medic. That's what I was, a *medic*. Like you, Paulie. Like Paul Whelan, like my friend Paul Whelan." He stuck out his hand and Whelan ignored it, grabbing him in a bearhug. He could feel the ridge of Mick's spine, the points of his thin shoulders through the cloth of his jacket. He smelled of old cotton and cigarette smoke. Whelan hugged him and patted him on the back and when they finally freed one another Mickey gave him one final shrug and said, "See you, Paulie."

"Listen to me, Mick. If I don't get a call or a note or a card, I'm coming out to find you. And that's one thing I can do. I find people."

Mickey Byrne nodded and gave him one last final wave and then was walking north on Broadway toward Argyle Street. He moved fast on his stiff leg, like a man accustomed to covering long distances on foot, and Whelan stood there and watched till he could no longer make him out in the distance.

They had to page Mrs. Pritchett for him at the hospital and she sounded just this side of annoyed when she picked up the phone.

"This is Evangeline Pritchett," the voice said. It wasn't her home voice but he believed it was just the voice that would make a wardful of nurses and aides and orderlies jump when it was time for them to jump.

"Paul Whelan, Mrs. Pritchett. Sorry to bother you at work, but I thought—"

"Mr. Whelan, oh, I'm glad to hear from you. Have you found anything about Tony?"

"Yes, ma'am."

"Is he alive, sir?" The voice dropped down another notch,

tougher, ready to deal with things.

"Yes, he is."

"Oh, thank the Lord. Where is he—or can you tell me that?"

"Right now, he's staying with some people a little north of your place. Nice people, but it's only temporary."

"And he's all right?"

"Physically he's fine. Who knows about a kid's mind?"

"Oh, this is wonderful. You're a smart man, Mr. Whelan. I need to pay you what I owe you, sir."

"We can talk about that later. I want to talk to a couple of people about him, and then I think we should meet and discuss the boy. I'm hoping I can get him to come in to see me. We can go over the options he has available, the three of us. If he doesn't come in, well, maybe he'll at least get in touch with you."

"Mr. Whelan, I thought sure that boy was dead."

"Tell you a secret, so did I, but you have to keep looking to know for sure. Anyhow, I'll get back to you."

When she hung up, he wondered what he'd do if the boy didn't contact him. He thought of the Indians in the hills of Mexico who hunt by pursuing their prey for days, literally running down the deer till the animals are exhausted from the chase.

I'll run you down, kid. You better show up.

He spent much of the afternoon on the phone, with Abby and Father Collins from St. Augustine's Indian Center and with several people that they put him in touch with, and when he was done he thought he had something solid to offer Tony Blanchard. In the long run, he knew, there were no guarantees. Tony Blanchard was still just a street kid and for all Whelan knew, these things he was trying to accomplish were just ways of buying the kid time. There was no guarantee the kid would have any kind of a life. Whelan thought about Marty Wills for a moment: nobody was buying Marty any time. He wasn't on the street but anybody who got a good look at Marty's older brother would have a pretty fair idea what Marty's prospects in life were going to be. After a moment's reflection, Whelan decided it wouldn't hurt him to drop in and see the foul-mouthed, sulky boy sometime.

Finished with business, he sat and stared at the phone, trying to convince himself he was not nervous about making one last call. He got up and poured himself a drink from the water cooler, then had another. When he was back at the desk, he lit a cigarette, took a puff, then picked up the phone and began dialing her number. His finger slipped and he had to start over, irritated. The whole world was going Touch-Tone and Paul Whelan was still rotary.

The receptionist forced him to identify himself and he waited a long moment till Sandra MacAuliffe came on.

"Hello, stranger. You know that song, Paul?"

"Yeah. Barbara Lewis. I'm sorry."

"It's all right. You said you'd be busy wrapping things up. I thought you might call late last night but…it's okay. How are you?"

"I'm all right. It took me a little longer to wrap things up and they didn't go as smoothly as I had hoped. It was…shit, it was messy. It wasn't pleasant, and I didn't call because I didn't want to talk to anyone, not even you. But I want to talk to you now."

"You said you were all right but you're not. Is…how is your friend?"

"Mick? He's all right, he wasn't part of it. He's…I'll tell you about him over dinner. I mean, are you free?"

She laughed. "I was going to tell you I was busy but that's not playing fair. Sure, I'm free. If other guys call me I tell them I'm busy."

He blinked and wrestled with this information. "Do they? Do other guys call you?"

She laughed again. "Oh, once in a while they do, yes, they sure do."

"Oh."

"We can talk about that some other time. Is the boy all right?"

"More or less. I was feeling pretty pleased with myself but this kid and his friend Marty, they're just a couple of sad cases.

The only thing I did was make sure they didn't get killed. I didn't do a thing to ensure that they're gonna have good lives."

"Who can?"

"Nobody, I guess. So how about dinner?"

"Where?"

He thought for a moment and then nodded. "Someplace where the service is slow and I'll have your company for a long time."

"Nice comeback," she said.

He closed up the office early and drove to Waveland Park, then parked in the long narrow lot nearest the tennis courts. He lingered for a while at the edge of the big saucer-shaped depression used for the baseball diamonds and watched a high school team practicing. Then he headed for the rocks.

The wind had died down and the dark green water of the big lake slapped at the rocks and rolled off again. Whelan found a dry spot at the very edge, a square white rock with a red heart painted in its very center. The heart proclaimed that Andy loved Amy. The date was July 4, 1975. He wondered where Andy and Amy were now, and figured the chances were pretty slim that they even knew each other's whereabouts.

The only company he had were a pair of fishermen, one white, the other black, both in their sixties, who sat a few feet apart and watched half a dozen lines for any sign of a bite. They had identical white plastic buckets and the same number of lines in the water, and as Whelan watched them he could see that they were talking, without ever taking their eyes off the water.

He looked around and remembered steamy days when the boys from his street came scrambling over the rocks after a long game back at the diamonds and tossed themselves into the waves. He could see those boys, filthy with the infield dust and sweaty and jubilant, all talking at once as they spilled down onto the last line of rocks and into the water. Yelling and laughing and calling out to one another, all confident that the summer would never end and they'd probably live forever. In his mind's eye he could see them all, the Marklin boys who fought constantly and Hansie Becker always struggling to hide a German accent, and Bobby Hansen and Paul Whelan and poor Artie Shears and Rory Byrne, and standing at the very edge of the rocks, testing the water with one skinny foot, he could see Mickey Byrne.

MORE FROM MICHAEL RALEIGH

DEATH IN UPTOWN

A killer terrorizes Chicago's diverse Uptown neighborhood. Private investigator Paul Whelan's specialty is tracking down missing persons, but when his good friend is found slain in an alley, Whelan is steered down a path of violence as he searches for answers.

His investigation is interrupted by the arrival of an attractive young woman, Jean Agee, who is on her own search for her missing brother. But as clues lead Whelan to believe the two cases may be connected, the body count rises quickly, and he finds himself racing to catch a killer before he strikes again.

A BODY IN BELMONT HARBOR

The body of a small-time drug dealer washes up in Belmont Harbor among the yachts of Chicago's wealthy. Convinced that this murder connects to her husband's suicide two years prior, wealthy widow Janice Fairs hires private eye Paul Whelan to investigate.

Whelan's investigation takes him into the rarefied air of the wealthy, where he begins to discover unlikely connections between the two men in the harbor. But Whelan isn't the only one snooping, and he discovers himself an unwitting player in a game of cat-and-mouse, with deadly consequences.

THE MAXWELL STREET BLUES

Chicago private eye Paul Whelan is hired by an elderly jazz musician to find a missing street hustler named Sam Burwell. As Whelan delves into Burwell's past, the world of street vendors and corner musicians, he uncovers old enmities and love affairs, but his search for Burwell comes up empty. That is, until Burwell is found murdered.

Soon Whelan is swept up into a whirlwind of old feuds, dark pasts, unlikely romances...and a killer hiding in plain sight.

THE RIVERVIEW MURDERS

Margaret O'Mara's brother disappeared thirty years earlier, so when his last known associate is found murdered, O'Mara hires Chicago PI Paul Whelan to investigate.

Whelan makes the rounds through seedy bar and dilapidated apartment buildings where he discovers connections to a long-gone Chicago amusement park where another murder took place forty years prior.

Soon, Whelan finds himself navigating his way through dark pasts, deep secrets, and a mystery that may cost him his life.

Printed in the USA
CPSIA information can be obtained
at www.ICGtesting.com
JSHW031710140824
68134JS00038B/3620